11.99   102-826-206-+

ESSENTIAL BEGINNINGS

Surviving Ashes, Book One

Kennedy Layne

ESSENTIAL BEGINNINGS

Copyright © 2015 by Kennedy Layne
Print Edition

E-Book ISBN: 978-1-943420-00-1
Print ISBN: 978-1-943420-03-2

Cover Design: Sweet 'N Spicy Designs

ALL RIGHTS RESERVED: The unauthorized reproduction or distribution of this copyrighted work is illegal. Criminal copyright infringement is investigated by the FBI and is punishable by up to 5 years in federal prison and a fine of $250,000.

All characters and events in this book are fictitious. Any resemblance to actual persons living or dead is strictly coincidental.

DEDICATION

Jeffrey—you are my essential beginning. Thank you for being by my side on this journey.

ACKNOWLEDGEMENTS

Sylvie Fox—for helping a fellow author out in the research department when I was in need of some expert advice that I couldn't find on the Internet.

Dr. Matthew A. d'Alessio—for taking the time to answer questions regarding volcanoes and earthquakes. Any mistakes or liberties taken pertaining to these subjects are solely on my part.

CHAPTER ONE

"A YEAR SEEMS to pass by quicker the older I get." Maverick Becket took a drink of his strong black coffee before setting the heavy ceramic mug back down beside his freshly cleaned plate. He gathered up his utensils and placed them on the dish, raking his mouth with his napkin one last time before dropping it center mass. The older leatherneck sitting across from him was right. Time didn't used to get ahead of a person back in the early days when they were in the Corps. It used to be time stood still and you were lucky if it started back up again while they waited to rotate back to the world from some godforsaken shithole halfway around the world. The truth of the matter was that everything had changed. They had no choice but to accept the fact that they were aging faster than they wanted to. Keeping up with the younger troopers tended to get harder with each passing year. One couldn't wage a war against the wear and tear the Corps, and now his employment with the state police, had put upon his body. The life of service was thankless. Mav relaxed back against the smooth red vinyl of the diner's booth, not ready to leave the sanctuary of this quiet diner quite yet. The fact was that he was more comfortable here in Lost Summit than he was back home in Illinois anyway. Each year his trip back to this remote small town made it more like coming home.

"That it does," Mav replied in agreement, studying the man who was more like a father to him than the one who had barely claimed those rights. His biological father had passed away long ago and Mav had little remorse for his death. Master Gunnery Sergeant Ernie "Tank" Yates had stepped into those shoes whether he'd intended to or not. "Which just means that Mabel is not going to wait around forever, you old Devildog. Don't think for a second that we all missed noticing that Stanley Ratliff was paying extra attention to her at Friday's fish fry."

Tank was now over sixty years old and had no trouble keeping up with the six younger former Marines who'd been under his command twelve years ago. His blue eyes sparkled with life, standing out even more so due to his silver hair. The weathered wrinkles around his eyes were more from hard won laughter than age, but he could be a tough son of a bitch if the situation warranted it. What he needed was a woman by his side that softened his harder edges while enjoying the rural country life he'd managed to carve out for himself here in Lost Summit, Washington.

"You know I'm right," Mav insisted with a smile, liking to rile up the old man every once in awhile. Too bad the guys weren't here to join in. "Rat might as well have been up her skirt the other day at the church kitchen. We supply the beer battered fish and he makes a play for your gal while you fry them up."

Ernie raised a bushy eyebrow and thinned his lips. Not even his grey mustache could hide his contempt for Stanley. The ongoing feud between the two men was becoming legendary. Rat had taken a personal affront when Ernie had moved to the northernmost part of Washington nine years ago to open Lost Mountain Lodge, a small fishing and game resort made up of a dozen log cabins surrounding a sprawling main lodge. The lodge consisted of ten smaller private accommodations, a great hall, a commercial kitchen with a dining room, not to mention a well-stocked taproom and bar. Rat considered Ernie to be competition for his bait shop and family campground located southeast of town near the Pine Peak Silver Mine. They were two separate businesses and yet Rat couldn't seem to stem his animosity. It wasn't a contest, but Ernie had stood by and let the man talk shit to anyone who would listen, which only added fuel to the fire.

"Mabel is smarter than to fall for a common fool like Ratliff," Ernie exclaimed gruffly, sliding a look over to where the woman in question was refilling coffee cups for a couple of older men at the counter. She was the owner and operator of Summit Diner, the only café in town that served breakfast, lunch, and dinner—zero six hundred to nineteen thirty hours every day but Sunday. She'd lost her husband years ago and Ernie was taking his sweet time in courting her, regardless that she'd been giving hints to him for some time now. It was tough to imagine that the hardened, crusty old man who'd once been a tank commander in the Marines when they rode M60s would be uneasy at the thought of asking a beautiful woman out to dinner. "And you're one to talk, son. I'll be in the grave by the time you and Henley decide to actually do something other than argue about the sky being blue."

Mav was wise enough not to rise to Ernie's bait, and now he was the one grateful his buddies weren't present. Henley Varano wasn't a subject he was ready to discuss. She'd left her small hometown for the fame and fortune that Hollywood offered, only to show back up out of the blue a few years ago and ask Ernie if he needed a manager for the lodge. The old coot wasn't one to turn down a pretty lady in need and she'd settled into the administrator role as natural as could be, thus freeing Ernie to focus on being a fishing and small game guide for those city folk that needed one. That was all well and good with the exception that Henley wasn't as gracious in her dealings with Mav as she was with the other guys—and those jarheads sure liked to rub it in his face at every opportunity.

Berke Daniels, Owen Quade, Mason Sykes, and Van Overton were his four fellow former Marines who were missing from this breakfast. They used to be his brothers in arms, the men who had his six during their numerous combat tours together, and now they were lifelong friends who met up once a year at Ernie's lodge to drink too much beer and drown the latest lures Ernie had uncovered from local Native American lore. All four of them had left early yesterday while Mav had stayed behind for one more day. He'd like to leave town with his ego somewhat intact, so he reached for his wallet only to have Ernie already laying down a twenty-dollar bill that would more than cover the cost of their breakfast plus a healthy tip.

"That's what I thought," Ernie said wryly with a trace of humor lacing his words when Mav wouldn't engage. He ignored Ernie as he reached for his cheap dollar store shades and keys. It was time he hit the road back home, if that's what he could call it. Low murmuring arose from the men at the counter, along with what sounded like a cry of alarm from Mabel. It was that high resonance that had Ernie standing first to see what the problem was. "Mabel?"

"Ernie, look," Mabel directed with a finger, her voice shaking in what Mav could only describe as apprehension. He unfolded his large frame from the booth and joined Ernie at the counter, where everyone had their eyes glued to the ancient standard resolution tube television that hung from the ceiling in the corner. The thing was as big as an ice chest and four times as heavy. "I need to call Derek."

Derek was Mabel's son who was currently living in Wyoming. While Mabel grabbed the cordless phone that was always positioned near the cash register, Mav focused on what the newscaster was saying and the words sliding across the bottom of the screen. The picture quality was so poor that you had to concentrate to make out the words.

6.1 Earthquake at Yellowstone National Park.

"Turn it up," Elijah Burch said from his usual spot at the counter. The eighty-two year old gentleman was a fixture at Summit Diner and was known for telling tall stories about his time at Pine Creek Silver Mine until it was played out some forty years back. He was born here and he would die here in all likelihood, just as he'd always intended. "I didn't put in my hearing aids this morning."

Ernie was the closest to where Mabel had set down the clunky worn remote, so he picked it up and pressed the button repeatedly until the newscaster's booming voice echoed throughout the diner. By this time everyone had stopped eating and had made their way over to stand behind the men at the counter to hear firsthand what was happening.

"...*animals leaving Yellowstone National Park in herds. It's unprecedented the numbers that have been caught on video in this mass exodus. We also have footage from our affiliate station KBZK out of Bozeman, Montana of a massive crevice that has formed inside the park as a result of the earlier earthquake. With us right now is seismologist Julie Cramer. Julie, can you explain to our listening audience what is taking place at Yellowstone and what the odds are of this being the start of a catastrophic event or if this is just another in a long line of earthquakes near the park?*"

Mav took a couple steps back and leaned against the table, crossing his arms and settling in to hear exactly why this was bigger news than the fact a certain Middle Eastern country had seized a United States flagged cargo ship in the Strait of

Hormuz. He'd yet to see the follow-up story to that breaking news featured at zero five hundred, but he'd bet his left nut that the Pentagon had already deployed a destroyer or frigate to that area out of the 5th Fleet in Bahrain. Ask anyone who has lived in California...a six point one earthquake was nothing more than the rattling of dishes and setting off everyone's car alarms. They didn't even delay school for a six point one on the Richter scale.

"This could be it." Ernie had stepped back away from the counter as well, the beat-up remote still in his hand. He leveled his solemn blue eyes on Mav as he shook the device toward the television. "I told you it was only a matter of time, son."

"Tank, I know you built that massive shelter up at the lodge for a natural disaster or national emergency, and honestly that was a pretty smart idea back during the Cuban Missile Crisis. But this is nothing more than a tremor compared to what happened in Nepal earlier this year." Mav and the guys had helped Ernie over the last ten years build what he called a *necessity*. The bunker was actually quite large and ingeniously self-sustaining. It could accommodate a couple dozen survivors for an extended period. He'd gotten the idea for the ultimate prepper's wet dream after retiring from a lifetime in the Old Corps and living through difficult situations in austere hostile environments that most people couldn't begin to imagine. He had spent years researching all the available documentaries and then studying everything he could get his hands on about surviving all types of natural disasters and emergency situations. One of Ernie's favorite calamity scenarios evolved from the 1980 Mount St. Helens eruption, famous for its massive ash cloud and the now infamous pyroclastic flows. Everyday people had started talking about volcanic activity under the United States and the Yellowstone caldera topped the list. The BBC had even produced a made for television docudrama back in 2005, realistically portraying what the likely consequences would be if the place finally popped its cork after all these years of relative stability. Ernie had predicted on numerous occasions that the supervolcano underneath Yellowstone would erupt sooner rather than later. "An earthquake is a far cry from a massive eruption."

"This is how it starts," Ernie cautioned, widening his stance and settling in to watch the live broadcast. Sure enough, the camera cut from the newscaster and his guest to footage of the park. At first the images were beautiful—mature trees, vivid greenery, and a sparkling lake that would make the most amorous fisherman envious. It wasn't long before the newsfeed cut from the stock footage of the park to a rather shaky airborne clip of an exposed crevice that was quite vast, but that's all it had been showing over and over since the story broke. There was no steam; nothing to indicate it was anything more than a big crack in the surface of the earth. "The tremors and swarms of seismic activity will rise. There will then be hypothermal events until eventually one or two vents will open, releasing an incredible amount of pressure, but it won't be enough to forestall the collapse. Ultimately the…"

Mav inhaled deeply, listening to Ernie explain in detail the ins and outs of volcanoes as if he'd been a geologist instead of a tank commander. He'd probably read and cataloged more information about Yellowstone National Park than the employees who worked there, but that still didn't mean that a catastrophic event was about to happen. Mav had heard the stories for the past ten years, and the one thing that stood out was the fact that there was only one chance in seven hundred thousand of the caldera experiencing a cataclysmic eruption. That was close to the odds of getting struck by lightning. They wouldn't see something like that in their lifetime, but it was easier to let Ernie have his quirks than it was to debate with him over the future of the planet. He and the guys had all agreed to help out their old Master Gunnery Sergeant when they visited the lodge each year on vacation. Over that timespan they had built new additions and improved the facility according to Tank's master plan while squeezing in some fishing and more than a little drinking. Needless to say, they had all jokingly agreed that if the shit ever truly hit the fan they would all haul their asses up here. Mav suddenly found that he wasn't smiling anymore when it came to reflecting on Ernie's obsession.

"Tank, I've got to hit the road," Mav said, checking his watch. It was going on zero nine hundred and he still had a twenty-five hour trip ahead of him. He'd have to stop somewhere tonight, but his shift at the barracks didn't start until

Wednesday morning. The national news was revealing nothing besides the fact that an earthquake had struck the region. There were no fatalities, although a few hikers had a couple of minor injuries. If nothing else he'd turn on the radio instead of listening to the music on his phone so he could be kept up-to-date. "Why don't you walk out with me?"

"Mav, would you like a coffee for the road?" Mabel asked, calling out to him from behind the counter. She must have spoken to her son and realized that everything was all right. She had a smile on her face and her eyes kept shifting toward Tank, but she'd look away by the time the old man took notice. They were worse than teenagers. "We don't want you getting drowsy on the trip back."

"A coffee to go sounds good, Mabel." Mav flashed her a smile and then nudged Ernie in the arm, but that went unnoticed as well. His gaze was fixed on the screen, even though nothing more had happened. The newscaster was recycling the story until Mav was sure he could recite the coverage word for word. "Tank, I don't know how much more of an invitation that woman can give you. She—"

"You shouldn't leave." Ernie set the remote on the table behind Mav and then continued to put him in an awkward situation. So much for making a clean getaway. "You'd be driving just north of Yellowstone and that's the last place anyone should be traveling right now. I know you and the boys have been placating me over the years, but I'm asking that you stay a day or two until this thing settles down."

"Tank, come on." Mav could see Mabel putting a lid on the disposable Styrofoam cup she'd poured his coffee into and he figured she'd be coming around the counter at any moment. He didn't want her to hear what Ernie was spouting, or else she might think he'd gone around the bend. "Don't do this. I'm scheduled to work on Wednesday morning. It would be almost impossible for me to get another officer to take over my shift at this late date. I'd have to work Christmas and New Year's to even tempt another trooper to cover me on so little notice. Don't you think that if this was an indicator of something bigger that FEMA would be on television advising everyone to evacuate the immediate area?"

"What is there to evacuate over a hundred mile radius from the park? Where would they all go?" Ernie was like a dog with a bone and now Mav found himself wishing he'd left yesterday with the others. This wasn't the note he wanted this trip to end on. "It wouldn't surprise me if FEMA actually gave a press briefing saying that this earthquake has released the pressure of the plates and things were back to normal. FEMA knows that any acknowledgement of the Yellowstone Caldera erupting would only cause widespread panic throughout the whole country. Hell, it would create mass hysteria."

"Exactly," Mav said, trying to point out that all the research Ernie had done over the years had done exactly that. It obviously didn't penetrate because he kept talking.

"One more day then," Ernie requested, his voice lowering when he caught sight of Mabel coming their way. At least he was smart enough to keep her from hearing his irrational theories. "Give me tonight to show you some calculations and if by morning nothing else happens or you think I'm crazier than old shithouse Rat, you can hightail it out of here and still make your shift."

"Here you go," Mabel said, handing Mav his regular cup of coffee—tall, black, no sugar, and no cream. "I spoke to Derek. He and the family are just fine. They didn't feel a thing and didn't know anything about the earthquake until I called with the news."

"And how is that cute grandbaby of yours?" Ernie asked with a finesse that surprised even Mav. "The last picture you showed me had to be over a month ago."

"Well," Mabel began, a flush settling over her cheeks, "you've had the boys here and I didn't want to intrude on the nights you came by for dinner. You only get to see them once a year and I know they're like your family."

Something on the television must have caught Ernie's eye. He looked over Mabel's shoulder, getting the older woman to turn around, and then pointed up at the screen. Mav was grateful for the reprieve because he didn't want to make Ernie upset after he'd already made his decision to head back home. As much as he'd have liked to stay—the reasons being anything but Yellowstone—he had responsibilities to get back to and he wasn't one to thwart them.

"...do confirm that there has been unusual seismic activity over the last week, but it's been relatively quiet since this *morning. The Teton Fault borders the Yellowstone volcanic plateau and may have been only relieving the pressure between the two, which is actually good in preventing anything noteworthy of happening beyond this morning's event. We can determine from the reports that we've been receiving that things are now status quo and the park can return to normal operations with certain minor exceptions."*

Mav gritted his teeth when Ernie made a sound of confirmation for his benefit. He didn't need the reminder that Tank had believed that FEMA might actually say those exact words. It was probably the damned truth, and yet he couldn't shake off the uneasy feeling that Ernie might be right this time.

Everyone in the diner seemed to lose interest after that and they finally returned to their meals. The low murmurs of conversation started back up and life in this small town got back to normal, leaving Mav to struggle with making a decision he'd thought he'd already made.

"We'll miss you, Mav," Mabel said, turning back and lifting her arms for a hug. He returned the gesture, ensuring that he had a firm grip on his coffee. The older woman even kissed his cheek before pulling away. "You have a safe trip back home."

Ernie waited until Mabel walked back around the counter with a promise to show him some pictures when he stopped by the diner for dinner tonight. Mav was just about to slip his shades on when the bell above the door chimed, revealing Henley Varano in all her glory. Damn, but that woman was a downright natural beauty. Devoid of any makeup he could detect, her innate glow only served to accent the light in her eyes. Her long, dark brown hair hung down her back in waves and her shade of olive sun-kissed skin gave a hint of her Italian heritage. She had perfectly arched eyebrows, classically high cheekbones that most women only wished they'd been born with, and a dash of freckles across the bridge of her nose that gave her an impish appearance. She was anything but mischievous and he usually bore the brunt of her razor sharp wit. Her radiant green eyes met his before she immediately looked away, taking the light with her.

"Ernie, I figured you'd still be here," Henley said, jingling the keys in her hand. She stayed near the door. "I'm stopping over at the grocery store to pick up some fresh dairy and produce for the new guest that's arriving later this afternoon. Is there anything you need?"

"As a matter of fact, there is. Let me grab a pen and a piece of paper from Mabel. I'll let Mav fill you in on what's happening."

Mav held his coffee in one hand while his keys and shades were in the other. He studied Henley and noticed that she'd crossed her arms, her own set of keys closed tightly in her fist. He didn't understand why he made her so defensive when he'd made a point to be kind to her and not spar with her this year as he'd done in the past. She'd been a rather well-known fashion model back in her day, so he would imagine that she was used to men appreciating her beauty. He'd never been lewd and Ernie would have hit him upside the head if he'd been anything other than a perfect gentleman; however, it was in Mav's character to be a bit of a challenge to warm up to. Henley always appeared so relaxed around the other guys and her superior attitude toward him was starting to give him a complex.

"Yellowstone experienced a six point one earthquake earlier this morning," Mav said, taking the time to explain to her what was going on, and not only because Tank had instructed him to either. Henley lived up at the lodge in one of the cabins on the back of the property, so she was well versed in Ernie's obsession with prepping. He wasn't the type that would ever consider going on that television show about doomsday people, but Mav was pretty damn sure that he would receive a perfect score on their readiness scale. "He thinks it's going to be a catalyst for the caldera springing a leak."

"Let me guess," Henley said with a trace of a smile. "He doesn't want you to leave today."

"I wish I could stay longer to ease his mind that I'm not going to get taken out by an eruption, but I'm back on duty at the post on Wednesday. FEMA has already come out with a statement that everything's fine." Mav didn't know why he was explaining his reasoning to Henley when she most likely didn't give a shit what the hell he did or didn't do. He looked over to see Ernie scribbling his list on Mabel's pad, but Mav couldn't bring himself to leave without saying goodbye. "Tank's going to give you an extensive list of items that he already has ten of, but he's going to stock up a little more to top off the pile. Do me a favor and have dinner with him tonight, all right?"

"Have you thought that maybe he's using this morning's events to keep you here just because he doesn't want you to go?" Henley asked, her gaze also landing on Tank. The green of her eyes softened and Mav suddenly saw a side of her he hadn't witnessed before. "Look, Mav, he loves you like a son. He gets lonely up here sometimes, but especially right after you and the guys leave. It gets harder for him every year."

"I know that," Mav admitted, honestly surprised that Henley would share that with him. He didn't know what made him say the next words, but they'd come out before he could stop them. "Which is why I'm considering moving here sometime next year. Sheriff Ramsey mentioned in passing that he was considering retirement next spring and I've already spoken to him in private about my interest in the position. I would appreciate it if you could keep that quiet until Ramsey's spoken to the town board."

"You're moving here?" Henley seemed shocked more than anything and Mav wasn't certain how to react to that question. It wasn't like she would have to deal with him any differently than she did now. His local presence didn't necessarily require her to change her perspective. She usually left him and the guys alone when they were in town anyway. "I guess I didn't take you for a small town kind of man."

"And why would that be?" Mav asked, genuinely wanting to know why she would think that. She hadn't taken the time to get to know him, so that presumption was a little out of left field. "Because I work around the city of Chicago?"

"There's just not a lot to do around here. Not a lot of action," Henley replied with a small shrug, appearing uncomfortable with his question. "It's home for me, but I like the quiet."

"And what do you think I do on Friday and Saturday nights?" Mav couldn't keep himself from pushing her just a little bit further. Did she think he partied it up every weekend? Is that why she had such a low opinion of him? "Do you think I'm out on the town drinking until I can't stand up and stirring up shit?"

"No, I didn't say that. You can do that here at Miner's Bar." Henley was shaking her head in defense and she'd furrowed her brow in displeasure at his misinterpretation. His curiosity was somewhat appeased when she continued to elaborate and her frustration was rather endearing…not that she would agree. "What I mean is the only women here are either married or over seventy years old. You'd get bored within a month and—"

"I'm sorry," Mav said, not apologetic in the least and damned tired of tiptoeing around the subject that they'd both been avoiding. He held up his coffee to gesture toward Ms. Stein, who was more in her early sixties than she was in her seventies. "I think you're over exaggerating. I also wasn't aware you knew my taste in women. How do you know I don't prefer a woman with a little more experience?"

"What?" Henley asked with an exasperated laugh. When Mav didn't even crack a smile, her own faded until those naturally shaded rose lips were in a perfectly shaped O. Her eyes switched over to Ms. Stein, who was sitting in the corner of the diner with her eyes glued to the television. "I-I didn't...I mean, I never thought—"

"No, you didn't. You should try it sometime," Mav commented, unable to keep up the ruse any longer. He stepped closer until he could feel her body heat and she had to tilt her face up to his. He would have given anything to kiss her, but this wasn't the place or time. "Henley, the only woman I'm interested in has been you, and when you finally come out from under that cabin tucked back at the edge of civilization and return to the land of the living...at least you know I'll be close enough to hear you when you change your mind."

"Here, Henley," Ernie said, coming at just the right moment to save Henley from replying. Mav stepped away, allowing her to grab the small piece of paper out of Tank's hand. It wasn't hard to notice that there was a slight tremor in her fingers, and Mav patted himself on the back for finally managing to get a spark out of her that wasn't tainted with irritation. Maybe Ernie was right. It was time Mav took a step forward and pressed Henley a little harder. "I'll meet you over at the store in around twenty minutes to help carry out the bags. I want to make a quick stop at Marvin's Hardware Store."

Mav figured Henley purposefully didn't look his way again

as she and Ernie finished their conversation. She'd schooled her features with a half-smile that was only meant for Ernie. Mav would have given anything to know her thoughts, but it wasn't long after that she departed and tipped the bell above the door. Mav was left behind to stare at Ernie's weathered face and sharp blue eyes, bringing them right back to where they'd started…shit.

"Do you really want to take the chance of leaving Henley here?" Ernie smoothed down his mustache as his focus became even more precise. "All I'm asking is that you stay another day to play it safe, Marine."

"Henley is safer here than any other place in the United States according to you." Mav finally slipped his shades on and stepped around Tank, holding up a hand to the residents still eating their meals or watching the news. "You all behave until I make it back here this winter. I'll be back for the holidays if I don't have to work."

A round of goodbyes echoed throughout the diner as Mav exited the door with Ernie on his heels. Mav hadn't even bothered to look at the television. He was torn between returning home to his responsibilities and caving into the demands of a worried man who was more like a father. He did his damnedest to steel his mind against his wavering decision. He made it to his fully outfitted Jeep Rubicon before turning to make Ernie understand why staying behind over a common natural occurrence wasn't feasible.

"Son, I try to never ask of you anything that you can't deliver," Ernie said, beating Mav to the punch. "If I have to bring up the favor you owe me then it might as well be now…so I'm calling in my chips."

Mav barked out a humorless laugh and leaned back against the door to his somewhat dirty vehicle. He never would have imagined that Tank would bring up something that happened when he was a green recruit out of boot camp.

Mav had started out hanging with a couple of fellow Marines in his new command that were headed down the wrong path and Master Gunnery Sergeant Yates had pulled Mav's young ass out of the CO's line of fire when he roasted Mav's running partners at NJP. An Article Eleven hearing so early in his career would have certainly ruined any chance of Mav getting ahead in the Corps. MGySgt. Yates had seen something in Maverick's character that caused him to call in a favor. The CO had deferred to his MGySgt. A lieutenant colonel in the Corps rarely took counsel from anyone outside a select few that have earned his loyalty. Mav had benefited from the fact that MGySgt. Yates held the CO's trust and confidence. Unfortunately, that meant that Mav had attracted the MGySgt's ire and would have to pay the piper for his earlier poor choices.

As Mav's mentor, Ernie had ridden him hard and made a fine Marine out of the young wayward youth. It had directly determined how his career in the Marines had played out. He owed Ernie his career and start in life. It wasn't something he could dismiss out of hand. Ernie never cracked a smile; his subdued features made it obvious he would resort to any level to get Mav to stay.

"I'd say that was a low blow, but you and I both know I could never repay you for saving my ass." Mav took a deep breath, trying to figure out some excuse he could tell his sergeant back home that he wouldn't be making his shift on Wednesday. And now he would owe another trooper a big favor—so much for having the holidays off. "Fine. I'll stay for one day. But I head out tomorrow if nothing happens by morning."

"Good." Ernie wasn't triumphant in any way. What concerned Mav was the fact his mentor appeared rather assured in his judgment of what was to come. "Walk with me to Marvin's shop and then we'll help Henley carry out the items I'm having her pick up at the grocery store. The list is extensive, but when the town realizes that the world is about to plummet into ten years of winter...it'll be people like Rat who will clean off the shelves intent on schilling his neighbors out of any chance at surviving the week while not giving a good goddamn about anyone other than himself."

"You'll show me these calculations you're talking about?" Mav asked, pushing himself off of his Jeep and falling into step beside Ernie. "I'm going to need something a little more concrete than those docudramas you keep watching, and that includes all that conspiracy theory horseshit too."

"We'll make an evening of it," Ernie promised gruffly, pulling a battered baseball cap out of his back pocket and sliding it over his silver hair. "After you come to see and believe that what I've said over the years is in fact the truth…that's when you'll sound like the zealot and not me."

"Why is that?" Mav inquired, not understanding where Ernie was going with this. Mav didn't want his coffee to go to waste, so he took a drink of the now lukewarm liquid and grimaced. He tossed the cup into the trashcan when they finally crossed the road with regret, knowing he would need the caffeine later. "You think I'll drink the Kool-Aid, Master Guns?"

"Oh, you'll drink it all right. Every last drop, son." Ernie pulled open the door to Marvin's hardware store but stopped to look at Mav. "And that's when you'll be calling the rest of our Marines to haul their asses back up here before it's too damn late. By that time we'll have to defend what we've got."

CHAPTER TWO

HENLEY STILL COULDN'T believe that Mav had caved into Ernie's demands regarding staying for another day. It shouldn't have mattered to her, but somehow it did. To add on to her bad day, the old coot had talked her into having dinner with both of them this evening. She would have tried her damnedest to get out of it, but it wasn't like they didn't know she didn't have anything else to do. She had considered an outright refusal though, but that would have certainly have made her look like the bitch Mav undoubtedly thought she was. She did have two reasonably solid justifications for not going, but it wasn't like she could tell Ernie she didn't want to hear his nonsense regarding a supervolcano and she certainly couldn't convey to Mav that she wasn't going to deal with the underlying attraction between them right now. She was screwed no matter how this evening ended, but she could make certain it wasn't in the literal sense.

It was quite cool here in the evenings despite it being spring, so Henley had changed into a pink lightweight fleece sweater. She didn't want Mav to think she was going to any extra lengths in her looks just because he was going to be there, so she purposefully didn't put on any make-up and used a hair tie to secure the long strands in a semi-bun on top of her head. She took one last look in her bathroom mirror before she was satisfied with her appearance.

Henley made her way into the living room after having closed the blinds in her bedroom and turning on her small bedside lamp. The sun was just now setting, but it would be dark by the time she returned. The small cabin was only one of two out of twelve cabins that contained a modern indoor bathroom. Ernie claimed the other at the front of the property. Her cabin was the last in line uphill from the main lodge. The remaining ten cabins were for guests and they used separate two-hole outhouses behind each unit. The idea was that log cabins provided a rustic and primitive experience, yet each had electric power and a natural gas heat pump. The outhouses also used a shared septic system and were heated since they were also equipped with a shower stall and sink—so much for truly roughing it.

Ernie had capitalized on the fact that people wanted the facade of primitive camping, but without the inconvenience. Two 400kw military surplus generators, converted to burn natural gas, powered the entire Lost Mountain Lodge complex. One was designated for primary power with the other in standby as one hundred percent backup. Ernie had purchased them—along with enough replacement parts to build three more—at a Defense Reutilization Marketing Office (DRMO) auction back in Twenty-Nine Palms, California. It cost him nearly as much as the auction to truck the entire lot of gear north to Washington and up to the top of his valley below Lost Mountain.

The lodge and ten of the log cabins had already been on the property when he bought the place nearly fifteen years ago, but it wasn't the land that closed the deal for Ernie. It was the plentiful native mountain spring water source and the natural gas well that provided enough fuel and water to sustain the camp indefinitely.

Henley loved the simplicity that the fishing cabin gave her, especially after having lived a life where she was basically on call twenty-four seven. The paparazzi that had surrounded her back then hadn't even allowed her to go to the grocery store without having her picture plastered all over the gossip magazines and websites while sporting no make-up and crudely asking the public if she'd gained weight in the jeans she'd been wearing. Never mind dressing in a dress or a skirt. They would line up to take pictures as she'd exited her vehicle in hopes of catching a shot of her panties. Unfortunately that had happened one too many times. The anxiety had eaten away at her until she'd literally lost those pounds they'd been referring to and she'd ended up in the hospital with esophageal ulcers. It had been a constant battle with her self-esteem and in the end…it just hadn't been worth the effects on her personal well-being.

And that was the problem with Mav. He didn't see her as anything other than a woman on the front page of the magazines. Henley remembered meeting him as if it had been yesterday instead of three years ago when she'd returned home with only one suitcase to her name, leaving everything else behind in California. The group of men he'd been with had been so nice, Mav included, and she'd thought of no one other than him that entire first year…until he'd returned for his annual visit.

Finding a couple of magazines with her picture plastered on the front pages in the back of his truck had caused her more pain than what she'd felt in her stomach when she'd been in the hospital. Those magazines had been issued a couple of years prior, so he must have gone to some lengths to get a hold of them. One of the issues had even been recalled due to slander, although luckily at the time it hadn't been about her. She'd thought Maverick was different, but even he saw her as nothing more than an object. She'd asked for that life and she'd gotten it, so she had no one to blame but herself. It had been easier—still was—to keep her distance from him. The pull she felt from him made her want things that she knew she could never have without giving up a part of her pride. That wasn't going to happen.

"One dinner and then he'll be gone," Henley whispered to herself as she slipped out the front door and strolled down the gravel path toward the main lodge. "You can do this, girl."

The large building occupied the center of the camp. It contained her office and a check-in desk off of the foyer. The rest of the first floor facilities were centered around the great room with its massive river rock fireplace. It had an old log cabin charm on a grand scale and yet contained a rustic tasteful décor. To the right of the fireplace toward the back of the room was an archway leading to the taproom and bar. It had all the amenities of an English dart tavern, which was always well stocked with virtually any liquor or beverage imaginable.

To the left of the fireplace was the passage to the restaurant and a truly splendid commercial kitchen. Farther left was a spacious main area with several French doors leading to a long, glassed-in four-season room filled with comfortable pine deck furniture and multiple overhead fans running off of an old-fashioned pulley system. Flanking the main room on the right were two separate archways leading to either end of the library and game room. Inside these walls were lined shelves, floor to ceiling, stuffed with a great number of volumes spanning hundreds of subjects. Quite to Ernie's amusement, many of the guests had never bothered with his unique library, preferring to utilize the room's billiard or gaming tables covered in their green felt rather than enjoying a good read in one of the many overstuffed high-backed leather chairs.

Opposite the check-in desk and Henley's office in the foyer was the stairway leading to the second floor balcony overlooking the great room and granting access to the more modern guestrooms in the main lodge. The remainder of the guest cabins were arrayed around the main lodge in a semicircle, but all of them could be seen from the thin lane she was walking.

Henley continued toward the lodge, ignoring the early spring mosquitos that wanted a fresh meal and the sounds of the horny crickets in the surrounding forest. She was not able to stop herself from looking over to the right where Mav usually stayed, his lodging tucked in amongst the foliage. Why did it stand out more than the others?

Henley finally reached the main entrance and she sighed to herself as she opened the door before she could change her mind. The one thing that prevented her from running back to her cabin were Mav's earlier words. He thought she'd buried herself in her cabin and wasn't living her life? She felt more at peace here than she ever had in front of the runway lights, so he didn't have the right to judge her. Why then was her heart pounding and the blood rushing in her ears? She didn't have anything to prove to this man or any other. It was because Mav's earlier words continued to haunt her and she didn't want that hanging over her head for another whole year. She'd face him head on and make him see that she was just fine here in Lost Summit. This was her life and she damn well loved it.

"Henley, we're back in the dining room," Ernie said as he emerged from the passageway leading to the restaurant.

There were a couple of doors to storage and utility areas on either side of the hallway leading to the open dining area. Mav was sitting at one of the dozen unused tables looking at some papers that were strewn all over it. He peered at her with his sensual brown eyes, looking exactly like he had the day she'd met him the first time at this very place. As a matter of fact, he might even be wearing the same cargo pants and faded brown USMC T-shirt. He was at least six feet tall, with a broad chest and biceps bigger than her thighs. His brown hair was closely cropped on the sides, but was thicker and longer on top and swept to the side in a casual wave. His jaw was square and his lips were what people in her old business would call downright sinful. Sexual frustration was what she was suffering from, but he wouldn't be the one to satisfy it.

"You need to see this data that Ernie has collected."

Henley crossed the threshold into the room and resisted the urge to run her palms down the sides of her denim. Mav was watching her too closely and she didn't want him to know that he affected her in any way. It was one of the reasons she enjoyed having the other four men around. They were a buffer, although she truly enjoyed their company. Mav, on the other hand, got under her skin worse than the ticks that caused Lyme disease around these parts. That would probably be preferable over this underlying tension between them. He knew exactly what to say to rile her and he seemed to take pleasure in doing so. She'd been proud of herself this morning at the diner when she'd walked out without rising to his bait. She'd do the same this evening and looked forward to when she'd be able to breathe a little easier come tomorrow morning. There was no way that Ernie would be able to talk Mav into staying again.

"See what?" Henley asked, walking right behind the service counter to the glass-topped beverage cooler to pull out a bottle of water. Mav shifted to the side and rested his arm on the back of his chair so he could see her. She had to look away when he lifted the beer bottle to his lips. "I've had the radio on since we got back from town and nothing has happened that would indicate something more major than a natural series of smaller aftershocks."

"Tank has collected enough data over the years to have a valid point on what would happen to the United States if the caldera at Yellowstone erupted," Mav replied, although his eyes said something completely different. It appeared he still wasn't convinced that Ernie was right about it occurring anytime soon. "You should read this stuff and make your own best judgment."

Henley really didn't have a choice but to join both men in front of the open table facing a small row of three booths against the opposite wall, so she slowly made her way over to the nondescript dining table as she unscrewed the cap on her water bottle. Ernie would hire local workers to staff the dining room during the height of tourist season—a couple servers and a cook who managed a decent breakfast, lunch, and dinner service. Anything outside of that and the guests had to rely on the diner in town or use the kitchen as long as they cleaned up after themselves.

Once Ernie finished preparing the side dishes, wrapping the potatoes in foil with a bit of salt and butter, and placing the steaks in a black pepper marinade, they would carry their preparations over to his cabin. It was the same as hers with basically three rooms—the living area, the bedroom, and a small bathroom that only allowed for a stand-up shower. The main room contained a couch, two chairs, and a coffee table plus a kitchenette. It was simple, homey, and efficient, just the way Tank had intended it to be.

Tank emerged from the kitchen and asked for some help getting everything back to his cabin. Mav made sure he carefully packed up the stack of papers detailing all of the information Ernie had put together. They arrived at Tank's place after a short walk.

The fireplace was the focal point of the cabin, with multi-colored river rock forming the hearth. The rough-hewn thick wooden mantel contained pictures of Ernie and the guys from their annual vacations, but there was one with only Tank and Mav that was front and center. Both men had on their sunglasses and were wearing smiles as they held up their catches from the day on one of the local lakes. It had been a beautiful morning and one that had been captured on film as a reminder of how close the two men were.

"You don't think it will erupt from the sound of your voice." Henley leaned back in the chair after having delivered everything she'd carried onto the counter and made herself as comfortable as she could, considering Mav's smoldering eyes had made the room rather stifling. She fiddled with the cap on her water bottle again, not really thirsty. "Like I said, there's been nothing on the news."

"I wouldn't be making assumptions without looking at the

evidence first," Ernie chastised, taking a seat next to Mav after shooting him a sideways look. Henley smiled for the first time since this morning, loving when Tank got his feathers ruffled. Mav hid his own grin, probably figuring he was closest to Ernie and not wanting to get backhanded in the head. Tank shuffled through some of his papers and sorted them into some kind of order until he found the one he was looking for and handed it over to Henley. She secured the cap and placed the bottle in between her legs as she leaned forward to take it. "This is a report that documents what can occur if an earthquake was large enough to be a catalyst, a precursor to a major event."

Henley shared a look with Mav, whose brown eyes held a bit of skepticism at what Ernie had just given her. She could see Mav's hesitation in saying he didn't quite believe what he was reading, but she'd decide for herself and then give her honest opinion. Scanning the document, she didn't see anything that stood out. It took her around ten minutes to read the report and by the time she was done, she understood Mav's uncertainty.

"Tank, I admit that this is a pretty dim view of what could happen." Henley did find it a bit peculiar that there was a Yellowstone Volcano Observatory at the University of Utah, where the caldera was monitored every second of the day. She hadn't known that and she doubted most of the public was aware of it either. "I do see where you're coming from, but the geologist who wrote this also states that he doesn't expect

Yellowstone to explode for another one hundred thousand years."

"The odds are one in seven hundred thousand every year." Ernie pointed to the paper still in her hand. "Those are the same probabilities of getting struck by lightning."

"It's still just sheer speculation unless certain specific events follow a large quake. None of which has happened," Henley argued, not willing to let Ernie's paranoia get out of hand. She was surprised that Mav wasn't saying more, but then again…she wasn't sure why he stayed in town either. "We can't live our lives in fear worrying about what might happen in the future."

"It's not the future I'm worried about," Ernie shot back, leaning his elbows against his knees. "It's the present, and the two of you are putting your lives in danger if neither one of you can see that a six point one earthquake followed by swarms almost just as severe *is* the catalyst all these scientists have been talking about for the last few years."

"Going on the assumption that you're right, where are the events that your research said would follow?" Henley asked as she leaned forward and placed the report on the table. "Is there really anything we can do about it if it did happen? There would be virtually nothing left of Wyoming, Montana, or Idaho should the caldera explode from the facts given in your report. After that it's only a matter of time before the ash cloud travels and sulfur dioxide is released into the atmosphere."

"Together they would cause temperatures to plummet,

pushing us into a volcanic winter for years," Mav added on, taking another swig of his beer. "Nothing that we've read gives an indication of how far apart the catalyst would be from the main event. Are we talking hours? Days? Years? Tank, even you can understand that we can't put our lives on hold for something that may never happen."

"While Mav starts the grill up, why don't you show me why you think we'd be okay up here in Lost Summit?" Henley suggested this for a few reasons. The main one was to give Mav something to do besides stare at her. That didn't mean she wasn't thinking of Ernie in this situation. She really was curious as to why he felt their small valley would be protected from an apocalyptic event that would affect the entire world, unless he thought he could fit every resident in that bunker of his. "I don't know about you guys, but I'm rather hungry from all the extra errands I ran today."

"Sounds like a plan," Mav replied with a relieved smile as he unfolded his large frame from the couch. He went to the small refrigerator to retrieve the steaks that Ernie had marinated, along with the grilling utensils. She had a hard time looking away from his muscles as they moved underneath his shirt, but then Tank leaned forward and pulled out a large map from underneath the other papers, spreading it out on the coffee table and demanding her attention. "When you guys are done in here, come outside with another beer and join me as I master the grill."

"Look at this," Ernie instructed as he ignored Mav's intention to lighten the mood. Tank used his callused index finger to circle a large area around Wyoming, Montana, and Idaho. Henley breathed a little easier when the door closed behind Maverick, allowing her to concentrate on what was in front of her. "This area will be eradicated rather quickly once the eruption occurs. No one within hundreds of miles of the caldera could survive the initial blast, and then that's when the ash will begin to spew into the upper atmosphere to be carried by the prevailing winds."

Henley sat in her chair and listened as Tank went on to explain that most of the United States within seventy-two hours would be covered in ten centimeters or more of ash. Most people think of volcanic ash as the same as that on the end of a cigarette, but that wasn't the case. It is made of pulverized rock and glass shards. It would limit visibility and worse, especially should it rain, the ash would double in weight by at least fifty percent, if not more. The massive weight of ten centimeters of wet ash alone would collapse the roofs on most houses. The list of what volcanic ash could do was downright frightening, including contaminating the water supplies and having the ability to affect radio and satellite communications to the outside world. The worst? Breathing in the ash could coat the inside of their lungs and when the residue mixed with the moisture inside one's body, it could basically turn into a cement-like substance. It would be a horrible smothering death and if Ernie was trying to scare her, he was doing a damn fine job of it.

"Tank, you're telling me we're safe here in Lost Summit even if all of this were to happen," Henley said, softly laying her hand on his arm. She finally had his attention. "That would depend on Mother Nature quite a bit and from what you're showing me, going north into Canada might be a better choice. I know what you're trying to do, but Mav and the rest of the group cannot put their lives on hold to move here based on a chance of something happening. What would they do? How would they support themselves? It's not like the silver mine is open for them to have a place to work. We are basically a tourism town and the only thriving business is this fishing lodge and the camping grounds that Rat owns. Anyone that had small children moved out years ago, leaving behind the older generation that didn't want to leave their home. There's no industry here for them to support themselves."

"If that earthquake this morning was the catalyst, the boys need to start this way tonight," Ernie exclaimed, effectively shutting down this conversation. He was adamant that he was right and there wasn't anything that she or Mav could say to change his mind. He stood up in a huff and grabbed his favorite coffee mug that he used every single day. It was chipped and faded, but the decal of his medals from his years in the Corps could still be seen. It had been a gift from Mav. "I'll meet you outside."

Henley sat for a moment and watched Ernie as he walked to the counter and went about making another pot of coffee. It was easy to see his frustration at the fact that they didn't believe him, but it would be different if he could only give them something other than a half-assed guess. Earthquakes were common and FEMA had already come out and said that everything was fine. What was it about this specific occurrence that had Ernie all keyed up?

She really didn't want to be alone with Mav, but this might be a good opportunity for the two of them to figure out how they were going to address this situation. Ernie was the most grounded man Henley had the privilege of knowing. He wasn't prone to illusions of fantasy and, although he had been constructing a survival bunker for many years for that worst-case scenario, it hadn't consumed his entire life. She'd always viewed it as a hobby and his way of being prepared, but now she wasn't so sure.

Henley left the papers on the coffee table and made sure she had her bottle of water as she headed for the door. The sun was now setting off to the west and creating a beautiful skyline that she'd come to love watching each and every evening. Those horny crickets were out in full force and having their own particular conversation. Walking around the corner to where Mav would be manning the grill, she didn't look his way as she sat at the picnic table Ernie used in the evenings for dinner. It was rather chilly and she regretted not bringing a heavier jacket.

Mav had the radio turned to a news channel and from what she was hearing the talk of today's earthquake had already run its course. The announcers had moved on to a nuclear materials ban that several countries were trying to negotiate. Commentators from both sides were giving their viewpoint.

"I'm not saying he's wrong, but I don't think it's going to happen today." Mav's deep voice cut through the drone of the radio and Henley finally looked his way. With the tongs in one hand and a basting brush in the other, he looked ready to do battle. She almost smiled at his appearance, but she caught herself in time. Besides, his words were nothing to be happy about. "Hell, I don't think it will be in our lifetime."

"You need to tell him of your future plans," Henley suggested, starting to peel off the label on her water bottle. "It will make Tank feel better knowing that you'll eventually be here for good. Plus, it will get him to ease up on you tomorrow morning when it's time to leave."

"Sheriff Ramsey has another year to do toward retirement before I'd be able to replace him." Mav set the basting brush down and the tongs on the plate that he had positioned on the side shelf of the grill. He closed the large chrome cover, grabbed his bottle of beer, and then took the seat across from her. The picnic table instantly became miniature, but she never broke eye contact with him. She refused to let him think he got to her in any way. "I had wanted the move to be a surprise, but I can see that I'll have to tell Ernie now. The way he's pushing this though, I don't think it will be enough of a reassurance."

They fell into a somewhat comfortable silence, although Henley was on edge that Mav might bring up their previous conversation they'd had at the diner. She didn't want to talk about this underlying attraction between them when it had no place to go. Honestly, she was rather surprised he *had* brought it up this morning. She knew exactly where he stood and how he thought of her. Being armed with that information was half the battle, but she didn't want to even enter the battlefield.

"He loves you." Henley didn't hear Ernie exiting the house yet, so she looked around wondering what they could talk about that kept them on neutral ground. They'd just covered that he should tell Tank about his intentions to move here, so there was really nothing else to say. She certainly wasn't going to talk about her past and she didn't want to know him any more than she already did, so she chose the safest topic. "I take it you were able to get your shift covered?"

"Yes, although it wasn't easy finding someone on such short notice." Mav rested his elbows on the old wood of the picnic table, the bottle of beer in his right hand. His brown eyes had settled on her face and she tried not to regret that she hadn't worn make-up. There wasn't a need to impress him. "We've never done this in all the years that I've been visiting."

"Done what?" Henley asked, unable to prevent herself from asking what he meant. She could feel herself walking into a trap, but her pride wouldn't allow it to happen any other way. He couldn't be talking about eating a meal out on this patio since they'd done that at least once every time he and the other guys would arrive for their annual vacation. She always let the group have their time with Ernie while she kept her distance after the first night. It had worked out perfectly, so she was curious as to what Mav could be talking about. "Discuss a supervolcano?"

"Have a conversation," Mav replied, not even bothering to smile at her humorous attempt to lighten the mood. The intensity of his stare was a hell of a lot more effective than any photographer could have captured on camera. "You have discussions with Berke, Owen, Mason, and Van as if they were long lost friends. You don't do that with me. In fact, you're usually berating me over doing something that isn't up to your impossible standards."

"That's not true. You're usually catching up with Tank when you get into town and I don't want to be the one to interfere in that." Henley was being drawn into a web when she'd rather be flying away from the sticky subject Mav had just broached. She'd peeled off the label on the water bottle and started to fold it up in a little square. "Besides, I know all there is to know about you from Ernie. I've heard all the stories and then some."

The vise on Henley's chest eased when the corner of Mav's mouth lifted in a half smile at her reminder of his time underneath Tank's command. The men had shared good times and bad, but they'd relied on each other and would now have a connection throughout their lives. She was somewhat envious of their close relationship.

"You might know the things that happened during our tours, but you don't know *me*, Henley. All you have to do is simply ask and that could change," Mav said, his voice an octave lower and instigating a shiver that ran down her spine. He wasn't willing to let this go and she wavered, wondering if he really saw her for who she was. She breathed a sigh of relief when the sound of Ernie's cabin door opened and he walked around the corner of the house with his cup of coffee in hand. "Tank, five more minutes on the steaks."

It was at that moment that the radio announcer's voice came through the evening air and cut through the chattering of the crickets. They fell silent. The only other sound was that of the steaks sizzling from the heat. Ernie was now standing at the end of the table where he'd set his mug down on the weathered wood. To his credit he didn't look smug or issue *I told you so's.*

"A vent has opened up in the Yellowstone caldera, but the initial reports we are receiving say that it is only high-pressure ash being released and that the hole was considerably smaller in size than what would be considered a significant threat. Officials have confirmed that they are vacating the park as a precaution, but that residents in Wyoming, Montana, and Idaho have nothing to fear for now."

The report continued on, but no other relevant information was being given. Ernie slowly lowered himself beside Henley as she and Mav exchanged looks of concern. She was positive that Mav had expected the evening to pass by uneventfully, but this threw them an inside curve. It was apparently one that Ernie was willing to swing at.

"Mav, I think it's time you call the boys."

CHAPTER THREE

MAV GLANCED AT the green digital display on the microwave and noted that it was going on twenty-three hundred hours. The evening had gone to shit from the moment the radio news announcement had been made regarding the initial states of volcanic activity at Yellowstone. Henley now appeared to be recognizing this was not a theoretical exercise any longer and she was treading on tires right alongside Ernie. Hell, Tank had taken her back inside the cabin and went into further detail regarding the caldera while Mav finished grilling dinner over his own active heat source, cursing the way his night had just gone to hell. He'd finally been having a moment with Henley and it had come to a complete screeching halt just when he thought he was making a bit of progress. Shit, after joining the duo inside Mav now had more knowledge of earthquakes and volcanoes than he had interest in learning.

Mav figured Ernie would be monitoring the radio for the rest of the night, and by that same reasoning there was no way that Henley had gone right to sleep after being told the next thousand year ice age was about to get underway...that was if they actually survived the aftermath of the massive supervolcano with its own ten years of volcanic winter. Ernie hadn't diminished the gory details and he'd certainly strung together a colorful sentence when Mav had opted to call Berke in the morning rather than right away. When Tank said that he would take care of it, Mav had reminded him of the men's reaction to Ernie's most recent improvements to the bunker complex...that had gotten a different response with the same meaning. It was better to wait for additional information before calling the four other men to tell them Ernie thought a monumental natural disaster was in their foreseeable future and they needed to drop everything to return to the place that they had just left the day before.

Mav didn't feel like being alone, but then again he couldn't be in the same cabin as Tank mumbling about how all the fucking politicians were going to be eating crow before too long. Ernie had become more insistent as time wore on and Mav didn't want to say anything he'd regret. The odds of what Tank was saying weren't even remotely in his favor. How had the situation gotten so out of hand so quickly? Mav should have left town this morning like he had originally planned and maybe he wouldn't have encouraged Ernie to be literally thinking that Yellowstone was about to have a major eruption.

Stepping outside into the dark of night, Mav used the light of the moon to lead him to the back of the camp where Henley's cabin was located. For some reason the gas lamps along the path hadn't been turned on tonight. The gravel path was easily visible in the available moonlight and Mav continued walking, taking notice of how cold the early spring night air had become. This season tended to bring out Mother Nature's hormones and while she had hot flashes during the day, she had ice in her veins at night. The few early mosquitos he had seen must have decided it was a little too cold as well, for they were nowhere to be seen or heard now. Mav found himself thinking it was odd that even the frogs and crickets had turned in for the night and he questioned his own sanity regarding the potential natural disaster and its effects it might have on nature as a whole.

Mav was only feet away from Henley's door when something stopped him in his tracks. He didn't know what it was at first…he couldn't put a finger on it, but there was a stillness around him that was ominous. He took a moment to look up toward the sky that didn't contain one single cloud to obscure the stars. The moon was large and bright, as if to shed light on something only it was aware of. Not even the leaves on the trees were moving. It was as if the outside world was holding its breath and had ceased its relentless march in time. He knew this feeling…it called out to him from the past, the agonizing pause just prior to kicking off combat operations. Knowing full well that the guys would ridicule him for what he was about to say, he still reached into his cargo pants to pull out his cell phone. He didn't waste time accessing the display he needed and then connecting to the first person listed on the preprogrammed speed dial list.

"Mav, I'm going to have to call you back," Berke said as he finally answered his phone. He spoke over the additional voices in the background, which had to be at the shooting range he owned and operated in Texas. Mav was surprised it was open this late at night. "You'd think I was gone for a goddamned year instead of a week. It'll take me days to get this mess sorted out."

"Berke, have you been listening to the news today?" Mav asked in a low voice, not wanting Henley to know he was outside her door quite yet. "Radio? Television?"

"Shit, don't tell me another terrorist attack happened in the States." Berke continued talking to someone in the background, but Mav could picture him walking into his private office in the back of the building as the voices finally faded. "Hold on."

"There hasn't been an attack, but this could potentially have much worse consequences."

"Well, this isn't exactly how I thought my day would go when I got up this morning." Berke must have seen a headline on his computer for him to make that comment. He had always been the one in the group to lighten the mood with some humor. It failed miserably this time, mostly because Mav didn't think this was something the media was blowing out of proportion. Quite to the contrary. They were downplaying every aspect of the developing situation as if they were taking their orders directly from FEMA. Ernie had definitely gotten to him. "Yellowstone? Don't tell me that Tank thinks a run of the mill earthquake and some pressure releasing is going to morph somehow into a gigantic apocalyptic event."

"You might say that." Mav had always been one to listen to his gut and walking outside to the deathly silence when only an hour before had been filled with wildlife told him something was approaching. Nothing good would come of this. He could feel it in his bones and he had to laugh at the fact that he now sounded just like Ernie. "Listen, we all know that Tank's been harping on this for years and we've been placating him, but what if he's right this time? What if the earthquake that occurred this morning is a catalyst for something much more?"

"Then I'd say on the upside we're looking at an early winter with above average snowfall on the slopes."

"Berke, I don't think we should risk our lives even on a five percent chance of this thing hitting the fan. Tank wanted me to call each of you this evening but I was able to hold him off. I'm calling now because there's something in the air that I can't explain. It's like when we were over there—that feeling that things were about to go sideways. It's in my gut. I just know all of a sudden that something's going to happen very soon."

"We risked our lives every damn day in the service, Mav. Besides, it's not like we can do anything to stop something of this magnitude if it went."

"Don't count on having enough notice to travel here safely, buddy," Mav said, taking his eyes off of the line of trees to the

ESSENTIAL BEGINNINGS

right of Henley's cabin to where a series of pipes, exhaust vents, and cabling emerged from an underground bunker complex which now existed courtesy of a lot of blood, sweat, and tears. It was tucked deep into the hard mountain rock, where many of the entrances and exits started out as part of an old commercial silver mine that finally played out back prior to World War II. "You need to get your ass back up here with the rest of the boys."

"Shit, you're talking about that damn bunker that Tank's been working on for years, aren't you?" Berke pulled the phone away from his mouth as he called out for someone, most likely to show whomever it was what was taking place. "How many times has the media exaggerated events only to have them fizz out to nothing? It's all hype. Smoke and mirrors, brother. There hasn't been another earthquake today, at least anything large from what the media's been reporting—just a couple of minor aftershocks."

"Just wait and see. Be prepared to bug out," Mav warned, figuring Berke had yet to see the segment of news regarding the lone vent that had opened up at the park.

Silence was Mav's answer and he paused for Berke to make another crack, but it didn't come. Berke and the rest of the guys had lined up behind him when Ernie had requested help building certain rooms and capabilities into the bunker. It was originally Tank's hare-brained idea against a nuclear attack from some rogue nation, but over the years it had changed purposes to be used for defense against natural disasters or any type of national emergency. Ernie had taken the good-natured jabs in stride and eventually they'd gotten the facility up and running.

They'd installed generators into a branch tunnel off the main line and then added piping to the natural gas well output into tanks for storage and processing in the lower levels of the mine. As it was, the entire camp ran off of less than sixty-five percent of the primary generator's operational output. The natural gas well had been drilled to five thousand, one hundred and eighty-six feet as a commercial endeavor in the 1970s. The pocket of gas that was tapped had turned out to be sweet non-associated gas almost completely free of hydrogen sulfide. The downside was that the well never produced enough gas to pay for the initial investment. The equipment associated with the project was sold with the property for pennies on the dollar to a land developer.

The then newly retired MGySgt. Ernie Yates bought the entire resort after many years as a marginally successful fishing and hunting camp, the surrounding land all the way up to the top of the valley, and also secured the mineral rights under the land he now owned. It had taken his entire inheritance from his family's lumber mill and sale of the business' interest in old-growth timberland throughout several northeastern states. Whatever the shortcomings of the property as a commercial entity, the well did produce more than enough raw fuel to power the generators and cover the camp's needs.

A concrete shelter with a heavy steel security door now

protected the equipment servicing the wellhead and pump system that transferred the raw natural gas to the mine's lower levels. Over the years Ernie had toiled to convert the mine into a self-sustaining facility with access to water from a natural mountain spring, plentiful fuel to power the generators, and cool dry storage areas where food and supplies could be kept.

"Tank said it would happen just like this, didn't he?" Berke asked without a trace of humor in his tone. He eventually barked out a laugh. "I'm turning into a loon right along with you two. I call the billeting chamber next to the armory if we do end up in that bunker. No one but me could maintain the weapons the way I would and it has more head room."

"Do you still have contacts at USGS?" Mav inquired, ignoring Berke's usual comical attitude. Mav recalled that his friend had briefly dated a woman who'd been in south Texas doing work for the United States Geological Survey organization. She'd only lasted with him as long as her stay, but she was still a point of contact they could use. "Is there a way we can find out what the facts are without the built-in FEMA filter? We might be able to get something accomplished besides sitting on our hands trying to guess if Tank might actually be right about this. I'm starting to feel like it's me who's losing his freaking mind."

"I haven't spoken to Paige in close to a year, Mav. It's not like I can just call and ask her if we're about to go extinct."

"It's not just about this place, Berke." Mav turned when he heard Henley's door open and he realized he must have raised his voice sometime during the conversation. She stepped outside and immediately wrapped her arms around her waist to ward off the chill. He would have done that for her, but he assumed she wouldn't have welcomed his gesture and he aimed to change that soon. "Tank spent the evening showing Henley and I the prevailing wind direction and speed that comes in off of the coast. Lost Summit should be somewhat protected taking in the estimates for at least five to seven days. Ernie thinks we'll be fine here, but at least we'll have the option to take the route up to Canada once everyone gets here. The farther north we're able to go the better…at least while the eruption continues."

"Canada? You can't be serious." Berke's disbelief came in waves over the line and Mav didn't blame him one bit. The reality of everything they'd ever worked for being gone within days wasn't something easily acceptable, especially when they didn't have definitive scientific proof of Tank's theory. Berke was the type of man who needed concrete evidence that a situation had gotten out of their control. Mav took things at face value and reasoned out the objectives on the fly. He made the best decision possible with the available information at his disposal at the time. It had taken him a while to get to that point and he would certainly look like an idiot if nothing happened beyond one vent releasing minimal pressure. Berke continued to try and reason why this was an impossibility. "The odds of that caldera erupting are practically nonexistent. Geologists and seismologists wouldn't have been able to keep that kind of information from the public. Secrets get out and big secrets rise to the top even faster. There are people who monitor this kind of crap twenty-four seven. Public organizations. Let's face the facts—you can't hide shit from social media these days. This is just the news channels stirring the pot and—"

"Let me talk to him," Henley said, holding out her hand. Mav was intrigued that she would insert herself into his conversation, but today had definitely been one of those days full of surprises. He cut Berke off and then handed her the phone. "Berke, it's Henley. Listen, Mav is right. Ernie sat us down tonight and showed us exactly what makes him think today's earthquake is a catalyst for a massive Yellowstone eruption. I'm not prone to hysteria, but even I can see the writing on the wall. We have been overdue for this eruption for nearly forty thousand years. Time has caught up with us all. If what Mav said earlier is true and you have a contact at USGS, then you need to call her now. If this is nothing we can tell that to Tank and ease his worries…then everyone can get on with their lives."

Mav couldn't hear what Berke was saying on the other end of the line, but Henley's lips pursed and her knuckles whitened as her grip tightened on the phone. It was more than apparent that Berke didn't want to make the call. While she continued to listen to his refusal she looked past Mav to the view of the mountain over them in the moonlight. It would most likely be the barrier to diminish the ash that would eventually coat the two-and-a-half mile long sheltered valley.

"We're practically begging you to call her, Berke. That is, if you can get over your personal baggage." Henley wrapped her free arm around her waist and Mav could understand the defensive gesture. "Now…and please call us once you get some answers. It would be nice to get on with our lives if we're all panicking over nothing."

Henley continued speaking and Mav was amazed by how comfortably she spoke with Berke. Why couldn't she be that way with him? What was it about him that put her on edge and had her wanting to take his head off at the slightest innocent comment? It was evident that Berke would be calling them back shortly by the end of their phone conversation. She disconnected the line before Mav had a chance to speak with Berke and then handed over the phone.

"Berke said he'd call Paige and then relay what she has to say to us."

Henley didn't seem too inclined to invite Mav inside and he had to grit his teeth at the apparent brush-off. He'd thought they'd been making progress, but now he felt like they were right back at where they'd started. She stood there with no sign of moving, but he certainly did.

"Henley, how did you know Paige's name?"

Henley's green eyes studied Mav warily and he appreciated that she was second guessing herself. Ernie had told him for the past few years that he'd been taking too long to do something about the underlying attraction between him and

Henley and there was no time like the present to correct that mistake.

"Berke told me," Henley said, like it was an everyday occurrence that Mav's friends divulged personal information to her. "Why?"

"What was the name of the girl that I last dated?" Mav inquired, wondering if she'd catch on to where he was leading this conversation. "The blonde lawyer that gave me her number."

"How would I know?" Henley asked with a snappish tone, waving her hand to add emphasis. "Mav, where are you going with this?"

"What is it about me that puts you off?" Mav put it out there and waited, his heart beating faster when her green eyes deepened into a dark mossy color. Henley parted her lips to say something, but then thought better of it. She slowly shook her head in an attempt to not answer, but he was done letting her run from this. He slid his phone into his front pocket and then stepped forward before gently laying his hands on her shoulders. "You're not comfortable with me like you are with all of them. You stay clear from any situation where we would have to talk to one another privately."

"Mav, don't do this now," Henley whispered, not unraveling her arms from around her waist. As a matter of fact, it appeared that she held herself tighter. "Berke should be calling back and we can find out if there's anything to worry about or if Ernie has us worked up for nothing."

"And what if Berke tells us there is a real threat? I don't want any regrets should that happen."

Mav lowered his head and paused right before his lips met hers. Henley's sharp inhalation gave way to her surprise and he gave her ample time to pull away. When she didn't he brought his hands up to cradle her face and then gently kissed her. Time stood still for the second time that evening. She tasted as sweet as the iced tea she made in the summers. The cool air no longer felt chilled and everything about her seeped into his pores, from the scent of her lavender fragrance to the feel of their heat mingling as she gradually laid her palms on the fabric of his shirt…only to gently push him away.

"Don't." Henley placed the back of her hand against her rosy lips, not yet swollen from their kiss the way they should be. "You shouldn't have—"

"I damn well should have," Mav said, no longer willing to pretend that there was nothing between them. "It's apparent that I've done something or said something that's offended you. This has been going on too long. Tell me what that is so I can fix it."

"Fix it?" Henley asked in the same angry tone she usually spoke to him in. "Mav, you think of me as nothing but a sex object in a picture come to life. There are still magazines in your Jeep from three years ago and I'll be damned if I let you fuck me like one of your other bimbos and then say I don't live up to your idea of who I should be."

Mav was rarely shocked into silence, but then Henley had

the tendency to do that to him on more than one occasion. She thought the magazines in his truck were for him? Hell, he hadn't even realized they were still in there. He'd love to know if she thought he jacked off to them every night, but the fact that she had such a low opinion of him stopped the words from rolling off of his tongue. He let the anger circle inside of him until it was nothing more than a ball he could contain in his chest and he did the only thing he could to stop himself from saying something he'd regret…Mav left her standing there alone in the moonlight.

CHAPTER FOUR

HENLEY RAN COLD water over her face, but it did nothing to erase the exhaustion that had settled into her shoulders and produced the bags underneath her eyes. It was going on eight o'clock in the morning and the lodge had a scheduled guest showing up in an hour. Within the next couple of weeks they would be filled to capacity for the spring season and then it would most likely stay that way throughout the summer. She didn't have time to dwell over what had transpired between her and Mav last night. It wasn't like he could say anything in his defense after she'd finally called him out on finding those damn magazines. It disgusted her that he viewed her as nothing but a sex object, yet she didn't feel any better having it out in the open after stewing over it for so long.

There had been no other events last night, not even Berke calling back, so Henley should be able to breathe a sigh of relief knowing that Mav had most likely already left town. The only problem was she wasn't comforted by that fact and that stressed her out all over again. At this rate she'd be getting an ulcer and that was the last thing she needed to deal with right now. She blotted her face dry with a towel as she walked back into her bedroom with every intention to forget what happened and push it under the rug—at least until next year when Ernie's gang of former Marines arrived for their annual beer fest. Unfortunately, a knock sounded on the door and it didn't take a rocket scientist to figure out it was one of two people.

"Coming," Henley called out, tossing the towel onto her dresser and pulling out a lightweight long-sleeved white shirt. She quickly pulled it over her head and settled the hem over the waist of her denims she'd slipped on earlier. Grabbing a brush, she gave her hair a couple of strokes before reaching for a hair tie and heading for the living room. She breathed a sigh of relief when she heard Ernie tell her to hurry up. Yanking open the door, she found out she'd celebrated too soon. "What is that odd look for?"

"You can march yourself into town and stop Mav from leaving." Ernie lifted his worn ball cap up and then fitted it back onto his head in frustration. Henley wasn't going to go into detail about why his request wasn't going to be granted and she could only hope that their guest arrived sooner than nine o'clock. "I've never heard the likes of this bullshit and now of all times is not the occasion to be battling each other over petty horseshit. I know it's all over a stupid misunderstanding."

Henley could tell that Ernie was baiting her into telling him the entire truth, because she highly doubted Mav had said anything. The two men might be as close as father and son, but Mav wasn't the type to divulge something so personal. And wasn't that just a double standard? She'd accused him last night of basically being depraved and yet she was assuming he was reputable enough not to share details that had passed between them.

"Ernie, Mav told you he had to leave today." Henley gathered her long hair and finally wrapped the black band around the strands, letting it hang down her back. Her own anger was starting to show and she didn't have time for this crap. "I have nothing to do with his decisions, but I do have lodge business to attend to…your business. The caldera didn't erupt and life is going on as scheduled, which includes a guest arriving in less than an hour. I already stocked his refrigerator, but I need to go over the room one more time to make sure I didn't forget anything."

"Go ahead then," Ernie said, his voice gruff as he turned away. The morning sun shined through the trees, giving a glimpse of the bright day ahead and yet it was dim right where she was standing. She'd hurt his feelings and he was letting her know that. "Take care of business."

Henley inhaled deeply and counted to ten, telling herself not to call out to him. He'd said the word *business* as if she didn't know that Mav meant more to him than this fishing lodge. She tried to remind herself that Tank was baiting her, but seeing his hunched shoulders as he walked away was just too much.

"Tank, you know what I meant," Henley called out, leaning against the doorframe in defeat. Ernie stopped and only turned enough so that he could look over his shoulder at her with disappointed blue eyes. "I know you believe that Yellowstone will erupt at some point, but it's not going to be today. Mav knows that too, which is why he's heading back home where he has responsibilities...just like we do right here and now."

"Putting that aside, do you really want to let a year pass with this festering between the two of you? Mav can be stubborn when he feels dishonored or betrayed, but I thought you handled things better than he did. To be honest, your differences are what I thought would bring the two of you together."

"Dishonored?" Henley asked, shocked that Ernie would use such a severe word. She was now questioning exactly what Mav had told the older man last night. She pushed herself off of the doorjamb, took a step outside onto the small porch, and then crossed her arms in anger. "Betrayed? He was the one who had magazines in his vehicle with me plastered on the cover as if I was nothing more than a sex object. Don't stand there and make it sound as if that's okay. It's not. They weren't recent covers either, Ernie. They were from my younger years and it made me feel filthy. He doesn't want *me*. He never wanted *me*. He wants what those photographs represent and she never existed. I do. I'm here, flesh and blood just like everyone else, and I damn well deserve more respect."

"You are just as stubborn as he is," Ernie muttered with a shake of his head as he removed his cap. Henley was practically out of breath from her tirade. She recognized a trap when she fell into one. She tilted her head back and looked up at the sky in exasperation, her frustration not dissipating at all. Tank shouldn't be concerned about her personal life and using it to keep Mav here in town because of his obsession with an apocalyptic event wasn't fair. "Is that what's got your panties in a twist? Old magazines? Did you ever think to ask Mav why he had them in the first place?"

"No, because it's wrong no matter how he answers," Henley exclaimed, turning to walk back into her cabin. She left the door open because she figured Ernie would just follow her inside anyway. "And that's not even the issue right now. You want him to stay, so you're going to use whatever means necessary to do that—even me, which let me tell you is downright manipulative, old man."

Henley stopped at the counter and yanked the coffee pot off of the burner, pouring two cups of coffee before she realized what she was doing. She was so used to having Tank join her in the morning to talk about their day that she didn't think that this was basically an open invitation for him to continue this conversation. She slid the pot back into its rightful place and then grabbed both mugs after she'd heard the door close.

"Mav isn't a recruit that needs to be told what to do anymore." Ernie took one of the mugs out of her hand but didn't bother to sit down. Instead he walked over to the window located on the right side of the living area and stared out at the mountain that she'd loved since she was a child. "He's decided to leave and there is nothing I can do about it but hope for the best. I don't doubt that the caldera will erupt soon, but the two of you might be right about it not being now. Mother Nature has her own agenda and she keeps it close to her chest. That vent is still releasing pressure, but there haven't been any follow-up events big enough to keep Mav here or bring the rest of the group back home. Bottom line, young lady, is that I love that boy like he was my own and seeing the hurt in his eyes when he came back to my cabin was hard for me. He's a good man, Henley."

"Good men can still have flaws," Henley pointed out, her annoyance leveling out to where she would finish this discussion without raising her voice again. She took a careful sip of the hot coffee, having gotten used to drinking it black years ago to cut back on calories. Now it was more out of habit than watching her weight. She closed her eyes to savor the lightly roasted rich flavor, urging the caffeine to do its job. "Ernie, there are shortcomings I can handle and there are those that I can't. I'm happy here. I'm content on my own, love this town, and am finally at peace. I don't need someone with me to make me whole. I do that all on my own."

"I'm not saying that you aren't complete, Henley." Ernie took a drink of his own coffee and then finally turned to face her, the knowledge in his blue eyes making her comprehend that he knew more about her than he was letting on. "But take it from someone who's been there. Life is so much sweeter if you have someone to spend it with."

"Then why haven't you asked Mabel out to dinner?" Henley took a seat on the couch facing Ernie, relieved that the conversation had progressed past her and Mav. Now this was a topic she could handle. "She's been waiting."

"I will ask her when the time is right and not a minute before," Ernie stressed, raising one of those bushy eyebrows of his and making it seem as if he was chastising her for meddling in his business when he'd been doing the same to her. She elevated her own eyebrow, letting him know he didn't intimidate her. "Now here is something you might consider to put things into perspective for you. If I recall Mav was supposed to have gotten some magazines signed by you for the daughter of a man he worked with back in Chicago. I remember him saying something to that effect after I told him I'd hired you, but then he called weeks later when that same little girl got real sick with meningitis and asked if I'd mail out a picture she could have instead. Could those have been the sick little girl's magazines that you saw in his Jeep?"

Henley froze, although the brown liquid in her cup was the only thing still moving. Memories of Ernie asking her for some stock photos with her signature came back to her, but she'd assumed they had been for Van's administrative assistant. Van had mentioned on more than one occasion that first time she'd met the whole gang that Kinsey had wanted an autograph. The reality of just what her misjudgment might have cost her hit hard, but she still had to verify this with Mav.

"Tank, why didn't he just tell me that last night?" Henley asked, pushing herself off of the couch and setting her coffee cup down onto the table. "I told him what I'd found in his vehicle and he walked away. How was I supposed to take that as anything other than a confirmation?"

"I can't speak for Mav, but I know how I would feel if Mabel thought that little of me." Ernie finished off his coffee and then walked over to the counter, rinsing out the cup and gently setting it in the sink. He still held his cap in his left hand as he walked to the door, leaving her to her own misery. "I guess I better make sure the boats are prepared for our guest. I'm sure he'll want to hit the lake later this morning and as you said…we have business to attend to. I wanted to check the supply side filters for the siphon pump at the spring and top off the storage tank before we get too many guests arriving for the season. I'll need to reset the on-demand storage to five hundred gallons with the increased number of visitors."

Henley followed close on his heels, grabbing the keys to the rusty old F-10 pick-up truck she'd purchased from Mrs. Geary after her husband had passed. It always got her to and from where she needed to be and Ernie had rebuilt the stake bed when it had rusted out. It could haul what she needed and would do the same now, only this time with a little more dust in her rearview mirror.

"I'll be back before our guest arrives," Henley called out, jogging to the driver's side door and yanking open the old hunk of metal. She didn't even bother to look over her shoulder, knowing full well there would be a smile on Tank's face. "If you so much as say I told you so, you'll be the one changing the sheets and cleaning the cabins before next week's group arrives."

Henley slammed the driver's door hard and then slid the key into the ignition, turning it until the engine rolled over and started. She nudged the gearshift into drive and then pressed her foot on the gas pedal. She didn't think an apology would change anything, but she'd always prided herself on owning up to her mistakes. Mav could accept it or not, but at least she wouldn't have to go the whole next year berating herself for a misunderstanding she'd let go on for far too long. She already had too many regrets and she didn't need this one added onto the long tattered list. Contrary to what Ernie thought, she wasn't nearly as stubborn as he was and she was about to prove it.

CHAPTER FIVE

MAV HAD ALREADY left the diner with his large cup of coffee to go and was currently gassing up his Jeep for the long drive home. He'd left Ernie up at the lodge, knowing he was expecting a guest today and would more than likely end up out on the lake with a fishing pole in his hand at some point. There wasn't a need to say goodbye to Henley since she'd already made up her mind about his lack of character. It stung and maybe he'd address it when he came back to town to stay. Maybe he wouldn't and he'd just leave her to her own devices. Either way, right now neither one of them would benefit from what he really wanted to say to her. He eased up on the lever of the fuel pump, letting the last drop fill his tank before he set the handle back into the cradle. The gas station was still quite old and didn't take credit cards at the pump, so Mav lifted his shades and set them on his head before walking into the store and pulling out his wallet.

"Good morning, Mr. Bassett." Mav snatched a pack of gum and set it down on the counter before looking over at the owner of Lost Summit's gas station. There wasn't even a convenience store attached to it, so the small square building was only big enough for a six-foot counter and a chair for Randy Bassett's best friend, Jarrett Moore. Both men had spent their youth in Europe during the last world war and had seen healthier days. Each of them were the better part of eighty-five years of age, if not older. The two of them had been attached at the hip ever since they had moved here after the war and both of them spent their evenings playing chess outside the hardware store so they could see the comings and goings of the town. "Jarrett, how's the heart this morning?"

"Still ticking, by some damn miracle," Jarrett came back with his usual reply before spitting his tobacco into a red solo cup. "We heard you might be taking over for Felix when he decides to retire."

"Sheriff Ramsey and I have discussed it," Mav replied vaguely, not wanting to give away too many details. He'd told Tank of his plans last night and while it was easy to see he was pleased, it wasn't enough to erase the worry of Mav heading back to Chicago this morning. Berke hadn't called and any attempt to reach him went straight to voicemail. Considering it was still quite early in Texas, Mav would touch base with him during the drive home. He figured the call would yield nothing since no other activity had been noteworthy and even Ernie had reluctantly admitted that there wasn't enough evidence of a major eruption to keep Mav there. Maybe now things could return to normal and they wouldn't need to send Ernie in for a psych-eval. "When the sheriff is ready to retire he'll let me know, I'm sure."

Randy announced the total and Mav took out his wallet from the back of his jeans, pulling out enough cash to cover the gas and the pack of gum. He would have been more comfortable in his cargo pants, but he hadn't gotten to leave yesterday and he'd spilled some steak sauce on them last night after grilling dinner. Denim and a faded black T-shirt was what he was stuck with until he returned home to wash some laundry. He wished it would be as easy to forget what happened on this trip as it was to dissolve the sauce stain in the fabric, but he doubted that would be the case.

"Marvin Jenkins mentioned that Tank sent Henley in for some supplies at the hardware store." Jarrett spit in his cup again, his curious eyes never leaving Mav. It was as if the older man thought Mav was hiding some important information that only he and Ernie knew. "Something we need to know about or is Ernie being Ernie?"

"That earthquake at Yellowstone yesterday made Tank a little nervous, especially after what took place in Nepal earlier this year," Mav replied nonchalantly, knowing full well whatever information he gave would go directly to Stanley Ratliff. "He just wanted a few more items to round out his emergency stash, but now that things have quieted down…it's business as usual. He has a new guest arriving at the lodge today, along with a large group in a couple of weeks. Spring sure has kicked off with a bang."

"Rat has a group of hikers coming in next week as well. They'll be down in town at the livery to rent horses before

Wednesday's trail ride up through Lost Mountain," Randy boasted, handing over Mav's change before taking a seat on the stool he'd positioned behind the counter. "It'll be good for business here about."

"Well, gentlemen, it was good to see you this trip." Mav returned his change to his wallet and then slid the worn old trifold into his back pocket. "Maybe next time I'll play a game of chess with one of you."

Jarrett barked out a laugh while Randy smiled, both men aware that Mav wasn't a chess player. Now poker? That was a different story and when the crew got together on their annual trip, there wasn't an evening that passed that someone didn't win or lose a pot of money. Mav pulled down his cheap shades as he walked out the door, heading for his Jeep. He looked down the road and spotted Henley's sun-weathered red truck and for a moment he paused before opening his door. Did he want to speak with her before leaving town?

"You're a fool," Mav muttered, shaking his head to try and get rid of the temptation to drive back over to the diner. "She made herself quite clear."

There was no need to continue to make a fool of himself. The taste of her still lingered on his lips and he doubted it would wash off any time in the near future. Mav hadn't been a Boy Scout and he'd dated his fair share of women, but he would gladly have thought about moving up his agenda of relocating if Henley had given him any indication that she'd wanted more between them than their connection through

Ernie. The pull he had toward her was strong, but she obviously didn't feel the same. If anything, she thought he was lower than dirt, but that wasn't anything he hadn't dealt with before. He was a fucking professional.

Mav opened his door and wedged his large frame behind his steering wheel. He'd left the keys in the ignition, so all he did was turn over the engine and then pull out of the gas station without a backward glance. As much as he loved visiting Tank, it was time to head home to the land of reality where burglaries, robberies, and murders were among the normal activities of his job. At least he knew what to expect there and how to handle it.

Mav had made it around a mile out of town when something caught his attention in the rearview mirror. What the hell? At first he thought Sheriff Ramsey might have been called to an accident on the outskirts of town, but then he recognized Henley's old stake bed pick-up truck barreling down on him. He felt a spike of anger when he realized just how fast she was driving. He was astonished when she pulled into the left lane and brought her rusty heap of metal alongside his, motioning with her hand that he should pull over. She'd gone certifiably insane. He eventually pulled over and slammed the gearshift into park before pulling on the handle of the door. He slammed his shoulder against the side and was out of the Jeep just in time to see Henley pull in front of him.

"What the hell do you think you're doing?" Mav yelled as Henley hopped out of her truck like she hadn't just been a menace to the roads. "You could have gotten us both killed. Sheriff Ramsey should ticket your ass up one side—"

"Oh, for heaven's sake, calm down," Henley snapped with a wave of her hand as she walked closer. Mav was lucky the vein in his head didn't explode and she was currently in a haze of red as the level of his rage rose. "It's not like anyone really travels this road except either to leave or arrive, and the one person coming into town isn't arriving for another half hour. I need to say something."

"You…are you kidding me? You have something to add on to what you said last night? Trust me, sweetheart, your point got across so loud and clear that my eardrums are bleeding," Mav gritted through his teeth, unable to accept that she didn't see how dangerous it was to drive on the left hand side of the road. "What if Ernie's customer arrived early? Did you think of that? Did it ever occur to you that someone could actually be driving through town in the lane they're supposed to use before you foolishly decided to take your life in your own hands?"

"I needed to confirm something before you left and I didn't want to wait until you returned," Henley stated, as if that validated her reckless driving. Mav ran a hand through his hair in disbelief at her carelessness and then was astounded when she had the audacity to bring up last night. "Why did you have those magazines in your Jeep?"

"You're asking me that now? I thought you already had that figured out." Mav turned to walk away with every intention of getting back into his Jeep and driving away, but stopped himself short. He whipped his shades off and faced her. "Three years, Henley. You had three years to ask me that question and you chose to either ignore me or draw me into arguments that I couldn't win. One snide comment after another for all that time and you need to ask me why? I'm going to go out on a limb and guess that you made assumptions about me based on your past experiences. Am I right?"

Henley appeared taken aback that he'd dove headfirst into the discussion she wanted to have. Either that or she actually expected an answer. He'd eventually give her one, but not until he had his say.

"Yes," Henley answered with another wave of hand as if she was dismissing his fact, "you would be right, but—"

"Then you've made up your mind about the kind of man I am," Mav said, cutting her off. He pointed toward her with one side of his sunglasses. "*You* made the choice to project other men's actions on me. I chose to see you in a different light, regardless of your fame or the fact that you have men literally falling at your feet. You think you had it rough in your high-rise penthouse in Hollywood, schmoozing with the other models and actors getting paid more than ninety percent of the average middle class American? Try living in the projects with a mother hooked on crack who spent every dime on drugs instead of feeding her kid or making sure he had clothes on his back. When she wasn't passed out on the floor, she was selling her body to the first man who'd line up with a ten-dollar bill. Do you think I judged you based on my past experiences? No, because you are your own individual person but in the end...it didn't matter. Your opinion of me was no better than hers and I realized something last night—you *should* be living in Lost Summit where the population is limited because you have no faith in humanity. So go ahead and stay buried up in the mountains, Henley. It sure beats the hell out of actually getting your hands dirty and helping those who need it."

Mav turned on the heel of his boot and marched back to his Jeep. He was literally nauseous at the information he'd just revealed, but she'd pushed him to the breaking point. Henley didn't get the right to be judgmental and he sure as hell didn't need to hear it. He opened the door without looking back and slipped his glasses back onto his face, not wanting her to see the vulnerability that had to be showing. He felt worse than when he'd been wounded during his first combat tour. It had been a relatively minor flesh wound at first, so the corpsman elected not to evacuate him with the rest of the casualties. A two-day long sandstorm had rolled in by the time it had become infected and prevented him from getting to the Cas-Evac Hospital. He had suffered from a one hundred and five degree temperature and slipped into shock before he'd arrived at the hospital. It was amazing that he'd survived at all. That had been a cakewalk in comparison.

Mav didn't waste time jerking the steering wheel and pulling the Jeep back onto the road, but God help him if he was able to prevent himself from looking in the rearview mirror. Henley stood there with her arms hanging at her side with her shoulders slightly hunched. He couldn't make out her facial features, but it didn't really matter. She would now look upon him with pity when that was the last thing he wanted.

He pressed the gas pedal, rolled down the windows, and tried his damnedest to think of anything else except what had just taken place. He ignored the vibrant scenery on either side of him, focusing on the double yellow line that would lead him home—home being a relative term considering he had no family there. He'd been born and raised in Chicago, so it had been natural for him to go back there after he'd finished his eight years in the service. Maybe he should stay there after what had just taken place recently and rethink his plans to move to Lost Summit.

Mile after mile didn't ease Mav's frustration or embarrassment at his impromptu revealing of his childhood, so he was grateful when he was finally in the vicinity of a signal an hour later and his cell phone chimed. He shifted in his seat so that he could reach into his jeans. He glanced at the display. Berke was calling and Mav was able to answer on the fourth ring.

"You took your sweet time getting back to me," Mav answered through the vehicle's hands-free link to his phone that sat down in the console so that he would be able to concentrate on driving. Too many states had different rules pertaining to cell phones while driving and he didn't want to take any chances. "I spent the night up at the lodge but hit the road first thing this morning. Nothing major occurred overnight so Tank's just going to have to wait a while longer for his apocalypse to happen."

"Turn around."

Mav must have heard wrong. Either that or the signal coming from the nearest tower wasn't as strong as he'd originally thought.

"Say again your last," Mav ordered, taking his eyes off the road long enough to glance up at the blue sky. Nothing appeared out of the ordinary and that's when he realized what must have happened. Berke had spoken to Henley and she said something about their encounter earlier. Son of a bitch. He certainly didn't want to look like a tool in front his friends. "Look, this situation is between me and Henley. She made up her mind about me long ago and nothing I say or do will change that. Hell, I don't want her to change her mind anymore."

"Mav, I don't know what you're talking about but it won't matter in a few short hours," Berke said, cutting to the chase. Mav could hear the tension in his friend's voice. "I called Paige like you wanted me to at the USGS. They aren't telling the public what they need to know—per orders from higher-ups."

Mav automatically lifted his turn signal and pulled off to the shoulder of the road, initiating his hazard lights. He reached for his cell phone and took it off of the car's handsfree link before placing the device to his ear. He was picking up sounds that he hadn't before and figured Berke was in the process of hauling ass from Texas to Washington. Mav had a ton of questions but went with the most vital.

"How long do we have?"

"Paige doesn't know and she went against a specific direction even telling me the truth, so our conversation was brief." Berke muttered quite a few foul words underneath his breath before continuing. "Tank's been right all along, Mav."

"Listen closely," Mav advised, swiftly bringing Berke up to speed on Tank's summary of how this would play out. "The population of Lost Summit is forty-eight, and that doesn't include Ernie and Henley residing up at the lodge. The bunker can't hold that many people for an extended amount of time, but I figure a lot of them will head north like I originally suggested. Those that stay could probably survive in town, but would fare better being up at the lodge."

"You've changed your mind about that?" Berke asked, somewhat surprised. "You think the area is that well protected?"

"Tank has obviously spent a lot of his idle time planning for something like this and although we might razz the shit out of him for it, he's come to some solid conclusions. In short, the blast radius of one hundred miles will initially be the worst area affected, but with the ash cloud reaching the east coast within seventy-two hours…eight-five percent of the United States is going to be buried under six hundred and fifty cubic miles of ash and debris very quickly. Lost Summit is reasonably protected from the blast and ash, at least until the winds of the northern hemisphere carries it around the earth...and even then we should be able to make do considering the valley has its own natural resources—natural water springs, Ernie's natural gas well, and a screen of very large mountains in all directions. The bottom line is there will be no safe place to go, but we have a better chance in Lost Summit than anywhere else. So get your ass here as fast as you can but steer clear of the blast radius. Call the others and tell them what's taking place while I head back to town. Take a circuitous route and bring what you can. Make sure you are well armed and bring all the reloading supplies from your shop if you can."

Berke acknowledged he'd heard Mav's request, but neither spoke the words aloud. Having a small arsenal on hand during times like these was the safest plan for them and their loved ones. The saying *it's better to have a gun and not need one than to need a gun and not have one* sprang to mind. His own stash was back in Illinois at the apartment he was renting. That wouldn't help them now.

Mav's gut tightened as he thought of the various reactions yet to come. Half of the town would follow Tank's lead, but the other half would either not believe him or allow fear to override their common sense and flee to the north. Panic wasn't an easy emotion to quell, especially when it was formed in a group mentality. It was the people with the intent to take advantage of a distressing situation that they had to worry about. Especially those that wanted what Ernie had built for themselves.

"I'll be there as soon as I can," Berke replied with no preliminaries.

"I don't know how long we'll be able to have contact with each other after it erupts." Mav finally shut off his hazard lights and shifted the Jeep into drive, making a U-turn in the middle of the road after looking both ways. "The weight of the ash, especially if it rains, will take out most of the electrical grid fairly quickly. Try to stay in touch until then so we at least know of your whereabouts when time runs out. After that use 14.275 megahertz during the day and 3.975 megahertz at night. We'll monitor those frequencies for emergency transmissions until everyone arrives. Get the word out to the others."

"I'll see you soon, brother."

Mav spent the next five minutes trying to get ahold of Ernie, but the older man had a tendency not to take his cell phone everywhere he went. The lodge's main line just ran and rang, indicating that Henley was still out and about. She wasn't answering her cell phone either and was probably seeing to the guest that was arriving this morning.

Mav finally set the phone back into his console, knowing and trusting that Berke would call the rest of the group while he took care of the residents in town. They had been a team before and they would be again, because the world as they knew it was going to change forever. The silence in his vehicle became stifling and he rolled down the window, allowing the breeze to fill the Jeep. The scent of pine and shrubbery enveloped him, reminding him that the earth had endured many obstacles. He spent the drive back imprinting the scenery in his mind for he knew it would never look the same again. Survival surpassed anything else, including his personal feelings regarding Henley. This moment and the years ahead were about life and death. Fate had given them a hand that they couldn't win, but it was in Mav's nature to stay at the table as long as he was able. This time he also needed to keep his fellow players in the game.

CHAPTER SIX

HENLEY FINALLY HAD time to herself and she took advantage of it by walking down to the river. Her attempt to talk to Mav had been a disaster and she was forced to face the type of person she'd become, which was no better than those people she'd left behind in her old life. Knowing that she'd stereotyped Mav for years without ever attempting to find out the truth didn't sit well with her and she was now forced to examine her life. Mav was right when he'd said she belonged here in Lost Summit, except it wasn't for the reasons she'd originally thought. Her home had not only become a refuge, it had become an unhealthy hiding place. She'd made it to the edge of the water where a large boulder she'd designated as her own was located.

The sound of running water was the only remedy for her frayed nerves. It had always been that way for as far back as she could remember. Lost River ran down from the Canadian side through the town of Lost Summit and paralleled the road that ran east out toward the campground and the lodge. Lost Mountain Lodge was actually situated in a valley between Lost Mountain and Snowy Peak on the north side of the river.

Ratliff's Summit Creek Campground was closer to town below the closed Pine Peak Silver Mine on the north face forward sloop of Salmo Mountain above the wide ravine that Lost River ran through. There were several major creeks that ran down off of both Salmo and Lost Mountains, all of which fed the growing river as it ran east toward the southern sloop of Snowy Peak.

Henley had walked the road leading down from the valley the lodge occupied. The gravel road followed the course of the valley's creek and crossed over it near where it joined the river's edge. It hadn't occurred to her until now that Whispering Creek must be fed by several mountain springs similar to their own. It was clear, cold, and fast moving. The rainbow trout collected in the deeper pools closer to the river. The climb back up the lodge's rock road over the bridge and up the gentle sloop would aid her in wearing away her tension so that she might sleep tonight.

She'd been eighteen when she'd moved to California, way too young to recognize that her parents had been right in asking her to go to college. She'd thought she knew everything and drove away in her partially restored 1964 white Karmann Ghia convertible with stars in her eyes. The most amazing thing was that she'd really made it and had become one of the most sought after fashion models in the industry. It hadn't been easy and by the time she'd realized the price tag of success, it had been too late and the damage was done. Little by little the leeches and predators of the industry drained her life force away until she didn't know whom she could trust or which way to turn. She'd become a shell of the young girl that had arrived with glorious hopes and dreams, leaving behind an isolated woman with health and trust issues.

The cold hard truth was that she'd had it easy compared to Mav and he had somehow come away without having a tainted view on the world. She couldn't imagine the childhood he'd had and yet he'd turned into a man of honor...just as Ernie had said and she'd been too afraid to open her eyes and view him that way. She hadn't wanted to see it because Mav affected her in a way that truly scared her. He made her want to be a better woman while he only wanted her for whom she already was. Maybe she didn't feel he should be burdened with her as she was. She honestly didn't know because her head still wasn't on straight.

"You gonna sit out here and mope?"

Henley closed her eyes at the cutting edge in Ernie's tone. She didn't need this now, not when she was already beating herself up. She would need to find a way to apologize to Mav and she'd have to make it count this time. She hadn't approached him in the best way earlier, but she didn't want to discuss making another mistake with Tank.

"I was just taking a short break," Henley said, doing her best not to sound defensive. She turned her head Ernie's way as she spoke. "Kellen Truman is set up in cabin five and he's requested the river fishing boat for five o'clock in the morning. I will say that there's something off about that man."

"I just met him and I agree with that statement, although I can't put my finger on it. I'll keep a close eye on him though." Ernie crossed his arms and widened his stance as he looked out over the flowing river. "I take it things aren't much better between you and Mav?"

"Tank, I don't want to talk about it," Henley 'fessed up, pushing off of the boulder. "I was wrong. I need to fix it. End of story."

"You should have fixed it three years ago, but you didn't."

Henley could have used the excuse that three years wasn't the issue. Mav had only been back to visit three times for his annual vacation and one additional time over a holiday. Basically she'd only seen him four times to personally ask about the magazines, but she'd chosen not to. She didn't need to be reminded of how she'd mishandled things.

"And you could have shared a little more about Mav than some war stories," Henley berated him, immediately regretting her words. Ernie wasn't to blame for her mistakes and bad assumptions. A headache was starting to form and it wasn't even lunchtime. "Tank, I'm trying. I really am, but nothing has gone right and I've only made things worse. You want the truth? Mav is different than the others for some reason and that scares me. I don't know why, but he is and how I reacted to that was wrong. I can't repair it overnight. I don't even know if I can ever mend the damage I've managed to pile up because I've questioned his integrity."

"Are you telling me that Mav told you about his childhood?" Ernie asked, facing her with a look of speculation. His one bushy eyebrow rose above to touch his baseball cap. "He doesn't share that with just anyone, Henley."

"I don't think he intended to, which makes it even worse." Henley slipped her hands into the back pockets of her jeans, just now seeing that Ernie had once again got his way. She was spilling everything and he would undoubtedly give his sage advice whether she wanted it or not. "My past troubles seem like a bed of roses after hearing a little of what he went through. I had loving parents, a town full of people who cared for one another, and I was accepted back without question. My trials and tribulations while I was away were infinitesimal compared to what Mav went through, and yet he's a hell of a lot better person than I am."

"You're mad at yourself and rightly so, but there's no point in crying in your beer about it. Mav will come around and when he does, you'll have an opportunity to make things right. And he'll let you because of who he is."

"Friendship, though," Henley warned, not wanting Ernie to get his hopes up. She highly doubted that Mav would want anything more after she'd made him feel like he wasn't any better than the mud on the sole of her shoe. The pain in her chest at her transgression was nothing compared to how she'd made him feel and the need to drive after him once more settled in, but she'd never catch up to him now. She'd call him later tonight and hope that he'd pick up the phone to let her speak. "I—"

The sound of a vehicle pulling up on the gravel lane behind them could be heard a ways away, stopping Henley from probably saying something she'd regret. This day wasn't really going her way, but she had no one to blame but herself. She hadn't been prepared to see Mav's Jeep pulling up on the road above or the butterflies that had decided to take flight in her stomach. Seeing him now that she'd come to her senses was a little overwhelming and she found herself really wanting him to accept her apology.

"Looks like your day is becoming a little brighter after all," Ernie announced, appearing happier with himself more than anything. Henley didn't comment as they walked up the slight incline to the roadbed. Something caught her eye farther up the valley beyond where Mav's Jeep had pulled to a stop and she saw Kellen leaning against a tree a quarter mile up watching them through field glasses. He was about Mav's height, with jet-black hair that went well below his collar and brown eyes that were almost as dark as his pupils. He was quiet, a little too quiet, and only spoke to her to answer any questions she'd had. He definitely didn't remind her of any fisherman she'd ever met. Something wasn't right about him, but she would let Ernie handle it. "Mav, what brings you back here so soon?"

"You were right, Tank," Mav said grimly, stepping out of his vehicle while leaving the door hanging open as he moved to lean on the wheelwell and hike a foot up on the fender of his Rubicon. He moved his sunglasses up to his head, briefly meeting her gaze before zeroing in on Ernie. "Berke spoke to Paige, the woman he dated from the USGS, and she's positive the earthquake from yesterday will be the catalyst to the caldera erupting in a major way."

"Why hasn't that come across the talk radio channels?" Henley asked, their personal issues immediately taking a backseat to the news Mav was presenting. All the dire scenarios that Ernie had brought to the table last night came back with a vengeance and she did her best to tamp down her panic. It was one thing to play with assumptions, but it was another to actually deal with the fallout. "I've been listening to the radio since I got back and there hasn't been a word of anything else happening."

"That's not true," Ernie denied, shaking his head. "There have been small swarms of activity occurring, but the state and government officials wouldn't want to cause a panic. Am I right?"

"Unfortunately, yes," Mav said, nodding his head and then running a hand down his face in frustration. "Berke and the others are on their way here, but who knows when this thing could blow. I gave them alternate frequencies for emergency communications once the grid collapses."

"Are you all talking about Yellowstone?" Kellen called out from the road above where he'd walked down to join them. Henley could see Mav stiffen at the sound of another man's voice and he narrowed his eyes once he saw Kellen coming down the drive toward them. "The broadcasters are discussing it now."

"Mav, why don't you drive us back to the lodge?" Ernie motioned toward the vehicle. "It'll be quicker."

Ernie and their guest had taken the back seats, leaving Henley to ride shotgun. The short ride was made in silence and when they all piled out, Kellen nodded toward his cabin. Mav took his time in shutting the door on his vehicle, eventually pulling up the rear and surprising Henley when he fell into step beside her.

"Is this the guest you were talking about?" Mav murmured, his voice low and deep. Henley wanted nothing more than to ask for his forgiveness, but she knew this wasn't the time or place. "What's his name?"

"Kellen Truman." Henley looked up at Mav, who had yet to take his eyes off of the stranger in front of them. "He claims to be from Utah but hasn't said what he does for a living. He wanted his own cabin, so that makes it easier since we haven't staffed the lodge yet."

"Military." Mav didn't hesitate when he answered, but the response didn't ease her mind. If anything it made Henley more nervous as they walked into the cabin. Everything appeared as it had when she'd prepped the place, with the exception of a small overnight bag to the right of the door. "I'm Maverick Beckett, a friend of Tank's."

The two men shook hands, but it was apparent they were sizing each other up. Ernie had already made his way over to the counter to where the portable AM/FM shortwave radio was plugged in, as there was in every guest cabin. He turned up the sound, preventing Kellen from having to reply.

"...honestly surprised FEMA or the White House haven't issued the surrounding states an evacuation order, Steve. We're talking about major cities being buried underneath ash all the way to the East Coast should the caldera completely erupt. We are not being told the truth and it's going to cost a lot of people their lives. The long-term effect of this will be devastating not only to the United States but those in the direct path of the prevailing winds. This is the big one the experts have been warning us about for years and I can tell you firsthand from the data that's been leaked that this is it."

"Julie, FEMA has already announced that the citizens have nothing to worry about. The White House is remaining silent on the issue while the USGS is apparently following suit. Could you explain to those tuning in exactly what the Yellowstone Caldera is, what causes this type of supervolcano to erupt, and the consequences of such a natural disaster?"

"Of course. A volcano of any type or size is..."

"We need to prepare the town," Ernie said, turning to them with determination and sorrow in his eyes. He understood best of all the devastation that was about to rain down on them. "Mr. Truman, it looks like this might be the worst and luckiest day of your life."

"I'm well aware that the government keeps classified information from the hands of the public, but not announcing that the Yellowstone caldera is about to erupt would be paramount to killing the residents within at least three states." Kellen was looking at Mav when he spoke. She couldn't figure out if it was a planned speech or if the man truly thought that. "Are you certain that your friend is right?"

Kellen had just confirmed Henley's suspicion that he'd been eavesdropping on their conversation down by the river and that didn't sit well with her. They already had too much to worry about with regards to keeping everyone safe than to have to worry about a stranger whose intentions were not yet known. She glanced toward Ernie to catch his reaction, but he was already walking to the door.

"Yes," Mav replied, surprising her when he grabbed her hand and pulled her behind him as they followed Ernie outside. "You're more than welcome to stay here, but we'll be in town getting the necessary supplies we need and alerting the residents."

"I think I'll stick around to make a few phone calls," Kellen replied as Mav and Henley were about to cross the threshold. "I have family in that area and would like to warn them."

"I understand," Mav said without turning around. He kept a hold of her hand as they walked to his Jeep. Ernie was already in his black Ford F-150 pick-up truck. Mav did turn back to say one more thing to Kellen, who was standing in the doorway. "I have friends coming this way and they'll be prepared to do what it takes to protect this town until we make a decision on what to do."

Henley could feel the tension radiating off both men as if the sun had suddenly exploded and she turned to see what Kellen's reaction was to Mav's statement. There appeared an underlying respect in the man's posture, but she'd been such a bad judge of character lately that she wasn't so sure she'd read his body language correctly. He nodded his understanding and finally turned, shutting the door to his cabin as Ernie sped by them getting a head start into town.

"You want to tell me what that was about?" Henley asked, almost afraid of the answer but not enough to ignore what had just taken place. "Shouldn't we be able to trust him if he's military?"

"He's had military training," Mav clarified, opening the passenger side door to his Jeep. "It's in the way he carries himself. We don't know a thing about the man and I wanted to make it very clear that this is our town. We protect what is ours by any means necessary. The bunker is secured, as well as the lodge. Leaving Truman here won't be a problem for now. Let's drive into town since we don't know how much time we have and see if Ernie can convince the other residents that it's safer here than to travel anywhere else."

"Are you still skeptical of that?" Henley asked, climbing into the seat and wanting to stop in at the diner to watch the news. They didn't have televisions in the guest cabins and although the emergency radio provided them news, she wanted something more visual than her imagination. "Do you think we should head north?"

"Canada has to be aware of what's taking place and I'm sure they even have their own geologists, scientists, and whoever else on their payroll to give them the information they need." Mav's gaze appeared somewhat solemn with his next sentence. "They'll be careful as to who they allow across their border since they'll also need to worry about their own citizens."

"Tank thinks we'll be safer here," Henley pointed out before Mav closed her door. She waited for him to get into the driver's side before she continued, her previous apprehension returning about their earlier argument. It was a silly thing to think about when their lives were about to be placed into eminent danger. "I'm inclined to agree with what he showed us last night."

"All of his information is based on the wind patterns and while that is still likely the case, I'd rather have multiple avenues to take should we need them." Mav started the engine and quickly made a U-turn, following Ernie's path into town. "The bunker is only made to hold a couple dozen people, thirty at most. That won't work if the entire town decides to stay based on Tank's theory, so he better be right."

Henley rolled down her window, the temperature hovering around fifty-six degrees. She wasn't sure they would hear something of that magnitude should the volcano explode, but she didn't want to take the chance of missing something. The fresh clean air was flowing in while Mav left a trail of dust in their wake. They were twenty minutes outside of town, but it wasn't like they needed to go over anything. They'd discussed it until they were blue in the face last night, which only left one topic. She was being given an opportunity to apologize before they possibly met their maker and she needed this resolved.

"Mav, I'm truly sorry for how I've treated you these last few years during your visits," Henley said softly, glancing in his direction. The only indication that he'd heard her was the tightening of his fingers on the steering wheel. She continued to stare at his large hands, her skin tingling as she remembered what his caress felt like on her face. "I didn't handle this morning very well. You were right about everything...I've come home to hide and I've done a piss poor job of dealing with my problems. I know you didn't mean to hurt me, but you said it like you saw it and I reacted in a way I'm not proud of."

"It doesn't matter now, Henley." Mav never once looked her way and Henley's heart hurt at the damage she'd done. "Nothing does except seeing that the people of this town survive the aftermath of what is to come. Our problems are insignificant compared to what we're facing."

"It does matter, though," Henley insisted, not willing to let this go. "I've wasted three years of a friendship that we could have had because I didn't want to put myself out there, to let myself be vulnerable. Yet you put not only your emotions out there every day, but also you risk your life. I didn't see your sacrifice until today and it opened my eyes to my own selfishness. I'm not saying that what I experienced in my life wasn't appalling in its own right, because there was little humanity in the life I lived. You were right about that, Mav."

They fell into a silence for another eighteen minutes, but it wasn't a comfortable quietness. The time stretched until Henley thought she'd burst from the thoughts that were running through her head about the two of them and the weight of what was about to happen in the upcoming days. She'd even parted her lips to say something else as they crossed into town, but Mav finally responded.

"It's not just friendship I want, Henley." She wasn't sure how to respond, considering earlier this morning he told her something quite the opposite. Mav pulled in front of the diner and parked, taking the key out of the ignition before looking directly at her to drive his point home. "You and I…we've been going round and round with this for three years plus. We've run out of time for any type of relationship and trust me when I say that survival is not an easy thing in what is about to become our reality. I've lived it and it changes a person. If you thought there was little humanity before you haven't seen anything yet. The only people I've been able to trust aren't here yet with the exception of Tank. I can promise you this—I will do whatever it takes to keep you safe because it's who I am. There is no ulterior motive other than we take care of our own."

Mav shoved open his door and Henley continued sitting in her seat as he walked around the front of the vehicle like the gentleman he was. From what he said it wasn't his mother who had taught him that. Henley was a little in awe that he still held true to who he was with everything that was going on. The gesture made her feel even more remorseful than she had before and she waited until he was really looking at her after he'd opened her door to speak.

"I know you don't have an ulterior motive, Mav. I hope one day you understand how sorry I truly am that my insecurities hurt you the way they have."

Mav studied her and then held out his hand, helping her down until she was standing in front of him. She wasn't sure if he accepted her apology, but this was a start. Henley rose up on her tiptoes and impulsively kissed his cheek, wishing she could erase the last three years.

"I don't want your pity, Henley," Mav said softly, waiting for her to step to the side so that he could shut the passenger door. She was surprised when he backed her against the metal, his body covering hers and reminding her that he'd awoken something dormant inside of her. Her eyes met his and like last night, time stood still. "I want you and no matter how angry I was with you this morning, that hasn't changed. You want another *friend*? Feel free to hit up Kellen back at the lodge. If you want a man…I'm right here in front of you."

"Mav, Sheriff Ramsey is bringing the mayor over to the diner," Ernie said earnestly, appearing out of nowhere and causing Henley to startle a bit. Mav stepped away and for the first time in years, she missed the warmth of a man's body. How quickly things changed and the chaotic events around them weren't giving her time to think them through. What struck her odd was that Mav didn't look like he expected a response as he focused on Ernie. "The White House is about to have a press conference."

A shiver of fear traveled down Henley's spine at the thought that Mav might be right about her view of people in general. She'd been living in a bubble and hadn't allowed anyone inside, even those who'd had the best intentions. Mav had always been an open book which she'd chosen not to read, but he didn't want her to just peruse the prologue. He wanted her to join him in his story and she didn't know if she could do that. Ernie had always respected her privacy and she'd grown accustomed to people keeping their distance because of her demeanor. Now her sanctuary was about to be invaded by nature and the instinct in these people to survive would kick in, bringing with it not only the kindness but the ugliness of humanity.

CHAPTER SEVEN

MAV STOOD BACK away from the crowd, surveying the occupants as they crowded around the diner's television. He wanted the chance to observe and see if there would be any trouble, but there was only one group that he was concerned with—Stanley Ratliff and his cluster of friends. It was standing room only and Ernie was currently near the front having a serious discussion with the Sheriff and Reggie Thomas, the mayor of Lost Summit. Rat and three of his cronies were sitting in a booth talking with one another while the others had their eyes glued to the screen in the corner. Henley was standing next to Mabel, trying to comfort the older woman who was worried about her son. She'd already placed a call in to him and tried unsuccessfully to get him to move the family to safety. It wasn't until Mav had gotten on the phone and convinced Derek it was in the best interests of his family to start heading this way.

"Are you sure we can trust this woman that Berke has spoken to? I don't like to cause the people in my town to panic based on a discussion that someone had with a third party I don't even know. We can't be telling everyone this is going to happen unless it's a proven fact."

Sheriff Ramsey had slipped away from Ernie and the mayor, making his way toward the back of the diner where Mav was now leaning against the wall. Felix was one of Ernie's closest friends and a retired army colonel. All would be well within Lost Summit should martial law be declared over the course of the next few days. Felix was a born leader, one who could maintain balance and safety in this small town. But he was one man and Mav figured it was only a matter of time before he was deputized. It wasn't necessarily Rat and his group that had Mav concerned, for they were really harmless in the grand scheme of things. It was the desperation of those outside that would kick in and cause them to seek out better shelter at any cost as they fled north.

"Yes, I'm sure," Mav replied, his attention being pulled over to where Henley was standing next to the coffee pot. She was holding it up and silently asking if he'd like a cup. He nodded his acceptance, pushing away his thoughts about the two of them. Now wasn't the time and he honestly didn't know why he'd tested her outside the diner. His emotions were still running high and he needed to get them under control. Their safety took priority, but damn if she didn't make him want to break that rule for the first time in his life. "Berke and the others are heading here now. Do you have a plan for when we are all left on our own once the governmental infrastructure breaks down?"

"You don't know that will happen," Sheriff Ramsey said

with caution with a slow shake of his head. He was dressed in a khaki uniform with his utility belt around his waist. His right palm currently rested on the butt of his pistol, letting Mav know he didn't believe his own words. "Officials have known about this threat for many, many years. I'm sure they have a contingency plan, which we will follow to the letter once it is issued."

"The Army taught you well, but we both know what will happen when the fear sets in. Even good Samaritans get desperate unless they have someone to lead them, which is you."

"That's a grim outlook you have there, Mav." Felix took his time looking around the room at the majority of the residents from Lost Summit. "I've known these townsfolk my entire life and I'm here to tell you that they are goodhearted people who would give you the shirt off of their back. They've all experienced bad times when the last of the mines went under and we all struggled to put food on the table. Each and every one of us knows what it takes to survive. Whatever is said in a few minutes or whatever happens, we will be just fine like we've always been."

Mav wasn't sure what to say to that so he kept quiet and thought over the sheriff's outlook. The town had managed to make it through tough times, but there was a massive difference between an economic depression and all out survival during a state of emergency involving the entire country, if not the world. Mav had experienced both and fought for his life in the latter, but it wasn't until now that he'd comprehended where his thoughts had gone. He would have laughed at the ironic turn of events. He'd just got done lecturing Henley about her view of people while he'd claimed to be holier than thou in that department. Listening to Felix shine a light on his own reservations made him realize that he wasn't as trusting as he'd always thought he was. His assessment of these people was as cynical as Henley's.

"There's nothing wrong with having all your bases covered," Mav cautiously suggested, ignoring the ominous feeling that what they were about to experience was something that no one here could fathom because it was somewhat overwhelming. Ernie had always told his platoon to rely on their gut in sticky situations and Mav had yet to be steered wrong by his instinct. "Just remember this, Chief, if you need my help or that of my brothers, we're at your disposal."

"I appreciate it, Mav." Sheriff Ramsey followed Mav's gaze to where Rat and his friends were now laughing at something someone said and acting like this situation was a common occurrence. "Rat is harmless. He's also a coward and will likely fall into line when the going gets tough."

In Mav's opinion, a coward was the exact type of person that needed to be watched twenty-four seven in this type of situation. They were unpredictable and downright capable of anything, including taking what wasn't theirs to begin with. This was the sheriff's territory and Mav would respect that, but he would also do what was necessary to protect himself and those he cared about. Speaking of which, Henley was now walking their way with two cups of coffee in hand.

"Here," Henley said softly as she handed over the mugs to Mav and Felix. "I thought you two could use some caffeine."

"I'd better get back to Ernie and Reggie," Sheriff Ramsey stated after having thanked Henley for her thoughtfulness. "We'll need to coordinate our efforts should the governor agree with the assessment of Berke's friend."

"Does he doubt us?" Henley asked skeptically, watching as the sheriff maneuvered through the people and back to where Ernie and the mayor were still talking. "If he does, what does he think the press conference is about?"

"The press release might be just what Ernie said it would be—officials telling the citizens everything is fine. Trust me, Paige isn't the only one willing to lose her job over telling family and friends what's about to happen. There will be no jobs to worry about. The media would no doubt pick up on that, leaving the government and the USGS to make remarks to calm the masses." Mav took a drink of his coffee, his mind immediately wondering if they should start conserving their resources this minute. He'd definitely entered into Ernie's territory into thinking the worst and they were about to find out from the murmur that arose. "Listen."

"Turn it up," Elijah called out from his seat at the counter as everyone quieted down. He tapped his ear. "I left my hearing aids at home again."

Mav couldn't see who held the remote, but the sound of

the television ramped higher until the broadcaster's voice could be heard over everyone. Henley took a step closer and Mav figured it was a subconscious action, not that he objected. He found it comical that they'd finally cleared the air and knew where each other stood at a time when it might not matter anymore. The thing of it was…she would always matter to him.

"…listen as we take you live to the Oval Office of the White House."

"Did you ever see that movie about the asteroid hitting Earth?" Henley whispered, a slight tremor to her voice now that reality was settling in. Mav could relate and his chest tightened in apprehension as he watched the President of the United States sitting behind his desk looking as if he'd rather be doing anything else than delivering this news to the American people. "I don't think I'm ready for this."

"None of us are."

"*My fellow Americans, as I'm sure you are aware there was an earthquake at Yellowstone National Park yesterday. Unfortunately, the caldera has been showing signs of eruption over the course of the last forty-eight hours, so it is with deep regret that I am confirming what you have seen across your televisions the past two days. Scientists at the Yellowstone Volcano Observatory have been monitoring ground movements and earthquake activity at Yellowstone for years. The rapid pressure and temperature are unlike anything they've seen before and they alerted the proper officials immediately, but we needed time to make provisions for the people that will be affected should the unthinkable happen. Numerous swarms of seismic activity coupled with other indications the seismologists have been studying have suggested a rate at which this supervolcano has awakened is unprecedented. I wish we were able to tell you if the eruption will occur today, tomorrow, or a week from now. We honestly do not know."*

The voices in the diner started talking over one another and the people started exchanging scared looks and glances. There wasn't anyone to ease their fears, not even the President of the United States. He didn't have the power to prevent such a natural phenomenon. They were on their own unless the government had a plan to evacuate millions of people before the eruption and Mav already knew the likelihood of that.

"We urge the American public to prepare to be on their own for approximately thirty days, if not longer—this includes canned goods, bottled water, first aid kits, and any survival items you deem necessary. For those closer to the affected area we ask that you immediately vacate to the East Coast or as far as you can travel before visibility is impossible. Unfortunately, a large-scale evacuation within the time parameters allowed will be impossible. Emergency assistance will not be available until the ash cloud has settled and we are left to evaluate the damage. Know this—we will not abandon you. We will send help."

"Oh my God," Henley whispered, putting her fingers to her lips. One would have thought that time stood still as the

President of the United States gave his speech. Mav swore he could feel the nails being hammered home as the weight of their situation actually settled over them. The words being broadcasted were a message that most people would see as hope, especially with the polished words and confidence the President conveyed while speaking to the American people. Mav understood it for what it was, as did Ernie who was now looking back at them. The concern in his eyes was heavy and although he'd predicted what would come, he hadn't wanted this.

"...*so what we are dealing with is apocalyptic in nature and unlike anything we have ever had to deal with in our lifetime. Under the provisions of the Federal Emergency Management Act, I hereby declare martial law. Anyone caught looting or acting contrary to the common good order and discipline of the community will be summarily arrested and imprisoned until such time as a trial can be arranged. However, your right to a speedy trial is suspended due to the nature of this catastrophe. Governors in the affected states are empowered to immediately use all federal and state assets, including the National Guard, to secure whatever shelter they need to maintain their local government. I leave you with this...love thy neighbor. Do not panic, do not prey on one another, and do not give up hope. We will come for you. We are American citizens. Our nation remains united. Godspeed and God bless."*

Ernie didn't waste time in clearing his throat and walking around the counter to garner everyone's attention. The danger they were about to face was a cold hard reality and the mayor appeared content to let Ernie take the lead on this. This wasn't going to last a day, a week, or a month. When Yellowstone erupted, it would forever change their lives and they would all be plummeted back into the Stone Age.

Call it coincidence or just sheer bad luck, but when the live feed from the local television station had switched back to show Yellowstone National Park, something was happening onscreen before Ernie had a chance to speak. Multiple vents could be seen within the span of the next few minutes. They had opened up and steam was pounding into the air. Cries, gasps, and screams echoed throughout the diner as the aired footage demonstrated that Yellowstone National Park was being systematically dismantled by a massive ground swell.

The image was unlike any other Mav had ever seen and Henley reached for his hand for the first time since he'd known her. She held on tightly as they witnessed the camera on scene shake, the ground crack, and suddenly the feed went to static that remained until the picture transferred back to a stunned national news anchor. As if they'd been transported directly to Wyoming to experience the eruption themselves…the blast traveled at the speed of light. The citizens of Lost Summit heard a distant rumble, followed by a horrendous crack, as if lightning had struck just outside. The energy from the blast echoed off the surrounding mountains and everyone felt the reverberation of the detonation that would haunt their nightmares for many years to come.

Henley instinctively turned into Mav's embrace, seeking safety from what they'd just witnessed and experienced. How was it that they could hear and feel something that happened over eight hundred miles away? The dishes rattled, the chairs moved, and the lights swung from the ceiling.

Jeremy, who was the son of Marvin Jenkins, reached out to steady Elijah. Ernie did the same with Mabel. The vibrations slowly evaporated, leaving everyone breathless, frightened, and irrevocably grateful that they were still alive. Everyone desperately focused on the television once the sound dissipated to see if any other visuals would return. Mav understood the need to see your enemy, so he focused on the screen as well. The camera was still focused on the newscaster who was currently trying to compose himself. The man's face was pale and it appeared that he was quite shaken, as were the rest of them.

"Folks, what you just saw was the Yellowstone Caldera erupting. I don't know how much longer we will have to bring you coverage. If what the geologists say is true, the eruption of the caldera will put between four hundred and six hundred and fifty cubic miles of debris in the earth's atmosphere. That will cause a volcanic winter to descend on the northern hemisphere for as long as ten years. The ash from the eruption will fall over nearly the entire continental United States, thick enough to collapse most wooden structures, especially if the ash was to get wet. Breathing the ash into your lungs will cause you to asphyxiate as it absorbs the moisture in your lungs and hardens

like cement. Please make every reasonable effort to move to a safe location to ride out the national emergency before us all. We will now attempt to return you to the coverage we have available. We are switching over to the operation feeds we have nearest the park and..."

Mav didn't need to hear the newscaster's description. It was there for all to see on the little twenty-two inch tube television, even with cracks in the screen on the other end that must have come from the initial explosion. Grey ash had already been shot into the sky as far as one could see, merging with the clouds and funneling out until it shaded out the blue filament. The vivid orange of the lava now joined the covering mass of residue, bubbling and sending massive balls of fire into the air with a force that a human couldn't possibly contemplate. The destruction left behind wasn't visible, but maybe that was a good thing. It left little doubt that the people of Wyoming, Montana, and Idaho didn't stand a chance to survive. Suddenly static filled the screen and it was apparent they'd already lost the satellite feed. Mav stroked his hand up and down Henley's back, needing comfort from what they'd just witnessed as well. The loss of life was never easy to witness.

"Henley, I want you to get up to the lodge now. Ernie and I will meet you up there, but that's the safest place for you to be. Make sure you have your level action Remington with you and plenty of ammunition." Mav could hear Ernie giving instructions and those that were in the diner were heeding his advice for the most part. Sheriff Ramsey and the mayor were backing him up and giving orders to those that had the ability to help. It was times like these that society sought out leaders and the residents had lucked out. Ernie "Tank" Yates was one of the best and Mav would follow that man to the end of the earth, which might be sooner than any of them wanted. "The wind is in our favor, so that will give us more lead time."

"I'm not leaving the town," Henley argued, stepping back far enough so that Mav's arms fell to his sides. She waved a hand toward the counter in despair while determination settled into her beautiful features. "Elijah is eighty-two years old, Mav. He'll need help, along with Mrs. Welsh, Mr. Roberts, and Mr. Powell."

Mav wasn't going to get Henley to change her mind, so he hastily considered their options before implementing some instructions. According to Ernie's previous calculations they still had time as long as the wind coordinates stayed in their favor. What the town needed was an emergency evacuation plan should things change.

"Fine," Mav declared, making a decision that he hoped he wouldn't regret. "Get everyone over to the Village Community Center. Send Jeremy house to house if you have to and don't let him forget to retrieve Mrs. Welsh's portable oxygen tank."

Mav signaled to Ernie, who was still speaking with the diners. The best course of action right now was to treat this like a military mission. Once the facts were known they would then be able to give the residents an informed opinion on the best course of action. He just hoped like hell there was one available.

"Henley is going to round everyone up and have them meet us at the community center," Mav advised Ernie as both of them walked out of the diner and into the bright sun leaving behind Henley, the sheriff, and the mayor to see to it that those behind would be walked over to the meeting site. It was still relatively cool since the average temperature in April was in the mid-fifties, but it was hard to believe that over eight hundred miles away Yellowstone was going to take that away from them and plunge them into a cold, dark winter for years to come. "I still think our safest bet is to get them over the Canadian line and move them as far north as humanly possible. We're taking a chance by staying here."

"Son, you and I both know that we can't outrun this." Ernie squinted his eyes as he looked across the road to the line of small shops. "This will test our wills and bring out our true colors. We either survive as a group or disintegrate one by one."

"What are you saying, Tank?" To Mav it sounded as if Ernie wasn't willing to fight against the fate they'd been dealt. It was unlike the man and Mav refused to believe he wasn't willing to find a way to survive. He stepped in front of him, cutting off Tank's path to the right. "A thick cloud of ash will descend right over us if the wind shifts. If the winds maintain their direction as of right now, I figure we have roughly a week before the ash travels the globe and ends up right here in Lost

Summit. You even said so yourself. Either way we're better north than we are here. The bunker the guys and I helped you build would only give us a few months of survival based on the amount of people here and then what? It would be impossible to travel with that much ash coating the area. And that's just a handful of us. Are you willing to choose who lives and who dies?"

"I don't think we'll have to," Ernie replied in a vague manner, motioning toward the post office. The patrons of the diner started to file out, following Henley past them on the sidewalk. Jeremy turned left to where the majority of the town's small residential area was located. Mav felt naked without his weapon, so he opened the back of his Jeep Rubicon all the while keeping his eyes and ears trained on Ernie. "I want to grab some more maps from the post office to see what we're looking at, but our town is located in a valley with its own natural resources. We have natural springs for water, lakes for fishing, a running river, and hardworking people to sustain a safe environment."

"For ten years? What about the ash? It'll eventually make its way into the lakes and rivers." Mav could see where Ernie was going with this, but they'd have to convince the people in Lost Summit. They would need definitive proof or some of these residents would panic and head for the hills. He unlocked the safety box he used to store his service weapon and then fastened the brown leather holster over his shoulder. "Tank, we shouldn't be the ones to make that call unless we're damn sure we can stay here and survive."

"I am sure, son. I put away more than you know. There have been some changes since you last saw the bunker and the latest improvements make it nearly self-sustaining for an extended period," Ernie said with conviction, not taking his eyes off of Mabel as she trailed Elijah, who was using his cane for balance. The majority of the residents were over sixty years old and it finally hit Mav that Ernie had taken that into consideration. They wouldn't have the wherewithal to travel the distance needed for additional safety. Vehicles would only get them so far before the ash arrived and left them stranded. "It's only a matter of time before we lose contact with the rest of the world. Make what phone calls you have to and I'll meet you over at the Village Community Center. We'll need all the help we can get to convince the people to stay."

CHAPTER EIGHT

HENLEY HAD MANAGED to gather most of the residents at the community center, thanks to the help of Jeremy. She had done an informal head count and they were currently missing Lola Murray and her daughter. The two women ran the Summit Inn together, although they rarely had occupants out of season. She was afraid to stop and catch her breath for fear of the situation becoming too overwhelming. The world as they knew it was over as of twenty minutes ago. She shook that thought away as she headed for the exit of the community center.

Sheriff Ramsey had been looking over maps to create a plan of survival, but now Ernie was trying to tell him they already had one. She hadn't caught sight of Mav since they'd been at the diner, but she wasn't worried that he'd gone and left them to fend on their own. He would never leave Ernie, or the town for that matter. He was a man of integrity and she didn't doubt that now, although she'd been damn slow in getting to that realization.

"Jeremy, I'm running back over to the inn," Henley said, thinking of the items that Ernie and the sheriff might need.

Her mind had been spinning since she'd seen the news and she still couldn't quite believe this was happening, regardless that she'd known deep down this was a real possibility. A disaster on this scale wasn't easy to comprehend, but she had a feeling they would all get a better look at what a true catastrophe was up close and personal before this was over. She was terrified, but she wouldn't show her fear to those who needed hope. "I'll be back as soon as I can. Please do your best to keep everyone inside."

Henley pulled a hair tie out of the front pocket of her jeans and gathered her hair back as she walked through the open door. Keeping herself busy was keeping her from facing the horror that was surely coming their way. Elijah had wanted to be positioned by the door so that he could see outside, so the entrance was now being held open by a rubber doorstopper as he sat just inside the doorframe. He'd nodded her way, his solemn grey eyes immediately returning to stare at the sky to the southeast. She tamped down her fear of the unknown and started to jog toward the post office.

Henley veered right instead of walking left onto Main Street and entered the empty post office. She didn't think twice about walking around the wooden counter to where a portable multi-band radio sat underneath on a shelf. It couldn't hurt to have another one. It had been there from the time she was a child and its newer replacement had still been there when she'd returned home from California. Grabbing ahold of the black cord, she yanked on it until the prongs came out of the socket and she was able to gather the little black radio into the crook of her arm.

Henley stood and gasped when she saw someone on the other side of the counter. She almost dropped the radio but managed to catch it just in time. She brought it close to her chest as she tried to even out her breathing.

"What the hell, Mav?" Henley snapped, walking to the side and throwing the half door open a little harder than necessary. She was already skittish about what they could expect at any moment. She didn't need any stress added on. "You scared the shit out of me."

"Sorry," Mav said, not sounding apologetic in the least. He'd armed himself and currently had his cell phone in his hand. Henley thought of her modeling days and how shallow that lifestyle had been, already knowing that a lot of them wouldn't survive the devastation that was about to arrive on their doorstep. She'd never been more grateful for her decision to move back home when she did, even though her parents were no longer alive. "I saw you walking in here and wanted to make sure you were okay. Is everyone at the community center?"

"Nearly, but I need to go over to the inn." Henley handed off the radio when he held out his hand. It amazed her to find that even with everything going on she could still focus on the warmth his fingers spread to hers. The defenses she'd put up were no longer there and she would have liked nothing better than to walk back into his arms like she'd done at the diner.

ESSENTIAL BEGINNINGS

She walked away instead and pushed open the door faster than she normally would have and cringed when she wasn't sure what she'd find. The sky was still clear and she breathed deeply, taking advantage of every clean inhalation she could. "I'll meet you over at the center. I want to make sure Lola and her daughter heard about what happened."

"I just came from there. They're walking over now and will join the others in a minute." Mav nodded toward their left and Henley was able to see Lola and Missy walking towards the building. "I also stopped by the hardware store to make sure Mr. Jenkins wasn't taking his sweet old time. Jeremy did a good job notifying the town."

"How could anyone miss what happened?" Henley asked, figuring the entire country felt the eruption. She shielded her eyes as she looked toward the sky, but so far there was no ash to be seen. Mav was a lot like Ernie and wouldn't sugarcoat anything, so she asked him point blank. "What are our chances?"

"At this point?" Mav started walking and Henley fell into step beside him. The sun's rays were warm, but next week? They'd be lucky if it wasn't below freezing. "Ernie's right. Going over our options…our best chance might be to stay here, but it's not like we won't be touched by what's coming our way. We'll just have it slightly better, which will improve our odds of survival."

Mav stopped Henley from entering the community center where everyone was now gathered. He'd placed a gentle hand on her arm and the look in his eyes caused her worry to spike further. She felt a sharp pain in her chest that had nothing to do with fear and everything to do with her previous anxiety issues. She'd stopped taking medicine over a year ago, but at this rate she'd be using up what she had left in her medicine cabinet.

"I spoke with all the guys a few minutes ago," Mav said, seemingly not concerned that Elijah overhead him. "There are things we'll need that Ernie hasn't thought of, so I split a list between Berke, Owen, Mason, and Van. They'll bring what they can, but them making it here safely takes precedence."

"How is it that Van can even make it here?" Henley asked worriedly, knowing full well that Van lived in New York. He'd have to literally cross the entirety of the United States to reach Lost Summit. "Or the rest of them, for that matter."

"I guarantee the FAA has already closed down the airports, so they'll have to take whatever means necessary—vehicles until the engines are affected by the ash, maybe motorcycles since certain models have air-cooled engines, or on foot if need be. I gave them frequencies for an HF radio that we can monitor for emergency signals from them." Mav still held the radio, but he slid his free hand down her arm until he had ahold of her fingers. "I have no doubt that Ernie will coordinate this town the way he commanded his platoon in the Corps. But what I'm asking you now is that you go back up to the lodge."

Henley would have immediately objected, but Mav

squeezed her fingers to indicate he needed her to listen. She would, but that didn't mean she would agree to what he was requesting. This was her home and while she might have hidden away up at the lodge for the past three years, that didn't mean she didn't care about these people. He couldn't stop her from helping them.

"I've lived in situations and seen the reactions of people when times become increasingly desperate," Mav said, finally letting her go to tuck the radio under his arm. He reached into his pocket and pulled out the keys to his Jeep. He placed them into the palm of her hand. "Take my vehicle and go secure the bunker. No one goes in. Everyone here knows about it and I won't allow them to take it away from Tank should things go south and it's needed. We'll be behind you shortly."

"No one is going to try and take that bunker for themselves," Henley said defensively, not willing to believe that anyone who still lived in town would be that selfish. Mav was overreacting and Elijah wasn't helping by humming his agreement every two seconds. "We should—"

Henley was interrupted by loud voices coming from inside the building and they both turned to find out what had prompted the outburst. She followed and noticed that Elijah had turned in his seat to get a better view.

"We're heading north and we'll take whoever wants to go with us," Rat declared, standing in the middle of the room with Randy Bassett on one side and Jarrett Moore on the other. All three men looked determined and it was more than apparent that they'd made up their minds. Ernie didn't appear too surprised at the man's announcement, but the sheriff was trying to get the three hard-cases to see reason. "Felix, we all know you'll listen to what Yates has to say, but how does he know that we'd be okay here? We're sitting ducks and you know it. Canada is our best shot and we're going to take it. Who's with us?"

"Rat, you and I both know the Canadian patrol officer up at the border and he won't allow you or anyone else to pass through unless he's been given instructions to do so," Henley warned, walking up and standing alongside Mabel who'd stood when Stanley had started bellowing his intentions. Mav had made his way to the front and had set the radio down next to the map that Ernie had flattened out on the hard surface. "Now the sheriff and the mayor have emergency contingencies in place and they'll give us our best options. It's not in our interest to take off on some wild goose chase when time is so short."

"Don't you start with me, young lady," Rat cautioned, shooting a sideways look toward Ernie before launching into a tirade that left Henley speechless and more than a little sick to her stomach. "You'd take Yates' side no matter what he said because he gave you a job when you came running back to our little backwater town with your tail between your legs when you couldn't make it in the real world. Everyone here knows about the eating disorder you had that led to your hospital stay and then the mental breakdown when you couldn't handle your own personal business. Your parents would have been ashamed of—"

"Say another word," Mav threatened in a low voice that Henley had never heard before, "and I'll drop your corpse over the Canadian border myself."

Mav had somehow managed to get from the front of the large room in a matter of seconds so that he stood inches from Rat with his arms at his sides. Henley lost all color in her face and she had trouble swallowing, not sure how to respond to calm down the deadly situation. Unfortunately Rat was right about most of what he'd said with the exception of her parents. They had loved her unconditionally and remembering that fact aided in her composure. Having Mav protecting her the way he was only added to her rising confidence.

"What Ernie has is compassion, unlike the likes of you," Henley spoke softly, not needing to raise her voice like Rat had during his condescending speech. She cursed that everyone could hear the tremble, but they had bigger things to worry about right now. "And you don't have the right to speak for upstanding honest folks like my parents. We are all scared. We don't know what to expect, but I do know that we need to listen to Ernie if we have any chance of survival."

"You have two choices." Mav's fingers curled into fists as he stated his demands. "You sit your ass down and do what the sheriff tells you to or you leave town now while you can still move under your own power."

Henley hadn't realized that Mabel had laid a hand on her

arm until she went to move toward the two men, Mav apparently not willing to let Rat's remarks go. She patted the older woman's hand to let her know that she was all right. Henley wasn't, but she didn't have the luxury of running up to the lodge and hiding out again.

"You best get out of my face, boy." Rat leveled a stare at Mav, causing Henley to finally understand what Mav had been saying all along. People resorted to desperate measures when their judgment was clouded with fear. She didn't think it was possible, but Mav managed to move closer to the man. That didn't stop Rat from talking. "Your friends aren't here to back you up anymore."

"Get out then." Henley stepped away from Mabel until she was side by side with Mav. She glanced toward the sheriff, who was watching the scene unfold but not doing anything to stop it. The reason why confused her until she saw that Ernie had his fingers on Felix's arm to prevent the sheriff from intervening. "Stanley, no one is going to stop—"

"I'm going to say this once more," Mav clarified in a deadpan voice that had even Henley taking a step back. "You either sit down or you get the fuck out. What's it going to be, shitheel?"

No one in the building seemed to breathe, as if they were waiting for an explosion to happen inside instead of dealing with the one eight hundred miles away. Stanley moved slightly side to side but it didn't deter Mav in the least from standing his ground. Rat was finally getting it into his thick head that he might have underestimated his chances when Randy and Jarrett slowly back away from him and took some empty seats behind them. Stanley looked sideways and evidently didn't like his odds anymore.

"I'll stay to hear what the sheriff has to say and then I'll make up my own mind."

Stanley was the first one to back up a step, but he didn't join his other two friends in the chairs. He took up position behind the townspeople instead and crossed his arms while still casting Mav a menacing glance. Henley was surprised when Mav finally turned to her, fury filling his brown eyes.

"Don't interfere like that again. You don't know him anymore," Mav said in a low tone so that no one could overhear him. This wasn't the man who kissed her last night. "Men like Ratliff are imminently dangerous and placating them only makes them see you as weak and as a target."

Mav walked away before Henley had a chance to defend her actions and she felt a spark of ire herself at his arrogance. It was she who was verbally attacked by Stanley and she could say what she wanted in response. She was an adult woman who'd taken charge of her life years ago and she would continue doing so. If he thought that just because they'd both laid their cards on the table that gave him the right to take over making decisions for her, he was sorely mistaken.

CHAPTER NINE

THE DRIVE TO the lodge was made in silence, and Henley had yet to really speak to Mav directly after he'd rebuked her for trying to reason with a man like Stanley Ratliff. He'd dealt with those kinds of men his entire time in the Corps and the only thing that kept them in place was someone they couldn't intimidate. Rat had no right to drag Henley's past into the forefront of the town meeting and it had enraged Mav to see the pain in her eyes. Now all he felt from her was an anger that rivaled his own.

"The situation had been about to get out of control." Henley's comment broke the quiet as if a two by four had smashed into the windshield. She shifted in her seat so that she could face him, but Mav kept his eyes on the road and the taillights in front of him. Tank had taken the lead back to the cabins after a long and drawn out meeting in which Rat and his cronies had stayed to listen. "It was easier to try and get Stanley to see reason instead of letting him wander off to die. You and I both know he'd never make it unless Cody up at the border allowed him to cross."

"Having Rat here is more dangerous to the people staying,"

Mav cautioned, not knowing how else to explain this to her. Ernie, the sheriff, and even the mayor had all come together to explain why staying in Lost Summit was the best course of action. The town had access to natural gas, numerous naturally filtered mountain springs, additional food supplies that had been bought with the upcoming tourist season in mind, and mines for shelter when the ash fall made the wooden structured buildings unsafe. The majority of the people were in agreement, but there were still some that were on the fence. Their instinct was to flee, but yet it was that same fear that kept them in place. This town was all they knew. "It's been ten hours since the eruption and in another sixty or so the ash cloud will have reached the East Coast. The emergency radio broadcasts have already confirmed mass casualties and it's only a matter of time before millions more are added to the list. Communications have all but ceased from the worst affected areas and it won't be long before we'll lose touch with the outside world. It's imperative that we stick together, but having someone like Ratliff here is asking to destroy what we're trying to maintain."

"Why doesn't it feel that way then?" Henley asked, causing Mav to look over at her to decipher her meaning. Her back was to the door and she'd taken the shoulder strap of the seatbelt and tucked it underneath her arm. Her brows were furrowed and she lifted her hands in exasperation. "Hundreds of miles away people have died already and yet we're in this bubble that feels impenetrable. It doesn't seem real. Rat shouldn't be excluded from that just because he's an asshole and you shouldn't get to choose who lives or dies."

"I'm not saying I do, but I will continue to protect those that can't protect themselves."

"I'll have you know that I can protect myself just fine," Henley bit off between clenched teeth. Mav could see this argument was getting them nowhere, but she continued before he could stop her. "My father taught me how to use a pistol at a young age and I used to carry personal protection with me back in California. Rat doesn't scare me so much as he's just a nuisance that has the ability to influence other people. We needed him there to listen and see reason, so that the people who do give him credence could see that the sheriff knows what he's doing."

Mav wouldn't argue that Sheriff Felix Ramsey had stepped up to the plate and done his duty in prepping his community for the harsh days to come. He'd made calls to the National Guard, the county and state police, and even the governor's office to let them know that he was having his residents hunker down until the worst of the disaster had passed. All that was left to do now was prepare and they had less than a week to do so before any of the most severe elements appeared.

"I think I liked it better when you ignored me."

Henley's lips parted into a perfect circle until she smiled. It was the first one he'd seen since last night and his comment had the effect he'd wanted. Mav didn't want to fight with her.

That was the last thing either of them needed and it was clear that they didn't see eye to eye on how to handle specific situations, but he would continue to keep tabs on Rat. Right now they needed to get back to the lodge so that he and Ernie could prepare the area for a secondary camp if need be. There was no way in hell they could fit forty-eight people there including Berke, Mason, Owen, and Van unless everyone doubled up and ate quite a bit less. Fifteen rooms in the lodge and eight remaining cabins were what they had to deal with right now. Mav didn't forget that Kellen Truman had decided to hunker down as well. They would need to take inventory of the emergency stores Ernie had in storage, along with everything else that could possibly be used to solidify their future.

"Trust me, you were hard to ignore," Henley all but whispered, causing the vehicle to heat up in a manner Mav was sure she wasn't ready for. He hadn't seen this timid side of her and he wasn't sure how to respond. He'd been up front with her about what he wanted and she'd all but stated she wasn't ready for anything other than friendship. Or was she? She hadn't had a chance to comment after he'd spelled it out for her. Henley cleared her throat as Mav met her gaze. Her throat moved gracefully as she swallowed and he deeply regretted that they were now in a situation that was bound to become life and death. He also lamented that she switched the subject to something safe, at least in terms of emotions. "It looks like we're home, so I'll go check on our guest and fill him in on what's happened."

"Truman likely already knows," Mav replied, letting their conversation slide for now. There was still quite a bit of work ahead of them to prepare for what was to come and he would feel a hell of a lot better once his fellow Marines arrived. They were the only ones he trusted outside of Ernie, and in all likelihood the two of them alone stood only a fifty-fifty chance if some of the better-armed residents in town decided to take the bunker by force. What they didn't understand was there weren't enough provisions down there for what was truly needed, leaving Ernie's theory of Lost Summit being naturally protected by the high mountains to the west being the best scenario they had. Mav hoped like hell it was true, but it wasn't like they had many options. "Stay away from the man until we know more about him. I'll talk to him and see if he's contacted anyone that might be headed this way. We need to be prepared for people to start coming this direction, which is why I'm glad that Felix has stationed Jeremy on the only incoming access road."

"Elijah's house is on the west side of town and he said he'd keep a lookout from his back porch," Henley said, unclicking her seatbelt as they finally pulled onto the lane that led to the cabins. She shifted her body back into the seat and looked ahead at something that caught her eye and she finished her thought somewhat vaguely. "It'll give him something to do so he doesn't feel useless. Mav, Kellen seems to be waiting for us."

Mav had already noticed the other man standing off to the

side where Tank had already parked his truck. There was a grim look on Truman's face, alerting them that something else had happened. Ernie was in the process of opening his door when Mav drove passed and parked closer to where Henley's cabin was located. He parked the Jeep and then quickly exited with the intention of opening her door, but she'd already beat him to it.

"Where are you going?" Mav asked, placing a hand on Henley's arm to stop her from walking any farther. He didn't want her anywhere near Truman. "We can't be wasting time, so why don't I meet you at the storage locker in back. You can get a quick count on the supplies, cots, and sleeping bags we have to distribute if we need to provide for more than what Ernie thought would be necessary."

"Mav, I already know our inventory and I can recite it to you by heart," Henley said in irritation, shaking off his hand to continue in the direction of Tank and Truman. She shot him a sideways look when he fell into step beside her, but he didn't rightly care. Her attitude was going to get both of them killed eventually, especially since Truman wasn't what he appeared to be along with her penchant for taking everyone that appeared at her doorstep at face value. He would have thought from her experience in Hollywood that she could see the masks that people usually wore, but it was as if she'd put a divider between her two lives. She was wrong if she thought that the townsfolk from her hometown were different. They weren't. Mav could perceive a threat a mile away and this man had a written warning label stuck to his forehead. He kept pace with her when she quickened her stride. "Let's face it, we feel useless by not doing anything and twiddling our thumbs. We have a *need* to do something other than sit here and admit defeat. I get it. But there is nothing more we can do with the exception of protecting our town and taking care of our own. Oh, and have sex. Would you like that in between our breaks of defending what's ours?"

Henley stopped and whipped around to face him, the anxiety within her eyes telling him how hard she was trying to keep her head together. She'd shocked Mav with her last exclamation, but that had been her intention. Everyone was dealing with this disaster in their own way and his was to take charge, protect, and keep them alive. Hers? Mav didn't know, because he hadn't taken the time to ask and now he felt like an ass.

"Come here," Mav murmured, taking her by the hands and pulling her to him. Henley resisted at first, but then she allowed him to envelop her into his arms. She fit perfectly with every curve and he held her tightly for the first time in three years. He rested his chin on her head as she laid her cheek against his chest and slid her hands up his back. There was a hint of vanilla he'd never breathed before. It came from her brown hair and he dipped his head so that he could press his lips against her silky strands. They stood that way for a moment longer, ignoring the two men not ten feet away. "It's going to be okay."

"You don't know that," Henley whispered, her fingers

digging deeper into his shirt and skin. Her voice trembled, but she didn't break down. "I thought I was fine up here, keeping to myself while only having Ernie to worry about. I really wasn't okay and now it's too late."

Henley slowly pulled away, looking up at him with those green eyes that had haunted his dreams for longer than he cared to remember. There was regret, fear, and a sorrow for what they were about to lose. She was right when she said it didn't seem real that Mother Nature had stirred awake and eradicated a hundred thousand people while they stood here seemingly unaffected. He knew it for the lie it was and he could only imagine the devastation to come.

"I'm afraid, too, Henley," Mav softly conceded, trusting that his admission would make her understand that she wasn't alone. He brushed the back of his fingers down the side of her face, wishing beyond hope that they had the means to endure this catastrophe. This wasn't a television show that allowed them to go on with their lives afterward. The fallout of this would go on for years, the infrastructure of their country would eventually fail, and it would forever be a different world. Even the country might be destroyed by this overwhelming disaster. One just couldn't comprehend every consequence in one day. "We all are, but I can promise you that I will do whatever is necessary to see us through this. And as for it being too late...it's never too late to struggle against the tide."

Henley pulled away at the sound of Ernie calling them over

to where he stood with Truman. Mav wasn't quite ready to let her go, but he didn't really have a choice at the moment. This morning before all of this happened he would have driven away and not returned until the end of the year. He would have gone through months of being angry over what she'd said, resentful that he hadn't handled it better, and bitter that nothing had been resolved. It was astonishing that emotions and actions could change so much in so short a time, but it all seemed petty to him now. They would have to talk about it as soon as he was done figuring out who Truman was and what he wanted.

"Kellen has just told me that he's been in touch with Fairchild Air Force Base down near Spokane." Ernie appeared skeptical and Mav took his lead, trying to maneuver himself so that his body shielded Henley. She had other ideas and stood directly at his side, measuring the situation and causing him to be slightly uneasy. Talk about a contradiction. For how cautious she was, she had a tendency to be spontaneous and he was afraid that would put them in a precarious situation. "They apparently will make room for anyone who can make it to the base."

"We'll let the residents know first thing in the morning." Mav carefully worded his statement so that he didn't give out any names of those in charge, specially the sheriff or the mayor. "We appreciate your help. What branch of service did you say you were in?"

"I researched the area before deciding on this trip and I

know that the population is close to fifty," Kellen disclosed, blatantly not answering Mav's question. The man had not only skirted replying, he'd carefully steered the conversation back to the town. Mav glanced around the wilderness and had to wonder if this man had truly arrived alone. "The base is their best chance at survival and the citizens should head there tomorrow based on the military's calculation of when the ash cloud will reach us."

"Like I said," Mav reiterated, having an itch to scout the area but he would take a more powerful weapon than his pistol, "we'll inform the mayor tomorrow of your offer and allow the residents to make their own decision based on all the facts."

"I'd like to go into town with you," Kellen replied, skimming his eyes over Henley, although not in a sexual manner. It was more of a measuring glance than anything. "I can give the mayor more information if need be."

"That'll be fine," Ernie commented rather tersely, ending the conversation. "Is there anything else you'll be needing this evening? If not, we'll see you at zero five hundred."

"Zero five hundred it is," Kellen agreed before turning back to his lodging. Mav noticed the man's gaze hesitated as they drifted across the back of the grounds where Henley's cabin was located. The action solidified exactly where Mav would be spending the night, after he reconnoitered the area of course. "Good night."

Mav, Ernie, and Henley stayed where they were as Truman

shut himself inside of his cabin, a single light shining from the lone window of the wooden structure. The man didn't appear too concerned that an eruption of a supervolcano had already wiped out thousands of lives and would continue to do so for years to come. He didn't fool himself into believing that Truman wouldn't be up the rest of the night monitoring them, but that didn't stop Mav from indicating to Tank that he wanted the keys to the bunker where there was a stash of proper weapons for emergencies such as these.

"Take Henley to her cabin so I can do my job," Mav said low enough for them to hear but not loud enough that they could be overheard in case someone was listening. He caught the set of keys that Ernie had thrown him and didn't pause to explain things to Henley. Ernie would take care of that, but Mav was angry with himself that he hadn't brought Jeremy up to the fishing lodge instead of allowing him to monitor the comings and goings of people that could pose a threat to Lost Summit. The three of them didn't have what it took to protect the lodge properly from a determined force, which was why it was critical that the guys show up sooner rather than later. "And Tank? Stick to our motto. Shoot first, ask questions of the next of kin."

CHAPTER TEN

Henley slammed the cabinet after she'd snatched two coffee mugs and did her best not to break them against the counter setting them down. How dare Mav treat her like some helpless female who didn't know her way around a damn cave? She wasn't some fragile woman who needed to be taken care of when she had that ability all on her own. Just because she apologized for the misinterpretation of his character didn't mean she was a doormat. They needed to have a major discussion to set him straight if that's what he thought. She'd been raised in this area, taught how to hunt and fish from a young age, although her agent had kept that out of her modeling résumé. The power players had recommended omitting that fact due to not everyone thinking being self-sufficient was appealing. She could handle a weapon just as well as the men in town according to her father. She was losing sight of why she was angry at Maverick and that just wouldn't do.

"We can't afford to lose any dishes or cups, so go easy over there, missy," Ernie grumbled while he stood next to the window listening to the shortwave radio he'd turned up not ten minutes prior. He had even repositioned it from the kitchen counter to the coffee table. She didn't even bother to look over her shoulder at him because she knew she'd find his back to her. "This Kellen Truman didn't come today by mistake. He had this planned and there must be a damn good reason. Did you notice any firearm cases in his luggage when he unloaded his gear into the cabin?"

Henley didn't point out that Kellen had made the reservation months ago. Ernie would come up with some conspiracy that the military had already known about the Yellowstone caldera and had been making preparations. She wasn't about to debate more half-assed theories with him. She'd been proven wrong in the most horrific way and for the hundredth time today she tried to push away thoughts of the people that hadn't made it out alive.

"No, all I saw was the overnight bag he put next to the door. Tank, we need to drive back into town and let Felix know about the base accepting people." Henley watched as the coffee maker finished its brewing cycle, waiting for the last drop to fall. She then pulled out the pot to pour the much-needed fresh java into the mugs. They hadn't broken when she'd set them down and she felt smug for just a second at that fact. Unfortunately, it made her realize how on edge she really was in feeling a sense of accomplishment that she hadn't broken the dishes. She took a moment to deeply inhale the delicious aroma, giving thanks to whoever was listening that she was still able to do so. "I'm sure their buildings have roofs that won't collapse under the weight of the ash. We need to be thinking about that."

"I already showed you my calculations. The measurement won't be enough to cause much more damage here than that of a heavy winter's storm with a full load of snow by the time it travels around the continents. The cabins and the lodge were constructed with twice that average load in mind when they were built."

"Other than what it will do to our air, soil, and ground water," Henley added on wryly, not even going to debate this with him. She'd lose and right now…she wasn't in the mood. She put the pot back onto the burner and then collected their mugs. "Our phones still work. Why don't you call him so that at least he knows and then let him make that decision?"

"Communications won't work that much longer with the exception of the single channel radio sets in the bunker, and I can guarantee that the sheriff is tending to his own family instead of sitting in front of that short range two-way radio in his patrol car," Ernie replied, finally looking over his shoulder. He'd taken his baseball cap off and it was sticking out of the back pocket of his dark grey pants that he usually wore fishing. His words stopped her in her tracks. "You would have known about the satellite relay coverage taking a crap if you'd been listening to Truman and me when we were having our conversation instead of taking a not-so-private moment with Mav."

"It wasn't a private moment," Henley snapped and all but

shoved Ernie's coffee into his hands. It was really hard to remember that he was in his sixties, especially at times like these. "And are you telling me we've already lost contact with the outside world?"

"I explained to you the chronological order of things last night." Ernie lifted the mug to his lips and took a sip, somehow the liquid not touching his mustache. "Now it's a matter of making the right choices to survive. AM radio maybe—FM is mostly line of sight or relayed over landline and transmitted for thirty to fifty miles in this kind of environment. SHF is toast, although UHF might still be working for airborne platforms in the unaffected areas and that will only last until the ash cloud arrives. VHF and HF are all that we have left. The military will soon assume control of the landlines that remain in operation, assuming newer generation microwave towers can still operate covered in ash and of course while the power grid is still working. Doubtful beyond the next three days at best."

Henley startled when a bang came on the front door, causing her coffee to slosh over the rim of her cup. She cursed and gave Ernie the honor of letting in Mav, who'd already announced his presence through the thick wooden planks. She turned and walked back to the small kitchenette for a hand towel.

"Well?" Ernie moved back and then closed the door behind Mav. He immediately went back to his station at the window, taking another long sip of his hot beverage. "Anyone out there?"

"Not that I can tell, but Owen always was a better tracker than me." Mav glanced over Henley's way but didn't address the elephant in the room. She gave him credit for being smart, because she would have lost her temper had he brought up the fact that he'd just treated her like a five-year-old girl. Right now he was carrying two Rock River LMT 4 .223 caliber AR style rifles along with two pouches containing five extra thirty round magazines and a Lula speed-loading tool for each. He handed off the spare rifle and the second pouch to Ernie. She knew the caliber, brand, and what it could do because she'd been taught. Mav needed to understand that she could walk by his side and not hide behind him. "It'll be good when they finally get here."

Mav had stressed the word *when* and had purposefully not used *if*. Henley understood his need to have faith in the fact that his friends would arrive here safely, but she still couldn't fathom having to travel the distance needed in the ever increasingly hazardous conditions. The harsh elements would make traveling all that much harder given that they wouldn't be able to breathe without a mask that would require a new, clean, unclogged filter every few hours, let alone dealing with groups of terrorized people in search of someone to help them—people that would take what they couldn't get by any means and kill for what they couldn't steal. Mav thought she wasn't listening to him, but she was.

"We'll tell the sheriff tomorrow morning what we heard

from this Truman character and then give traveling supplies to those who don't want to stay here," Ernie said with a tad bit of resignation. He couldn't make everyone see things as clearly as he did. Look how long it had taken him to convince her and Mav. "In the meantime we need shifts. We can't be caught off guard sleeping if Truman has ulterior motives. I'll take the first two hours and then we'll rotate. We'll figure out the angles needed to secure the property and the likely avenues of approach once the others arrive. We will subsist inside the perimeter until we have to retreat to the bunker. We can survive for years once we're inside if we have to."

"I'll be included in that rotation," Henley stated loudly, staring at Mav and daring him to contradict her. His lips thinned out but he didn't argue. She wanted to ensure that it would remain that way. "Mav, could I speak with you in private?"

"That's a good idea," Ernie commended with a nod of his head. Henley's irritation rose at the fact that there was little privacy, but it wasn't like it was something she could change. He started for the door but then added on one more thing before he left that lifted her spirits. "You two need to sort out your baggage because anything left up in the air will only pull us down."

All that could be heard was the low murmuring of the emergency radio, giving as much detail of what was occurring in the Midwest as possible. Volcanic ash was raining down from the sky, visibility was nil, there were high casualties in the blast area, and the people who had survived were either trying to drive their way out of those areas or staying put. Unfortunately, neither option was useful unless properly prepared. Mav's brown eyes sought hers and in them was a touch of helplessness, diluting their previous tension but not totally erasing it.

Mav slowly walked through the living area, the rifle still slung over his shoulder. He reminded her of one of those actors that had a distinctive swagger that let everyone know he wasn't one to mess with. She doubted he would take kindly to that comparison and truth be told, she knew from Ernie that the vast majority of those actors wouldn't have lasted a day in real combat. Mav didn't acknowledge or agree with anything that she or Ernie had said, but at least he wasn't arguing with her. It was progress.

"The coffee is fresh," Henley offered and followed that up with a wave of her towel. Mav didn't immediately head that way, but instead stopped directly in front of her and lifted the cloth off of her hand. His touch was hotter than the coffee had been. "Mav, it's fine. What's not fine is you thinking I can't take care of myself or help you when or if the need arises."

Mav sighed in resignation as he released her and then let the strap of his rifle slide down his arm. He set it carefully on the counter behind her and then poured himself a cup of coffee. She got the distinct impression that he was going to say something that would change things between them and she wasn't sure that's what she wanted. A lot of things had occurred over the past twenty-four hours and she honestly didn't like the whiplash she was experiencing. She stayed where she was and didn't follow him when he took Ernie's place by the window.

"Do you find that the past has made its way into every little thing we do now?" Mav worded that question as if he didn't expect an answer and Henley relaxed a little, walking slowly to the couch and sinking into the corner. It was the first time that she'd sat down since this morning and yet her body still felt on edge. It didn't take long to realize why and her previous unease returned. "This morning, well, I didn't mean to compare what you went through to my childhood. I diminished what you went through and that wasn't fair. We each have our personal battles and the only thing that matters is that we're here. We just need to do our damnedest to make sure we stay here."

"I take it your mother has passed on?" Henley almost regretted inquiring about such a sensitive subject, especially when his haunted eyes met hers in the windowpane. This really wasn't the time or place, especially when she wanted to clarify their earlier non-verbal disagreement about whether or not she could carry her own weight. "I'm sorry. You mentioned several times that you had no family, but I didn't know if it was by choice. That was too personal."

"Too personal?" Mav did turn around at that statement and then leaned against the wall. He slowly brought the mug up to his lips and drank, initiating thoughts at the wrong time and place. That whiplash was likely to leave her hurting. "I've been trying for three years to get to know you personally, so your question doesn't faze me. Honestly, I'm surprised Ernie hasn't told you. My mother died of an overdose when I was sixteen years of age. My biological father only claimed me because his name was on the birth certificate and I managed to be an all-star athlete in high school, despite that I had to work at the grocery store stocking shelves to pay for the transportation to and from practices during the summer. He stayed around for about a month until he finally got the hint that I didn't want anything to do with him. The only family I have is Ernie and the rest of the guys who I consider my brothers. My life started from the moment I turned eighteen and joined the Marines. That choice gave me more than you could ever imagine and I usually don't think of the days that occurred before that. At least until now."

"Because I remind you of your mother," Henley said regrettably, still holding the hand towel. She was glad since it gave her something to hold against the pain she'd caused him. "That wasn't my intention, Mav. In my mind, I made you out to be like everyone else. My past experiences clouded my opinion and I chose not to come to you to clear up my misconception."

"Why?"

A one word question that should have been so simple and yet the answer would expose her in a way that the camera never had. His life was more horrific in ways she'd never understand and hers paled in comparison. Yet for the first time she wanted him to hear what had made her this way and hope that he could explain how his past hadn't tarnished his view of others. Henley had been able to hide behind the lens and then basically do the same here, all so the public couldn't see how messed up she really was. Maybe Stanley Ratliff was right when he said her mental breakdown was what had brought her here. If so, Mav deserved to know.

"The majority of what Rat said was right," Henley reluctantly acknowledged, taking a deep breath and peering up at Mav through her lashes. His facial expression didn't change and there didn't seem to be any harsh judgments within those brown eyes of his. She slowly released her hold on the towel as she continued with her story. It wasn't one she'd ever told to anyone and if she were going to share it before the world came to an end…she was glad it was with Maverick. "The lifestyle got away from me and I became as obsessed as the fans of my work had become. If the media thought I was overweight, I'd lose a few more pounds. If a photographer said my skin needed to be darker, I went to the tanning salon. If my agent requested I date a specific actor, I went to dinner with him. The last time I saw my parents they asked me to see a psychiatrist because they were worried about my mental state. It leaked to the press around the same time as their car accident. A week later I was in the hospital with what I thought was a heart attack only to be diagnosed with esophageal ulcers. Everything—mentally, physically, and emotionally—culminated until I couldn't take it anymore. I didn't want to live that way and I found enough strength to leave, but apparently not enough to go forward with my life. I chose sanctuary over actually living."

Henley leaned her head back against the cushion of the couch and gave a dry laugh. She stared up at the ceiling because she wasn't ready to face the disappointment that had to be written all over Mav's face. Rat had been right. Seeing her in this condition would have caused her parents a lot of sorrow.

"I'm not the same person that I was. I'm not insecure and I finally chose to be who I really am—*me*. I'm still hiding though. My parents had been so worried about me, making as many trips to California as they could each year, that they didn't get a chance to live their own lives fully," Henley whispered, closing her eyes against the pain while acknowledging that she at least had parents who loved her. Her words had come out too fast and she realized how all of this must sound to him. She'd wanted to tell Mav her story so that he understood her a little better, but she'd failed miserably. It paled in comparison to what he'd gone through. "I'm sorry. I—"

"Why are you sorry?" Mav was closer than he was before and when she finally opened her eyes, it was to find him sitting on the coffee table directly in front of her with his elbows resting on his knees. His brown eyes held compassion and she chastised herself for not seeing this side of him long before now. "Are you sorry you had parents who brought you into this world through love? Are you sorry because you rectified how you were living? Don't be, Henley. I was wrong to say you hadn't. Cherish every memory you had with them, but please don't look at me the way you are right now. I don't need you to feel sorry for me. My life has made me into the man I am today."

"I don't—"

"Yes, you do," Mav corrected her gently, slowly reaching forward to take the towel away from her hands. He set the cloth next to his mug and then gently slid her fingers into his. "I'm a grown man, Henley. I'm not that little boy who questioned his existence. I'm an adult who was given confidence by a man who saw something in me that I couldn't see myself."

Henley had leaned forward when he'd taken ahold of her hands and she inhaled sharply when the air around them became instantly charged with emotion. There was so many things she wanted to say now—wanted to clarify—but he didn't give her a chance. He leaned forward and tenderly pressed his lips to hers. It was over too soon, and he pulled away before she could say or do anything to prevent him from standing.

"You need sleep." Mav bent to pick up his coffee and the hand towel. He walked around the couch to the kitchenette, leaving Henley feeling like they hadn't resolved anything. He was always making choices for her that she didn't technically agree with. It was frustrating, but if she were honest…it was the sexual frustration that was really getting to her. "I'll take the couch for a couple of hours before I relieve Ernie if it's all right with you. I don't think we should be separated right now."

"Wait." Henley stood and faced Mav, needing some closure and clarification before either of them did anything else. His brown eyes had become hooded, preventing her from seeing what he was thinking or feeling. She now felt like she was walking on eggshells, but damned if she would wilt under the pressure now. "I'll take the next watch. I can pull my weight and to set the record straight, while I did have some issues a few years ago, I'm more than capable of making sound decisions and contributing."

"Did you hear me say you couldn't?" Mav asked with a slight warning in his tone that she chose to ignore. "Let *me* be clear. I have never and will never put stock into what that idiot Rat says. I also have never thought you *weren't* capable, but I will stand up for you if I think you're being naïve or taken advantage of. As for me wanting you safe, that's not going to change. I'm a protector. It's in my nature. It's who I am and I won't apologize for it."

Henley sensed that Mav was talking about two separate issues and while he soothed her ruffled feathers in one area, the other was still filled with landmines where she needed to tread carefully. She could see the tension radiating in his broad shoulders. She wanted him to feel safe with her, but it was more than apparent that he thought she was still judging him. Oh, how the tables had turned and it was up to her to prove that she wasn't anything like his mother or those people that had made him feel less than appreciated.

"Like I said, I'll relieve Ernie in two hours," Henley stated, taking a deep breath and feeling more steady. She gestured toward the couch and the throw blanket as Mav picked up his rifle off of the counter. "I agree we should stick together, so make yourself comfortable. I'll wake you when you're up on rotation."

Henley made her way to the bedroom and sensed Mav's dark eyes on her the entire time. It would do her some good to be by herself, so she could sort through the varying emotions over everything that had happened in the last twenty-four hours. Their lives had inevitably changed and nothing would ever be the same. She hesitated at the door, looking over her shoulder to find that Mav was still standing where she'd left him. Her mother had always tried to look for the silver lining and Henley channeled that mindset…Maverick Bennett was her blue sky among the inescapable ashes.

Henley went directly to the closet after she'd entered her bedroom and took down a heavy cardboard box Ernie had given her a month ago as a present. She took it over to the bed and opened the top as if she were unwrapping the foil from a hot potato fresh from the oven. Inside were several items; chiefly among them was a navy blue plastic box bearing a symbol of three small circles and three upturned arrows inside a larger circle. Ernie had explained to her that she needed a weapon of her own and he'd managed to do some horse trading down at the bait and tackle shop for some antique lures he'd found up at the lodge when he'd first bought the place.

    Henley opened the blue case to find her brand new Beretta Px4 Storm .40 Caliber subcompact, still glistening with CLP from when Ernie had shown her its operations and cleaning procedure. Tonight, she would have the first occasion to wear the holster he had bought for it. Everything she knew had changed and she would have to change along with it. Not only would she have to be armed in this new world, she would have to be willing and able to use her weapon on a living person.

CHAPTER ELEVEN

AN HOUR HAD passed while Mav had sat near the window in a darkened room, peering out into the cloudy moonlit night watching for manmade shadows amongst the shimmering iridescent glow. Hard edges had been what they had taught all of them—look for the hard edges and definable features.

Heavier clouds were now rolling in that had nothing to do with the volcanic eruption, but it did hamper visibility deeper into the tree lines. Ernie had stopped back not thirty minutes prior with a couple of Midway two-way radios with a basic encryption set so that they could all keep in contact with one another without the other team listening in, even taking time to raid the coffee maker for the remainder of hours-old coffee that had been left in the pot to stew. The older man didn't ask what had been said between Mav and Henley, nor did he ask if things had been resolved. Mav would seek advice if he needed and now wasn't that time.

"I'll take the next shift," Mav said softly, having heard the rustling of Henley's jeans as she made her way back into the living room. He'd heard her lie down a while ago, but she'd been restless. He doubted that she'd even closed her eyes. "You haven't slept, so try to get some rest. I have a feeling you're going to need it."

Henley didn't reply, although she did surprise him when she continued to quietly walk his way only to maneuver herself in front of him. She sat directly in between his legs, gently took his arms, and then wrapped them around her waist while she leaned back up against him. Mav needed this intimacy as much as she did and he rested his chin on top of her head, breathing in her lavender scent and absorbing the heat from her body. They sat that way for quite a while, the silence comfortable for once.

Mav had gone through his adult life thinking he'd conquered his insecurities regarding his childhood and she'd brought them out as if the uncertainties had been hiding right below the surface. It didn't sit well with him. He couldn't help but wonder if it had been her past that had clouded her judgment or if she really did see something in him that had cautioned her to keep her distance. His concern brought back unwanted thoughts and feelings, which he wanted to turn off. He hadn't doubted himself on any level in so long that this was like a punch to the gut. He refused to be weak when others were counting on him to be strong.

"Tank doesn't believe Kellen when he says that the military base is offering refuge to any citizen who can make their way to the base," Henley said, her voice low enough that he had to strain to hear her. And there it was. Distrust. She was more likely to believe someone else and put in her life in danger if she didn't trust him. "I can tell you don't like him, but is there any way he could be telling the truth?"

"I'm more inclined to trust my instincts and Ernie," Mav answered cautiously, doing his best to shove aside his doubts. They wouldn't serve him well and could only end up hurting them in the long run. "Truman knows more than he's letting on and I don't think he booked this fishing trip out of the blue. There is a way to find out if the base is accepting people and that's to use the HF radio inside the bunker. I'll do that when it's my shift and we'll have an answer before we leave for town. I locked down both of the main entrances into the bunker from the outside. You can't enter from the cliff face truck entrance or the lodge utility tunnel anymore without having someone to unlock them from the inside. The Stump Tunnel and the NG Wellhead Security Door are on keypad now. I reset the primary codes to the secondary set earlier. If you use the Wellhead Tunnel, reset and engage the gate charging system each and every time. We have no clue whether or not Kellen is here to secure the bunker as part of an advanced team."

"I remember when he called to make his reservation and it had to be in January," Henley said, even offering up the fact that Truman had booked his cabin for four weeks with a likelihood extension of another two. Mav would have contacted someone back in Chicago to do a background security check had the lines been working. They were in the dark with what this guy's intentions were with that option out of the question. It was highly doubtful the men at the base would know Truman, but it couldn't hurt to ask. The most important thing right now was confirming Fairchild AFB was taking in those seeking shelter. "I find it odd that he would have known something like this was going to happen and now that it did, why send people away if he'd already figured out what Tank had about the area being a select region that might provide a chance at survival?"

"I don't know, but that just means we have to be even more careful and watch each other's backs." Mav wondered about his four buddies out there, maneuvering through what must be thirty millimeters of ash closer to the supervolcano. The only one out of all of them that would have a harder time of it would be Van. He'd been in New York with the bigwigs working at a financial institution and while he'd always made sure his home was well armed against intrusion, he didn't have access to survival items needed for this type of catastrophe. "We'll protect what we can until the guys get here and then reevaluate our situation."

"Should we move the residents here?"

"Yes, at least within the next couple of days. Preferably tomorrow," Mav replied, already knowing this place was easier to fortify than the entire town of Lost Summit. It was convincing the residents that it was for the best that would pose a problem. Jeremy and couple of his local friends who were in their mid to late twenties had come home to help their parents work the stores in town for the tourist season that came each summer and they would more than likely understand the need to set up a main camp and collect supplies. It was the older generation that would be harder to convince. They would probably refuse to accept that society in general had changed. It would be easy to have someone monitor the HF radio for any emergency calls from Berke, Owen, Mason, or Van on a rotating shift once Ernie and Mav had everyone transitioned up here at the lodge. "At least those that have stayed. Some may have moved off during the night."

Henley turned in Mav's arms at his declaration, her green eyes searching his. He'd turned off the lights at the start of his shift to simulate them knocking off for the night and allow his night vision. Now there was barely any moonlight. She wouldn't find the reassurance she was looking for so he stroked her arms, which were now covered in a heavier sweater than she'd worn during the day. She gently laid her palms on his chest and her warmth soaked through his shirt, reaching his skin.

"Are you saying you think a number of people have already left?" Henley whispered as if she were afraid to hear the answer. It wasn't a truth she could hide from and Mav was also troubled that people they cared about had fled in the middle of the night. "Where to? The border patrol agent won't let them cross, Mav."

"They need to find that out on their own and most likely the Canadians have already beefed up the main border crossings. The smaller outpost north of town may not be as secure. That road links up directly with Crowsnest Highway #3 on the Canadian side. Ernie will be listening to the police two-way radio and the shortwave, so we'll know if anything changes overnight. People might feel that they have the right to cross in spite of what the border patrol agent says." Mav's thoughts went in a totally different direction when Henley's fingers pressed deeper into his chest. He rested his hands on her waist, standing them both up and planning to finish this conversation so that she could go back to her bed…alone. "Look, you need to get some rest. Go back to bed and then I'll wake you up for your shift. We'll see who's still here in the morning."

Henley didn't reply or move, causing the tension in the room to rise. She slowly slid her hands higher up around his neck, her body pressing closer to his. He'd imagined this moment for a very long time, but never had it included an apocalyptic backdrop. Decisions in extreme circumstances were never made with rationalism. Mav should have pulled away for both their sakes, but he couldn't.

"Come with me." There was no hesitation in Henley's voice. "Come to bed with me."

"You're scared," Mav replied, justifying her request in a way that she could understand. This situation wasn't life and death at the moment and he didn't want her to regret this decision since they still had to wake up in the morning. It was better to wait and he did his best to alleviate the situation with some lightheartedness. "Learning that the world as we know it will never be the same can do that to a person. On the bright side, we don't have any zombies attacking."

How Henley managed to spike up the sexual tension in the room was beyond him, but she did. She lifted up on her tiptoes and pressed her lips on his ear, her breath sending electrical currents down his neck. Damn if he didn't want to throw sanity to the wind and see where this took them.

"Please come to bed with me, Maverick," Henley whispered before pressing a kiss to his jaw. "Don't make me beg on my hands and knees."

Visions of Henley pleading with him to make love to her while kneeling at his feet slammed into his mind's eye and he kissed his tactical sanity goodbye. Regardless that he knew this act was only to give them a temporary sense that they were still here, that they were alive and well, he quickly lifted her until her legs wrapped around his waist and captured her lips. A hard bulge on her waistline attracted his attention for the first time. She was wearing a clip holster with some type of subcompact pistol poking into his abs. They were going to have to talk about that later. He didn't need a flashlight to lead their way to her bedroom. He'd mapped it out in his head the moment he'd set foot into her cabin, just as he did with every room or building he entered since his training had started back in the day. This time…the deep-rooted habit came in handy for an entirely different reason.

By the time Mav had reached her rough-hewn pine log four-poster bed, he'd had the pleasure of drinking from her lips. His tongue had danced with hers and he'd memorized the shape of her swollen lips with his. With one hand wrapped around her waist, he used his other to take off her holster, remove her hair tie, and let her hair flow free down her back. Her legs loosened and then her tiny feet finally hit the floor, giving him the ability to grab the hem of her sweater. It was the release of her lips that had him catching his breath along with bits of lucidity.

"Henley, I don't want this to happen because you need someone to make you feel alive tonight or hopeful for the future," Mav murmured, his fingers brushing against the warm skin of her abdomen. He tightened his jaw to prevent himself from going higher until he'd received the answer he needed. He pulled away when she went to place her palm on his cheek. "I need to know you want *me*."

"I want you more than my next breath, Maverick," Henley replied, resting her hands on his arms as she stilled the rest of her movements. She looked up at him, but the room was too dark for him to make out what she was thinking. It was her next words that told him what he needed to know. "There is nowhere else I'd rather be than in your strong arms if we were to wake up to the end of the world. What's happened has put things into perspective for me and it has nothing to do with fear. It has more to do with desire. It also has everything to do with not wasting any more time. I want *you*, Maverick Becket. No one else but you."

The moonlight chose that moment to shine through the

clouds and highlight the truth in Henley's eyes. She truly believed what she was saying and Mav decided he wouldn't waste another moment second-guessing what he had waited years to hear her say. Without knowing what the future held, he wanted her by his side for the rest of the duration, however long that might be. With as much restraint as he could muster, he slowly lifted the soft sweater that he still held tightly in his fingers over her head. Her hair flowed through the opening but stayed behind her as the material fell from his grasp to the floor.

Henley looked up at him as his gaze touched over her body. She was wearing a plain bra without any frills. It was beige with no lace or trim and yet it cupped her rounded breasts perfectly, holding them up to him as if they were an offering to the gods. Her mounds were flawlessly aligned and he momentarily suppressed the urge to reveal what was underneath the material. He hadn't celebrated many holidays when he was younger and he found this was very much like Christmas morning. He wanted that feeling to last a little longer, so he unbuttoned her jeans instead.

"I can take off my—"

"Don't. Mine," Mav ordered, keeping his tone as low as hers. He didn't want to break the bubble of ecstasy around them. He swore he could hear it crackle due to the sexual tension being so intense. Henley had a way about her that he'd never before seen or felt from any woman. It was more than her physical beauty, though that was certainly there. It was the intrinsic nature of her feminine grace in this moment. Maverick wanted to savor it and sear it into his memory. "Give me this, please."

Henley must have understood his need because her hands slowly fell back down to her sides from her attempt to reach behind and unhook her bra. Her breathing had become somewhat uneven as he then continued to leisurely unbutton her jeans only to pull down the zipper one tooth at a time. The anticipation built until he finally slid the heavy material off of her hips and down her thighs as he knelt in front of her. He couldn't prevent a small smile when he saw the basic white French cut panties, as ordinary as her bra and yet the most seductive thing he'd ever seen on a woman.

Mav continued to pull down her denim until the material bunched at her ankles and then he had her step out of them one leg at a time, removing her long red fuzzy socks with them. He was currently kneeling on one knee, but he didn't stand right away. He leaned forward instead and brushed his lips against her thighs. Her fingers made their way into his hair and he could have sworn he heard a low moan of need escape her throat. Still not wanting to rush this, he gradually kissed along her panty line until he made it to the V in between her warm legs. She tightened her hold of his hair, letting him know that she was enjoying his attentions as much as he was. He inhaled deeply and it left him wondering how her lavender scent could be everywhere on her. He suddenly had a yearning to taste such a sweet fragrance, like licking the swirl off a freshly served vanilla ice cream cone, but he forced himself to trace the other side of her skin all the way up to her hip.

"Maverick, I don't think my legs can hold me up much longer." There was a need in Henley's voice that resonated with him and her hands finally fell away from his hair as he rose to stand in front of her. He couldn't take not seeing the emotions in her eyes, so he stepped away from her and made his way to her bedside table. "What are you doing?"

"I'm turning on your light so that I can see you." Mav twisted the small black knob, lighting the bedroom with a soft golden hue. He'd never taken his eyes off of her form, so he caught the vulnerability in her eyes when the room was finally lit. He could finally take his time to treasure the sight in front of him and her true beauty left him in awe. Beauty actually arises from the small flaws that make each of us different and Henley had them just like any woman did—the pinch here or the crease there, and of course the freckles that sprinkled her maiden form. He stayed where he was so that he could get his words out. "Whatever I say is going to be no different than any other man, but I can see further beneath your surface. You are a beautiful woman, Henley. Your physical appearance is stunning no matter how you try to hide it—whether by wearing no make-up, wearing plain underwear, or going around in a burlap bag. But that's not all. What I also perceive is a woman who is independent, intelligent, compassionate, with a dry sense of humor to match my own. You never back down when you think you're right and you're radiant when you force yourself to come out of that shell you have constructed around you. I could just live to see you smile...that genuine smile that you don't think anyone notices. I want to share in your vivacity of life, Henley, and not hide anymore. Are you willing to do that with me?"

Henley's green eyes had deepened in color until he swore he saw his reflection. She walked toward him with pride, every step showing her confidence in the body she'd grown to love. She was nowhere near that overly thin model on the pages of magazines. She was a woman who'd allowed her natural curves to flourish and he for one was grateful.

"Yes, but you'll have to undress, Maverick," Henley said with desire written all over her classically beautiful features. "In case you missed it, I'm also impatient."

Mav loved to hear his full name fall from her lips and he planned to hear it a lot within the next hour. He unfastened his own holster and carefully set it beside the lamp before discarding his shirt, never once taking his eyes from hers. He tossed his shirt to the ground and had sat down on the bed to work on his rough side out combat boots when she knelt in front of him, her fingers already pulling at the laces in their speed-lacing loops. Seeing her in such a submissive pose sent adrenaline pumping through his body at high pressure.

"Being impatient doesn't allow you to enjoy the moment, so let's see what we can do about that," Mav murmured, waiting to speak until she'd helped him take his boots off. He held out his hands and helped her to stand, bringing her close enough that she was snuggled in between his knees and he could finally reach behind her to unhook her bra. "Put your hands on my shoulders and leave them there."

"Why?" Henley asked with humor lacing her tone, all the while doing as he asked. "I want to touch you too."

"Because if you touch me right now you'll find yourself flat on your back with me buried deep within you," Mav replied candidly, glancing up to find her studying him with her eyes wide open with a ravenous look. She exhaled a trembling breath when she saw that he wasn't kidding around. "Keep your hands on my shoulders."

Henley's bronze skin broke out with goose bumps as the straps fell down her arms and into the crooks of her elbows. Mav didn't bother to follow the direction of the thin material because his gaze had stopped at the sight of her ample breasts and the hardened rosy peaks of her nipples. She was perfect.

"Maverick, please don't keep me waiting," Henley whispered breathlessly, her fingers digging into his bare skin.

It was the *please* that boiled his blood in desire and he leaned forward, pushing past her bra to allow access to his tongue, drawing a wet circle around her areola. He tenderly kissed the gentle curve of the side of her breast while caressing each globe in his firm hands. There was something addicting about being the one in control and Henley incited his craving by following his lead. He brought one hand around to the front of her in order to palm the underside of her breast and raise it to his mouth. He kissed, licked, and nibbled every inch of her with the exception of her nipple. He saved her nipples for last, pulling them into his mouth.

Henley cried out his full name when Mav finally drew her delicate peak into his mouth. He used the tip of his tongue to tease the hardened nub and it was only when she tried to get closer to him that he lightly used his teeth to graze the sensitive tissue.

"Okay, Maverick," Henley muttered eagerly, her right hand leaving his shoulder and moving to the back of his neck. He wasn't sure if she was trying to draw him closer or pull him away. "Finish undressing me before I come in my panties."

"In my own sweet time, sweetheart." Mav massaged her swollen flesh and he swore it became heavier the more attention he gave it. He pressed his other hand against her lower back, keeping her in place as he continued to suckle her nipple. He brought the delicate nub up to the roof of his mouth, dragging his tongue over and over it until her moans became longer and louder. Her whimpers were sweet music to his ears and he couldn't get enough. She'd tightened her hold on his hair until it was quite painful and he had no choice but to stop. "Here, let's get this off of you."

Mav pulled back long enough to bring both of Henley's arms down, finally allowing her bra to drop onto the ground. He took advantage of the moment and wrapped his hand around her wrists, pinning them behind her and giving him full access to the front of her. He paused to see her reaction, not wanting to push her too far with his need for control that she wasn't enjoying herself. Much to his gratification, Henley's parted her lips as she said exactly what he wanted to hear.

"I like this side of you, Maverick." Henley arched slightly, letting him know that she was his to have as he wanted. His cock strained against his zipper when she laced her fingers together, but he ignored the discomfort as he focused on the woman in front of him. "Show me more."

Mav decided that her other breast needed just as much attention as the first, but he wanted her pleasure to continue to be drawn out. He used the pad of his coarse finger to glide beneath the swelling of her flesh, outlining the underside until he reached her cleavage. He caressed upward, tracing her globe in circles until the movements became smaller and smaller, finally reaching her nipple. He took the sensitive peak in between his thumb and finger, massaging and rolling it until Henley pressed her lower half into his chest. She was radiating heat and while he couldn't wait to sample her delectable flavor, he didn't deter from his current mission.

"Do you like your nipples played with?" Mav asked, tearing his eyes away from what he was doing to her so that he could look up into her face filled with enticing desire. Henley's gaze switched from his to where his fingers were still rolling her nipple and he squeezed when it became apparent she wasn't going to answer him. "Henley, do you like when I play with your nipples?"

"Yes." Henley tried to pull against his grasp for the first time since he'd taken a hold of her wrists and pinned them behind her, but he wouldn't release her. "Why are you drawing this out? I'm more than ready, Maverick, and I'm not sure I can take much more foreplay."

"I like to take my time," Mav explained, not nearly done having his fill of hearing her small cries at his detailed attention. He was coming to understand that the men she'd been with hadn't done her justice and that was an utter crime that he needed to rectify. That insight made him even more determined to show her how good this could be between them. "Now, where was I?"

Mav released her nipple and then licked away the ache that he'd placed there with the pressure of his fingers. He drew on her swollen peak until it was distended, soothingly laving any throbbing that remained. His treatment didn't seem to be working from the way she was writhing against him. That didn't stop him for pleasuring her for the next few minutes and when he finally had his fill of her breasts, he decided it was time to move on to other areas of her body.

"Take a step back and then slowly discard your panties." Mav had released her wrists and was already standing himself, shedding his pants and briefs after he'd retrieved a condom from his wallet. He set it next to his holster before turning his attention back to her. Henley was devouring his body with her eyes, which wasn't helping his restraint. "Sweetheart, you need to take your panties off if we're going to continue."

"I needed a minute," Henley said shakily, as her arms remained at her side with what appeared to be no intention of doing as he'd asked. Her gaze had lowered to his hardened cock. "I think it's my turn to taste."

"Do you remember our earlier conversation when we agreed to change our bad habits? One of them was arguing all the time and I'm not about to get into another quarrel with you," Mav explained patiently, not willing to compromise on this. He'd waited a very long time for her and her haste to rush this to the end just wasn't going to happen. "There are different ways to use the straps on that bra, Henley. From the looks of your headboard, I could easily keep your hands tied while I continue to take my pleasure from your body."

That grabbed Henley's attention. She regarded him for a few seconds before apparently recognizing that he wasn't playing around. Her fingers slowly slipped into the waistband of her panties and he watched as she pulled them down her legs inch by agonizing inch. His balls were experiencing literal pain at not being able to empty their contents. By the time she'd stepped out of them, he could have easily bent her over the mattress and been buried inside of her before she could say his full name.

"Are you wet?"

"What?" Henley laughed out the word, although the sweet sound faded when she saw he wanted an answer. "You're so different from the others."

Mav continued to observe her, pleased with what she'd just stated. It was cute to see it dawn on her that she probably shouldn't have brought up other men while they were being intimate, so he smiled to relieve her anxiety.

"Bad timing," Henley said with a shake of her head. She bit her lip, making Mav want to do it. He stepped forward, closing the distance between them, and waited to kiss her until she'd let go of it. They were both breathless by the time he was through, but that didn't stop her from answering his previous question. "Yes. I'm very wet and would very much like you to do something about it."

Mav lifted her up off of the ground and had her deposited in the middle of the bed before her laughter had faded. He didn't think about what was happening outside of this cabin. He didn't contemplate what came after this. He focused on the here and now, because truthfully that was all they had. He looked down at her to find that her hair was sprawled out on the pillow as if she wore a halo. She was his angel in this time of uncertainty and he would gladly accept this gift.

"I'll see what I can do to satisfy your immediate needs, sweetheart," Mav said, with a promise in his voice that she couldn't miss. He rested his hands on her knees, separating her legs to reveal another present. She'd shaved completely and there was currently nothing blocking his view from her swollen, very pink clit. "Henley, I don't think we have enough time to give you all the orgasms you need, but I'll give it my best effort."

CHAPTER TWELVE

H IS BEST EFFORT? It wasn't going to take much more than Mav's mouth touching her throbbing clit to set off her release. Henley was still coming to terms with how different Mav was from the other men she'd been with and she'd immediately regretted her words, since she was well aware of etiquette when it came to mentioning past lovers. In her defense, it had been a damn long time since she'd been in this position. She just wasn't sure how to respond. Her body was doing that for her though. She hadn't been prepared to react with such deep and intimate responses and her thoughts were scattered. She was quite sure she wouldn't be thinking straight for a while.

"Maverick, I need you," Henley replied honestly while he lowered himself on the bed instead of overtop of her. Couldn't he see that she couldn't take much more? She could have wept with pleasure when his fingers separated her folds and his mouth descended onto clit. "Oh, my…"

Mav just hummed his reply, not that she knew what he meant by that. Her mind cleared as her reactions took over and when she tried to bring her knees up higher, it was his hands that prevented her from doing so. He pressed his fingers into her inner thighs and kept her spread wide open for him. The vulnerability this position placed her in, along with whatever he was doing with his tongue, triggered an initial release almost immediately. She cried out his name and arched her back, accepting the waves of pleasure as they rolled through her. Normally she would have been able to lie against the bed to recover, but Mav didn't give her that chance.

Mav's tongue caressed her entrance and then moved back over her clit, circling the throbbing tissue until he initiated another climb upward toward an even higher pinnacle than the one she'd just fallen off. He wasn't in a hurry and he took his time exploring, letting her know that he held her pleasure in the palm of his hand. All she could do was receive his intimate attention and it was freeing in the most fundamental way possible. Every time she thought she couldn't handle the pleasure and tried to close her legs, Mav was there to make sure she stayed open for him. When she started to pull on his hair he would take her wrists to hold them against her sides. His control was inflexible and she found that she responded more to that than anything else.

Mav was gently, slowly, and torturously building her release until she was afraid to let go for fear of embarrassing herself. He must have known because he used his right hand to spread her farther open to his mouth and then gradually inserted his middle finger into her pussy. She could tell which one it was by the way his index and ring finger tightened on either side of her clit. The pressure exposed the sensitive tissue to the roughness of his tongue and he stroked that sweet spot just right. She was grateful that she had a hold of the pillow underneath her head when she exploded, seeing white lights behind her tightly closed eyelids. Mav didn't stop to let her catch her breath either, but instead carried her higher and higher until one orgasm led into other multiple orgasms. By the time he brought her down he'd already sheathed his cock with a condom and was holding himself up above her.

"Let go of the pillow and pull your folds apart. Open yourself to me," Mav said softly, surprising her when he rose up slightly and used one hand to position her lower half so that his cock was at the entrance of her pussy. "I want to see your clit swell again when I enter you."

Mav's words alone could have triggered another wrenching orgasm. Henley struggled to get her fingers to do what he wanted and they finally released the goose down pillow. She knew full well that it would forever have the indentions of her grasp. Her hands trembled as she lowered her arms between their bodies, slipping her fingers easily into her folds and revealing her clit to him. He peered down and a guttural moan escaped his chest, vibrating both of them. It was the sexiest sound she'd ever heard a man make.

"Take all of me, sweetheart."

Mav's statement sounded so simple and yet Henley knew it wouldn't be that easy. For one, it had been a very long time since she'd been intimate with anything other than her one adult toy. Two, he wasn't just average size. His width alone made her wince at the stretching she'd have to do to accommodate him and his length already had her pussy leaking with additional cream. Mav pressed forward, his tip spreading her entrance to accept him.

"Beautiful," Mav murmured, obviously seeing what he'd expected and wanted. She couldn't, but there wasn't a way she could camouflage her reaction to her body accepting him. With each inch came a profound throbbing and a deep ache that she wasn't so sure could be satisfied. Her clit swelled and continued to do so as he worked his way into her. By the time she'd accepted all of him, she'd had to take her hands away and hold onto his shoulders for support. "Do you feel the bond?"

"God, yes," Henley replied, almost screaming the words out. Mav wasn't moving and it was agonizingly pleasurable to the point that she tried to move her hips only to have him stop her. "Maverick, I need to move."

"No, you don't." Henley had no choice but to stop and try to suck in some much needed oxygen. Mav leaned farther down until his elbows were on either side of her head, capturing her exactly where he'd wanted her. Their breaths mingled and time suddenly seemed to slow down, giving this moment to them. They were one, connected by more than just their bodies. From the look in his dark eyes, this was what he wanted her to experience—the intimacy that only they could share. She'd never had this before and it was something she wanted to hold on to. He raised a hand and gently brushed away some strands from her face. "Tell me what you feel."

"You," Henley whispered, taking the time given and allowing her body to relax into the insurmountable pleasure he was giving her. She ran her eyes over his face, studying his square jaw and the sensual lines of his cheekbones. His hair fell forward, covering his forehead and brushing the ends against his skin. There was a kindness in his eyes that resonated with her and made her want to protect him, much like he did her. How could she explain that in words? She'd try, but she was afraid she wouldn't give the truth justice. "Us. We're no longer separate. I feel comforted, cared for, and safe. You've made me a part of you."

Mav slowly pulled out of her only to gently push back in, giving her time to adjust to his size. Henley wrapped her legs around his waist, relishing in the pace he'd set that allowed them to enjoy one another. He was right about her impatience and she was grateful that he was giving her what she needed rather than what she'd wanted. He loved her leisurely, prolonging both of their releases. He never once looked away from her, their eyes connected the entire time he pleasured her. It was as if he was allowing her to see inside his soul and the purity within him astounded her.

Mav even kissed her, exploring her mouth with his tongue as slowly as his cock was entering her pussy. The climb was excruciatingly slow, but so worth the ascent that she didn't once try to rush them. Perspiration coated both of them and their bodies slid against one another in a sensual dance. Her clit rubbed slowly over his pelvic bone and with each intimate connection, it carried her further and further toward that abyss.

"Don't look away from me," Mav instructed in a low voice that mesmerized her into following his directive. This was also new to her, for she'd never allowed anyone to see her in such a vulnerable state. She'd always closed her eyes at the onslaught of pleasure, but she somehow managed to look at him as they finally reached the point of their descent. "Stunning…"

That was all Henley heard as she soared, unable to stop herself from arching into him all the while not breaking their connection. His brown eyes darkened to an almost pitch black as she witnessed his release, allowing her to see him at his most vulnerable as well. She realized what a gift they'd given each other and the foundation of trust became stronger. An unspoken acceptance emerged as they came down from that high. Mav moved to the side, pulling her with him and tucking her against his body. She'd never felt more safe and cared for than in this moment. Maybe that's why a sliver of fear moved in to signify that this bubble they'd just created could just as easily be broken. She vowed not to let that happen. She'd finally opened her eyes to the possibility of something more and she didn't want to return to the life of an unfulfilled hollow woman she'd been before.

Henley pressed her ear to Mav's warm chest just so that she could hear his heartbeat, reassuring herself that this was real and she wasn't dreaming. She pushed aside what the morning would bring and tried to focus on one single fact—whatever happened, they had each other now. It was bliss until a gunshot rang out and shattered the silence.

CHAPTER THIRTEEN

MAV ENSURED THE bunker was secure by checking the main entrance and the lodge access tunnel for signs of tampering and intrusion before making his way back to the main lodge via the NG Wellhead utility tunnel. The early morning was quite cool and he'd grabbed the Gore-Tex digital parka that he'd saved from his days in the Corps from his Jeep when it had been his turn up in rotation for watch. The sun was just starting to peek over the mountains at this early hour. He didn't miss the fact that the birds weren't singing and the crickets hadn't made an appearance since the other night. Mother Nature had made it known that something catastrophic had occurred and everyone and everything had taken notice. Nothing had overtly changed since last night in their valley, and yet his life had now been set on a different course after finally making love with Henley.

After he and Henley had scrambled out of bed thinking that Ernie had been hurt, or worse, they'd discovered that a brown bear had made its way down into camp. Ernie had fired a shot into the air as a warning, causing the animal to continue on without incident. It was probably looking for a cave to hide in for the duration of what was to come, but it sure as hell wasn't going to be in their camp. Mav had to excuse himself to clean up after finding out that the animal had been chased off while Henley managed to keep the flush on her face to a minimum. The thing was…Ernie was a hell of a lot sharper than she gave him credit for.

"Hi."

Mav looked to his left, surprised that Henley had been able to sneak up on him like that. He had just taken advantage of one of the many picnic tables scattered around the camp, plopping his ass down on the tabletop and resting his feet on the bench. It kept him up off the ground from its wet chill. He was on alert and had been keenly aware of his surroundings during his rotation, but maybe the lack of sleep was finally getting to him. Henley was holding a cup of coffee out to him and he took it, wanting to lean in and kiss her on the cheek. He didn't make the assumption that he could do that just yet. The time had come to talk about last night, because they might not have the ability to do so later. It was best to see where they stood before all hell broke loose for the day.

"Good morning." Mav stood and walked at a slow pace until she'd joined him on the gravel road that would lead them around to Ernie's cabin. He noticed that she was wearing a sweatshirt with jeans and her hair was pulled back with one of those hair ties she liked so much. Her cheeks still had some color but her green eyes were cautious, giving him an indication on what turn this discussion might take. He started out slow, because he wasn't ready for what they'd started to end. Being with her last night had given him hope in more ways than she could ever imagine. He was the type to take that and run with it, but they weren't in their everyday lives anymore. "Were you able to catch a few hours of sleep?"

"Not really," Henley answered with a shrug, holding her own travel mug filled with what he knew would be black coffee. She drank it just like the rest of them, which would come in handy once the ash cloud reached them. Dairy creamer wasn't likely to last for long. She licked her lips, leaving him wanting to be the one to do that for her, but not until he was sure she didn't have any regrets. "I keep waiting for you to tell me that we made a mistake. If you tell me that we didn't, my morning would go a lot better."

Henley's words brought him to an abrupt halt. Mav had waited three years for her to be as bluntly honest with him as she was with the other guys and it had been damn well worth the wait. She was always direct with them and now was no different with him, with the exception of where she wanted this relationship to go. He threw back his head and laughed, reaching for her hand and drawing her into his embrace. It felt so good to be able to do that without questioning whether or not it was the right thing to do. He heard her sigh into his neck and he held her tight, not ready to release her quite yet.

"Now that's a hell of a good morning," Mav said against her ear, the weight of his worry lessening but not eradicated. What if Truman talked Henley into going to that military base? He couldn't stand by and watch her be deceived into doing what could possibly lead to her death. "I've waited a long time for you, Henley."

"Then why do you seem so tense? Besides the fact that a supervolcano a couple hundreds of miles away from this very spot is about to plummet the earth into volcanic winter for a decade," Henley replied, her attempt at lightening the mood falling flat.

There was a lot Mav was concerned with, especially about the upcoming decision that she would have to make. He couldn't coerce her into staying here if Kellen Truman were to talk her into believing that the town's people would be safer on the base. It all came down to trust and even Mav wasn't so sure what the absolute right decision was. All he knew was that his gut was telling him that Truman wasn't who or what he claimed to be. His first instinct was to tie her to the bed in her cabin to keep her safe while he dealt with the residents today, but he could just imagine how that would go over.

"We have a busy day today, giving the residents their options and hoping like hell we're giving the right advice." Mav finally released her, but not before he kissed her properly. She tasted of coffee and mint and they were both breathless by the time they were through. He could get used to this greeting every morning, which only strengthened his resolve to make sure they had future mornings. "Are you still in agreement that staying here is the best choice?"

Truman was walking toward them before Henley could

answer and alleviate Mav's concerns. The man was dressed in black denim with a black jacket that appeared to be made of leather, but wasn't quite the same fabric. It didn't take long before Mav spotted the weapon's bulge on the man's left hip, indicating that he was carrying a concealed weapon of some type. If Mav had to guess he would say it was a M9 Beretta; however, if it was a Sig Sauer P226, then they could be dealing with a special operator of some sort and that spelled trouble. That wasn't really what concerned Mav. It was the phone still attached to the man's belt that was odd, especially considering that most satellites' relay coverage was down and cells were basically useless with the grid dropping. Was it special technology that gave him the ability to reach the outside world?

"Ernie is ready to head on into town and I'm all packed." Truman stopped a couple of feet away from them, his dark eyes going to where Mav's hand was still on Henley's lower back. "Have the two of you decided on whether you'll be coming to the base? It's the safest option."

"We'll hear what you have to say." Mav hadn't lied, but he felt Henley stiffen beside him. It was apparent that she didn't understand Mav's reluctance to admit that Kellen might be telling the truth, which also meant that she was wavering on whether or not staying here would be for the best. They'd gotten into a discussion about it during the brief period they'd switched rotations a couple of hours ago and he'd given her solid reasons why this man standing in front of them wasn't who he said he was. Mav had reconned the man's vehicle and found no fishing poles or tackle. He was carrying an overnight bag that in no way held one month's worth of clothing, let alone two. He had no compunction about eavesdropping on conversations and he definitely didn't appear surprised when Mav had shown up saying that a natural disaster was about to occur. As for being on vacation, even Mav didn't carry his weapon unless he felt he was going into an area where he'd need protection. "We'll follow you into town. The Village Community Center is located across the road from the inn. You can park your truck in the west lot, near the Village Garage. Did you mention you were stationed out of Fairchild?"

"No, I'm not Air Force, actually." Kellen leveled his gaze on Mav before clarifying. His expression was blank enough that Mav would never want to play poker with the man. "I'm with a special unit out of Joint Special Operations Command (JSOC) at Fort Bragg. The information about Fairchild AFB came from a trusted friend. Listen, the shortwave radio is saying the ash cloud has reached Illinois and it is falling at a steady rate. They also stated that regardless of the wind direction, Idaho, Oregon, and a southeastern portion of Washington have already received a fair amount of ash."

"What are they saying about the Canadian border?" Mav wasn't about to stand around and have a conversation when there was a chance the ash could reach this point, regardless of the odds being in their favor from where Lost Summit was positioned. Ernie had already provided Mav with the information broadcasted over the shortwave earlier, but there had to have been numerous updates since then. He didn't want to be caught unprepared. He took ahold of Henley's hand and led her down the gravel road to where he could see Ernie heading for his truck. "Have they ever confirmed if they are taking the U.S. citizens who can get there?"

"There's apparently some system in place, but they aren't manifestly opening their borders to anyone who shows up." Truman fell into step on the other side of Henley, which Mav didn't appreciate. He wasn't what he would call himself the jealous type, but he did protect what was his. Henley probably wouldn't understand that viewpoint, but he'd told her who he was yesterday and he certainly hadn't changed overnight. "That's not stopping people from trying to cross though."

"Tank, we'll follow you into town," Mav called out, veering to where his Jeep was parked. Ernie was well aware of the plan, since Mav had yet to reach out to Fairchild over the HF radio. He hadn't let go of Henley's hand and brought her around to the passenger side. He lowered his voice so that Truman couldn't hear him. "We're not leaving quite yet. Let them get a head start and then get out of the Jeep."

Mav closed Henley's door and then made his way around the vehicle, ensuring that Truman saw him open the driver's side. The man pulled out behind Ernie and the two of them drove down the lane, clouds of dust forming from the gravel into the air. Mav waited until they were out of line of sight before motioning for Henley to join him.

"Mav, what are you doing? We can't waste time," Henley called out behind him as she exited the Jeep. She slammed the door behind her and quickly caught up to him. "Everyone is going to be waiting for us in town."

"We're contacting the Public Affairs Office at Fairchild AFB to see if Truman is telling the truth." Mav planned to quickly make their way to the bunker via the stump tunnel and up to the bunker's highest level where a number of HF radios were set up in the radio room. An entire array of antennas and couplers were perched on top of the ridge above the old mine's ventilation shafts. The one particular array he planned to use was one hundred and sixty feet in diameter and stood just over eight feet tall with an omni-directional broadcast strength of a thousand watts. The morning sun was beaming down on them as they made their way to the tunnel, but with a little more heat than before as he no longer felt the chill in the air. "It's what we should have done yesterday."

"Do you think they'll answer us?" Henley asked, the skepticism evident in her voice.

"There's only one way to find out." Mav came to their concealed secondary entrance to the bunker. It appeared to be an old rotten stump when in reality it was cast from cement and concealed a hardened steel hatch, which led down into an access tunnel twenty-five feet below the surface. Mav flipped open a well-hidden cypher-lock keypad on top of the stump and entered the eight-digit pin. The hatch popped up a couple of inches and he leveraged it open to reveal the ladderwell down to the access tunnel. Once inside, Henley secured the hatch behind her and they descended to the tunnel floor and proceeded down the rock walled passageway for quite a ways, deeper into the second floor of the bunker. He made his way to where the freight elevator was located. He tripped the controls to bring the heavy car up from the third level below where he'd left it earlier this morning. The large wooden and steel car was twenty feet square and originally designed to move heavy equipment and people throughout the mining operation's multiple levels. It allowed them to travel up the two levels they needed to get to where they needed to be, which was home to the radio room, among other things. He made sure it was on the frequency that the watch officers would be manning at the operations center. "Fairchild Ops, this is Four Tango Whiskey Sierra Niner Foxtrot, over."

Silence greeted Mav's first attempt, but it didn't surprise him. Henley was standing so close to him that her lavender scent teased him and reminded him of their lovemaking last night. It wasn't enough and he looked forward to when he could actually take his time to pleasure her. She deserved that and more.

"Mav?" Henley's voice broke through the visions, but he didn't give her a reason that he'd lost his train of thought. Mav tried to reach someone at the base repeating his call-out one more time, with no luck of getting a reply. "We can't stay here all morning. Ernie and Kellen will be waiting, along with the rest of the town."

"They'll start without us," Mav declared, not willing to bet others' lives on the words of a man no one had met before or could vouch for. And if he wasn't willing to do that with the townsfolk, he sure as hell wasn't willing to do it with Henley's life. "We need to find out who Truman is associated with and why he's here."

"Master Gunny, we're a bit busy down here to shoot the bull today, over."

A jolt of satisfaction hit Mav square in the chest and he smiled at Henley, who was gesturing with her hand for him to hurry up and reply back. Mav pulled a chair closer and took a seat, trying to clean up the channel a bit by adjusting the sideband carrier a little more before responding. A bit of static filled the line, but it was quite manageable. All HF communications sounded like Darth Vader in a bucket of water when they were at their best. Henley set her hand on his shoulder and solidarity made itself known. He'd only ever experienced that with his friends, but it was a more than a welcome feeling.

"Fairchild, this is Echo Five Bravo calling for Master Gunny, interrogative. We require information on your operations accepting civilian personnel for emergency shelter on Fairchild. We have a DOD rep at our location claiming that Fairchild will provide shelter to citizens who are able to make it to your facility. Please confirm, over."

"Echo Five Bravo, that was the directive." The static was unusually heavy on this frequency and only a few words at a time were coming through loud and clear. "Fairchild has reached capacity. We are advising all personnel to billet in place and gather stores for thirty day sustainment, over."

Mav could sense that Henley relaxed somewhat at hearing confirmation that Truman had been feeding them facts when it came to the Air Force Base. Mav wasn't as trusting and he spoke into the mic once more, wishing there was an easier way to obtain the information he needed. Society had come to rely on technology too much and they were somewhat in the dark without access to the Internet.

"I'll relay your instructions to our town's leadership," Mav assured the man, before asking one last question. "The subject in question is Kellen Truman. Can you verify his credentials?"

"No, sir." The two words came across after a slight pause. "We have limited access to DOD personnel alpha rosters at present and that information would likewise be restricted to authorized personnel only. We advise you to stay in place until help arrives."

"Mav, Kellen said he wasn't with the guys at Fairchild." Henley squeezed his shoulder in reassurance, but it didn't relieve Mav's unease that something wasn't sitting right with Truman. "We need to go into town and let them know that the base isn't an option any longer. We need to let Kellen know that too."

Mav didn't like that Truman might opt to stay here at the camp, but he hadn't done anything to warrant being run off either. For some reason Mav didn't think the man would remain anyway. For his calm demeanor, there was an agitation showing through and it concerned Mav that Henley couldn't see it. Taking added precautions was essential.

"I want to stop at the hardware store and see if Mr. Jenkins has some automatic garage door openers and low voltage wiring for ground lighting systems. I can use them to improvise some perimeter alarms around the camp and on the road leading up the valley."

Henley followed Mav out of the bunker and back to the Jeep, where she pulled herself up into the passenger seat. The sparkle in her green eyes told him her thoughts weren't on securing the camp. She was thinking about their night together. Mav would have loved to be able to hole up in the cabin and spend the rest of the volcanic winter they had ahead of them with her, but first they needed to help those that were still in harm's way. They'd be running on nothing but caffeine by the time everyone who'd come to the camp were situated, but he'd at least be able to hold Henley while she slept tonight.

"We'll make it through this," Mav said softly, leaning in and pressing his lips against hers. She wrapped her free hand around the back of his neck and held him until he forced himself to pull away from her. He didn't like leaving this place unprotected, but he wasn't about to let Henley stay up here by herself either. She might be good with a firearm, but she'd be outmanned if more than one target came by to cause trouble. "Stay here for a minute. You should be carrying a weapon."

"Mav, I've already got my Beretta .40 S&W with an extra

clip," Henley argued, pulling away with a frown. "Regardless, I've known these people my entire life. They're wouldn't hurt anyone."

Mav could have stood here for hours telling Henley stories about people who thought the same thing. There were villages that his team would infiltrate to help where the locals swore their people wouldn't turn on them, only to find their closest friends or relatives had joined the rebel forces. People became desperate in times of need and would sell their soul to the devil if it meant their personal survival. That didn't even include those strangers that were bound to turn up soon, looking for an easier route into Canada and a source of supplies. He still took the time to go back into his own cabin and retrieve an extra box of .40 caliber S&W ammunition and a midway two-way radio with a clip that would fit easily onto her belt. He returned to the truck and handed the ammo and radio to her, neither saying a word as she took them from him.

Mav figured that Henley finally realized what he'd been trying to convey before as they pulled into town. Vehicles that were usually parked in front of people's houses or their garages were now lining the streets of Lost Summit. Mav counted at least twenty cars and trucks that were packed to the hilt and could name the owner's of at least half of them. They were trying to escape, but what they didn't comprehend was that there was nowhere to run.

"Mav, where are they going?" Henley asked, fear and surprise lacing her voice. She stuck her travel mug into the right side cup holder of his console as he pulled up outside of the hardware store. His intention had been to drop her off at the Village Community Center, but he knew her well enough that she would want try and talk to some of the people getting ready to leave. "They need to know we contacted the base and that our instructions are to stay here."

Henley had already opened her door by the time he threw the Jeep in park. Mav didn't even have time to say a word before she'd closed the door and made a beeline for Curt Rogers and Theo Powell. Both men were going over a map on the hood of Curt's car. Mav muttered a few choice words under his breath as his shoulder hit his door at the same time he pulled on the door's handle. She'd crossed the street before he could stop her.

"Mr. Rogers?" Henley was now standing behind the two men, who'd turned when she'd called out. "What are you doing?"

"Now, Henley, we've all been listening to the emergency channels. Our best bet is to get up to the Canadian border and cross into British Columbia." Curt nodded toward Theo, who'd already started to fold up the map. Mav came to stand next to Henley and he could already tell from the resolve written across both men's faces that neither he nor Henley would be able to change their minds. "Did you hear that the ash has reached southeastern Washington? It's not as bad as it is in the Midwest, but we can't stay here. We'd be better off farther north. Maybe even Alaska."

"We all know they won't allow you to cross the border," Henley said, throwing her hands up in frustration. "Didn't you listen to what Ernie had to say yesterday? The safest thing we could do is stay here, or better yet up at the camp. There is plenty of space for all of us and we have provisions. It's protected by the mountains, we have reliable sources of fuel, electricity, food, and water. We can provide safe shelter and protection from the elements for an extended period of time up there at the camp."

"Ernie is a good man, Henley, but it's all theory," Theo replied, his voice deeper than most due to his years of smoking. He gestured toward his car where his wife sat in the passenger side holding Snowcap in her lap. The Maltese would bite anyone who came near Mrs. Powell and he was watching all of their movements, debating on whether he should bark. Theo looked at Mav. "No offense, but we have to do what we think is best for our families."

"I understand, Mr. Powell, but I've looked over all the information as well and I believe Tank is right. I also spoke with Fairchild Base Operations and they're advising that we hunker down until the worst of it is over and they can get supplies to us then." Mav looked between the two men, already knowing that nothing he said would make a difference. They couldn't fathom staying and waiting it out. That didn't stop Mav from trying one more time. "I called Berke, Owen, Mason, and Van before the lines went down. They're making their way here and both of you know that means something if

Berke thinks this is the best place to be."

"Mav, do you really think they're still alive? How would they be able to travel any kind of distance in that shit?"

Mav gritted his teeth at the question and did his best not to say something he'd regret. Henley had audibly gasped at the inquiry and she laid her hand on his arm in comfort. He didn't need any because he knew his teammates unlike any other man on the face of this earth besides Tank. Those four Marines would not only make it here, but they would come bearing arms and the willingness to protect the sanctuary that Tank had created. It made Mav want everyone up at the lodge as soon as possible so that someone could be monitoring the HF radio for any distress calls.

"Listen, we have a guest up at the cabin who arrived yesterday morning. His name is Kellen Truman and he said he's with the military back at Fort Bragg," Henley explained, sharing a look with Mav. She tucked a loose strand of hair behind her ear and he could see the slight tremor in her hand. She was terrified for these people's lives, but she needed to accept that there wasn't anything that she or he could say to change their minds. "He thought that Fairchild AFB could take people, and that was true until they filled up. But like Mav said, he spoke with them this morning. It's best we stay here. Everyone else is over at the Village Community Center. Won't you at least come over there to see what we've come up with?"

Curt and Theo shared a look as they digested what Henley had shared. It was hope they were looking to grab hold of and as Henley continued to urge them to come to the Center to hear what else Tank might be able to tell them, Mav slowly disengaged himself to walk back across the street to the hardware store. Henley would be a while if she was going to notify the rest of the people that had lined the streets behind Rogers and Powell. He had to hand it to her. She had a tenacious spirit that would benefit all of them. When he reached the door to the shop it was locked.

"Dad's probably already over at the meeting." Mav turned to see Jeremy walking towards him from the south end of town. He had blood dripping down the side of his face and he had to be sporting a hell of a headache from where the drips were coming from. "We have a problem. Someone tried to ambush me from behind and did their best to take my rifle. I figured you might want to question him when he woke up."

CHAPTER FOURTEEN

HENLEY SPENT A good fifteen minutes talking to those folks who were lined up with whatever belongings they could fit into their vehicles. She'd shared everything she'd heard from Mav's conversation with Fairchild Operations along with the fact that Kellen Truman was currently with the rest of the residents inside the Village Community Center. People were panicking and she was right there with them, because her heart hadn't stopped racing since she saw how many residents were leaving town. She couldn't stand the thought of them stranded somewhere when the ash started to fall and from what the shortwave radio was saying…it was closer than they'd anticipated.

She'd convinced Mr. Rogers and Mr. Powell, along with Mr. Kahler to talk to Ernie once more before they chose to leave Lost Summit indefinitely. Right now she wanted to find Mav and but he was nowhere to be found when she'd returned to the front of the hardware store. She felt a twinge of anxiety at not locating him where he'd said he would be and she quickly made her way to the Community Center. Elijah had once again claimed his spot on a chair right by the door so that he could keep an eye on the sky and he patted her hand when she'd touched his shoulder.

"Have you seen Mav?" Henley looked around and could visibly see that only around three quarters of the population was still here. Sheriff Ramsey, Mayor Thomas, and Ernie were speaking with Kellen Truman toward the front of the large room. She didn't spot Mav and a weight settled into her stomach, causing her to locate Stanley Ratliff and his two followers. She saw them near the front as well, listening intently to the others. "He was supposed to be over at the hardware store."

"I haven't seen Mav this morning. Jenkins is inside with Mrs. Welsh, so I don't know how your man would have gotten inside the shop." Elijah turned and pointed to where Mr. Jenkins and Mrs. Welsh stood with their heads together, but Henley was curious as to why Elijah would have called Mav *her man*. It had been a whirlwind forty-eight hours and with the exception that the world would experience an apocalyptic event...she didn't regret a minute of it. She'd felt whole ever since she'd come clean with Maverick and then actually had the strength to drop the barriers she'd put into place. She'd finally let someone in—someone special—and now it was almost painful to be away from his side and not know where he'd gone. It would be so hard to put into words or explain that to someone looking in from the outside, but thinking that today could be her last had her holding on to what she'd been given with every ounce of strength she had. "I have my hearings aids in this morning. I don't want to miss anything that's said."

"That's good, Elijah," Henley replied, regretting that she sounded distracted when Elijah needed as much reassurance as she did. Henley turned around to look down the street, seeing a few people here and there as they turned their vehicles around and drove out of town. Mabel was walking their way with a carafe in one hand and a stack of Styrofoam cups in another. She looked haphazard, tired, and downright worried, which Henley figured was due to the fact Derek hadn't been able to contact her since the supervolcano erupted. "Let me go help Mabel."

"I've got it," Elijah said as he took his time standing, even using the edge of the doorframe to help his movements. He didn't have his cane today. "You go on up front. I've been picking up pieces of the conversation and it sounds like the mayor is in agreement with that new fellow to tell everyone to head to Fairchild Air Force Base."

What Henley wanted was to go look for Mav. His stories of not trusting people during desperate times was starting to worry her, even though she knew every single person in this town and was confident they wouldn't hurt someone out of fear. She'd just been about to tell Elijah that she'd be back when Ernie called out her name. Thinning her lips in concern and irritation, Henley reluctantly made her way to the front of the room.

"Ernie, I need to—"

"The mayor wants to move everybody who is still in town to Fairchild." Ernie pointed an accusing finger at Kellen, who stood there with his arms crossed in confidence. "That's four hours' drive south toward Spokane and that area cannot sustain that many people for the length of time needed. We're talking ten years of a volcanic winter and who knows what follows."

"It doesn't matter," Henley said, resigning to sharing what she knew so that she could go in search of Mav. "Kellen, we spoke with Base Operations at Fairchild less than an hour ago. They aren't taking anyone else. They're filled to capacity and his instructions were to stay here until someone from the National Guard could get to us with additional supplies."

Henley was now the center of attention, but that wasn't what made her uncomfortable. It was Kellen who'd become so still in studying her that it made her acutely aware of the danger Ernie and Mav had been referring to. She didn't back down and met his stare with a raised eyebrow. She wasn't about to let him know that he intimated her. Her white sweatshirt covered the weapon that Ernie had given her and it gave her a measure of false confidence that she could deal with anything thrown her way.

"You're more than welcome to stay in the cabin we've provided you," Henley stated to Kellen, raising her voice so that everyone could hear her. Ernie crossed his arms across his chest, evidently satisfied that someone was finally listening to him. She turned to face everyone else, already seeing the unwillingness to compromise on Stanley Ratliff's face. "As Tank mentioned yesterday the safest area would be the fishing lodge. Seeing that there are only around thirty some residents left, we have plenty of room between the lodge and the cabins, as well as accepting those who come to us for help as long as they don't show us any hostility. Whoever needs assistance we'll spend the day transporting clothes, medical provisions, whatever you need to carry you through until we start getting supplies from the National Guard."

"Curt and Theo, are you two still headed up north?" Rat asked, his booming voice cutting off anything else Henley had to say. She shared a look with Ernie, who remained silent. The mayor and the sheriff were quietly talking amongst themselves, but it was apparent that Felix was keeping an eye on the situation. "Did you hear that the borders are being sealed until the agents can verify that a person has family in the country before allowing someone to cross?"

"We didn't hear that." Curt didn't seem too put off at the news and after conversing with Theo, said exactly what Henley was afraid he'd say. "But that's not going to stop us. We'll be better farther north than here, so that's where we're headed. Ernie and Henley, we appreciate the offer and wish you the best of luck. We're doing what we think is best."

"Do you have enough supplies to last you if they don't allow you to cross?" Sheriff Felix asked, stepping forward and motioning toward Mr. Jenkins. "Marvin will open his store to anything you might need. The engines in your vehicles will suffocate or be clogged with ash within an hour once it reaches us and you'll be stranded."

"Then we better get moving," Theo muttered, despondent that this was happening and that he was leaving everything he'd ever known. Henley's heart went out to him while anger welled up inside of her that they even had to make these choices. Their lives were being ripped apart before the ash even arrived. It wasn't fair and she could have really used Mav here to try and convince them otherwise. "Good luck, folks."

Murmurs arose and the mayor stepped forward to walk them out while Felix stopped to speak with Mr. Jenkins. Several people were yelling out that they would need Ernie's help, while others were still debating on whether or not they were staying. Stanley was conferring with Randy and Jarrett, while both men appeared agitated. Henley made a move to leave so that she could find Mav when Kellen stepped forward and placed a hand on her arm.

"Did Base Operations at Fairchild say anything else? I should have known that Ernie would have an HF radio up at the lodge." Kellen cautiously removed his hand after Henley glared at the action like she used to have to do back in the day. She didn't like people thinking they could enter her personal space without her permission and that it was an acceptable practice. He wisely stepped back, but that didn't stop him from making her even more uncomfortable by his next question. "Do you think he'd mind if I use it to try and contact some of my team members?"

"Team?" Henley asked, torn between wanting to know more, finding Mav, and calming Stanley down now that he was in a full-blown argument with the sheriff. She couldn't afford to stay to hear Kellen's reply, but she'd asked anyway. "You have a team at Fairchild AFB? I thought you said you were out of Fort Bragg."

"No, I have a friend at the base," Kellen clarified, his attention being routed to Rat as well. His eyes were glued to the scene unfolding before them as voices rose and echoed throughout the large building. "My team is on leave and I was able to notify them before satellite coverage went south on us, but I gave them false information according to what you're saying."

"So they're heading to Spokane?"

Henley didn't hear Kellen's reply because now Ernie was in on the argument with Rat, causing a divide amongst those that were still inside the building. She could see Elijah at his post by the door, shaking his head at the commotion. Where the hell was Mav?

"What makes your lodge safer than my camping grounds?" Spit had come out of Rat's mouth when he asked the question. Stanley's issues with having to be better than Ernie was going to literally cost him his life. Mav would have said that was tough shit, but Henley couldn't just stand by without trying to get him to see reason. "I have access to the silver mine that's farther up the valley from my campground once the air gets too polluted. How many people can you fit up in that tiny test hole of yours anyway? Didn't they dig that hole back at the turn of the century? It has to be ready to collapse by now, or is it half flooded, Tank?"

"Now, Stanley, let's be reasonable," Sheriff Ramsey said, stepping in between the two men. Ernie didn't seem perturbed in the least, letting Felix take control of the situation. "Ernie's already shared with everyone the amount of protection that mountain can give us, along with the mountain spring water and natural gas well he's made sure the lodge has access to. He has the space and coming solely from a security standpoint—we're able to secure that place a hell of a lot better than this town, or an open campground for that matter."

"Security?" Rat scoffed after barking out a laugh, not getting a rise out of Randy or Jarrett. In fact, the two older men looked somewhat uncomfortable. "You'll be sitting ducks up in that mountain if a group of ruffians decide they want to take the site."

"Stanley, don't do this," Henley implored, gesturing toward the people surrounding them. She'd taken notice of those nodding their head in agreement with what Rat was saying. She would have thought they'd have been a lot wiser, considering they'd seen the man's pettiness over the years. Instead, some of the residents were actually listening to him. "You're only going to divide the town when we need to stick together. Everyone, you've known me since I was brought into this world. Sheriff Ramsey has taken care of this town for over ten years and he will continue to do so. If he feels that it's safe up at the lodge where we can all help each other out and be there for one another when the going gets tough, then we should heed his advice."

"That's a nice PSA, doll, but we all know that Tank and Felix are old buddies. It's not like you can pull one over on us."

"My friendship with Ernie Yates has never interfered with my duty to this town, Rat, and I don't have to stand here and defend myself from the likes of you when we're running out of time." The sheriff turned to address the townsfolk remaining. "I've done some research myself while we still had access to the Internet. I'm convinced that we'll all be safer up at the fishing lodge than anywhere else in the vicinity. This is still my hometown, this is still my jurisdiction, and we take care of our own. Any shitheels that want trouble and come up that pass are going to find it a bit harder going than old Rat here thinks. If you want to join him, just ask yourself if you would trust him with your life. That's what your decision really comes down to."

"I'll stick this out on my own land, Ramsey." Stanley took his time looking around, recognizably scouting for anyone to join him. Henley caught Jarrett looking her way and she slowly shook her head, imploring him to make the right decision. "I'm going to start moving things I'll need into the mine. Anyone who wants to join me, you know where to find me."

Stanley didn't wait around to hear if the sheriff had anything else to add and neither Ernie nor Felix tried to stop Rat as he made his way through the clearing that the crowd had made. Randy didn't hesitate to follow, although Jarrett was a little slower.

"He's never been known for his tact, Henley, but Stanley is a good man. He's helped numerous people in this town when they were down on their luck." Jarrett ran a hand down his weathered face, unable to wipe away the stress that this situation had placed on him. He'd seen his fair share of hardships during his life and Henley wasn't so sure he could handle another. "I'll be there to keep an eye on him and the others who join us."

"Jarrett, just come with us," Henley pleaded, feeling utterly useless that she hadn't been able to change this scenario. "You'll be much better off. We have emergency supplies up at the lodge, as well as generators that run on natural gas. It will see us through this ordeal."

"Don't think Rat doesn't have his own supplies," Jarrett informed Henley with a pat on her shoulder. "He's smarter than you give him credit for."

"Sheriff, do something." Henley couldn't believe this was happening, especially when she saw a few more other people follow behind Randy. When had this become about factions? She desperately tried to think of something that would stop this lunacy. "Can't you put them into protective custody or something?"

"Henley, they're grown men and women. They can make their own decisions and there is nothing I can do to stop them. They aren't looting, they aren't committing crimes. They're upstanding citizens doing what they think is right. They have to make what they believe to be the best decision for their own family." Felix looked around, as if noticing for the first time that Mav hadn't joined her. "Where is Mav? I'm going to need his help transporting some ammunition up to the lodge. I don't want to leave anything in town that someone may be able to use against another group."

"I don't know," Henley said honestly, looking behind her to address Kellen as well. He was gone. Vanished. That didn't ease her worry and neither did the fact that the town was basically being split in two. "I'll go looking for him while you start loading up. Does Patty know what's going on?"

"Yes, she's home packing what she can," Felix said, pausing when Mabel came up to the both of them. Ernie was off to the side speaking with Mr. Jenkins, who Henley wanted to talk to regarding Mav needing to get into the hardware store. If he wasn't there, then where could he have gone? "Mabel, are you all right?"

"I still don't know if Derek and his family made it out safely." Mabel wrung her hands as she tried to stem her distress. "I think it would be best for me to stay here in case he arrives in the next day or two. He won't know where I've gone."

"All you need to do is leave a note at home and also inside the diner detailing where you can be found," Sheriff Ramsey suggested, holding up a hand and stopping Ernie from interrupting. His conversation with Mr. Jenkins had ended and he'd had his eyes on Mabel the entire time. "Don't leave it where anyone can see it, but in a location that Derek would look. We shouldn't announce our whereabouts to just anyone scouting around."

"Mabel, does Derek have a key to your house or to the diner?" Ernie asked, apparently satisfied that Felix had given an answer that would protect those at the camp from looters who would just be looking out for themselves. Mabel replied that her son had keys to both, which was a blessing. "Why don't I come with you and we'll see what we can come up with."

"Sheriff, I'm going to go see if I can find Mav." Henley disengaged herself and jogged to the front of the building where she'd seen Mr. Jenkins exit the door. Elijah was still in his position, but his eyes weren't on the sky anymore. Instead, they were fixed on Stanley and a few of his friends who were trying to talk Paul Lockton into opening up the grocery store so they could stock up on canned goods. "Elijah, you're coming with us up to the lodge, aren't you?"

"I've always considered myself wiser than that fool Randy Bassett," Elijah grumbled as he pushed himself off of the chair. "Now is no different. I'll walk home to pack some things and be waiting out front of the diner if you could give me a ride up to the lodge."

"I'm glad to hear it, Elijah," Henley said, relieved that he was coming with them. She should now be in the free and clear to go look for Mav. "We'll meet you over there in a bit.

We'll drive over to your place if we don't see you out front."

Henley started toward the post office, noticing that some of the cars on Main Street were pulling away from the curb and heading out of town. She could feel their desperation as each of the families left one by one, wishing there was something she could say that would make them stay. There wasn't and that was like an open wound in her heart. She'd known these people all of her life and seeing them leave was akin to watching them march off to their death.

Fifteen minutes later Henley's chest was so tight with concern that she was having difficulty breathing. She'd walked all the way down to the Fish and Bait Shop, not finding any trace of Mav. She'd returned the way she'd come, intent on going to the last few places she hadn't checked when she caught sight of someone standing near the pavilion where the town held their farmer's market. Picking up her pace, she jogged to the left and followed the narrow street to the rotunda.

"Jeremy?" Henley called out, stopping abruptly when Jeremy turned to her with what appeared to be a fresh wound on the side of his head. "Are you okay? What happened?"

"Someone struck me from behind and did their best to take my weapon, but I was able to fight back." Jeremy tried to wipe away some of the blood, but the majority of it was now dry and stuck to the side of his face. "Mav searched him, but the man didn't have any identification. We're hoping he comes around soon."

"Henley?"

She hurried past Jeremy and saw Mav kneeling over a body behind the backboard of a table used by Mrs. Welsh to sell her canned grape preserves. There wasn't a mark on the prone figure that she could see, but it was obvious he wasn't waking up anytime soon. She got worried when she didn't see any movement in his chest.

"Mav, he *is* breathing, right?" Henley stopped by Mav's side, her fear rising with each passing second he didn't answer. "Mav? I just came from a lovely morning meeting where the town turned out to be divided because Rat doesn't want to come up to the lodge, so I really don't want to start the afternoon with a dead body."

"He's breathing," Mav answered, his voice grim as he waved a hand over the man. She needed to stop referring to this stranger like that or else she'd convince herself he *was* dead. "Do you recognize him?

Henley tilted her head to look at the man's face, but she couldn't identify him. He had blond hair that contained a slight curl on the ends with a scar that slanted diagonally across his nose and very thin lips. He wasn't handsome, but instead he contained that classic boy-next-door type of appearance.

"No, I haven't seen him around here before." Henley waited for Mav to say something else, but he remained silent. She looked over to find Jeremy scouting the open land behind her and she couldn't help but turn around to make sure nothing was there. She certainly didn't like the feeling that someone was watching them when they had more important things to worry about. "Mav, did you hear what I said about Rat? He's decided to stay at his campground, using the mine as a shelter against the ash...and people are actually joining him."

"If that's their choice there's nothing we can do about it now." Mav stood, appearing to make a decision that had nothing to do with what she'd just told him. "Jeremy, go get Dylan and Jason Wicks. We'll need their help transporting this guy up to the lodge."

"Dylan has a pickup truck, so we can load him in the back." Jeremy shifted the strap of his weapon over his shoulder, wincing when the movement must have jarred his head. "I'll go see if I can find them. They were at their father's farm trying to figure out what they were going to do with the animals."

"What are we going to do with *him*?" Henley asked, wondering where Mary McClend was at right now. She was a nurse that worked rotation in Metaline Falls, but Henley couldn't remember seeing her since they'd gotten news of the eruption. "Do you want me to find Sheriff Ramsey?"

"I'll talk to the sheriff." Mav turned to look at the field behind her, once again making Henley somewhat apprehensive that they were being watched. "Jeremy, tell Dylan to bring anything fit to butcher up to the lodge. We can use all the fresh meat we can get. It's unlikely this guy was alone, so the faster we get the townsfolk up to the lodge, the better. The predators are gathering quicker than I thought."

ESSENTIAL BEGINNINGS

Henley could see the worry etched into Mav's brown eyes, so she lifted a hand to his cheek. Her touch got his attention and he gave her a small smile of reassurance before leaning down to brush his lips over hers. The casual intimacy made everything seem okay and she leaned into him, placing her head on his chest. His warm arms wrapped around her and she hadn't realized she'd been so cold.

"Are you holding up okay?" Mav asked, stroking a hand over her back. Henley closed her eyes and nodded, taking a few moments to shut off her thoughts as he told her what had taken place. "Jeremy came to me when I tried to get into the hardware store and he told me what had happened. It's odd that he's not carrying any identification, and Jeremy said that he wasn't that good at fighting hand to hand. He was able to catch Jeremy by surprise, but he was able to get the upper hand when he turned around and used the butt of his rifle as a weapon."

"I haven't seen Mary, so for all we know she's still in Metaline Falls." Henley leaned back but she kept her arms around Mav's waist. She wasn't ready to let go of him. "I'm assuming Jeremy hit him pretty hard for him not to be waking up yet. What are we going to do with him once we get him back up to the lodge?"

"We're going to put him in the brig inside the bunker. Sheriff Ramsey can babysit him until he wakes up and tells us what we need to know." They both heard voices coming from the road and when Mav turned his body to the side, Henley was able to see that Jeremy had brought not only Dylan and Jason but the sheriff as well. "It looks like he already knows about his new prisoner."

"Mav, what's this about some stranger trying to knock out Jeremy?" Sheriff Ramsey walked closer and then slowed his steps when he saw the body lying on the ground. "Any idea of who he is?"

"No, but this isn't the kind of trouble we need right now." Mav kept his arm around Henley's waist, both of them standing side by side. "Neither is what Henley told me about Ratliff. How many people did he dupe into staying in that damn old abandoned mine with him?"

"Not many," Sheriff Ramsey replied, leaning down to take a closer look at the stranger. He studied the man's face before letting out a long whistle of astonishment. "Mav, I think I know this man."

Mav stiffened next to Henley and she braced herself for what Felix was about to land at their feet. There had been too much chaos in the last forty-eight hours that they didn't need anything else to add to their worry list. Felix looked up at them and revealed another setback, making her wonder what they were going to do next.

"If I'm not mistaken, this is Stanley Ratliff's middle son."

CHAPTER FIFTEEN

MAV DIDN'T LIKE leaving Henley alone to accompany Sheriff Ramsey to Ratliff's residence up at the campgrounds he owned and operated. Between Jeremy, Dylan, and Jason, they'd been able to load Trevor Ratliff's body into the back of Dylan's truck and then transport him behind the sheriff's vehicle. According to Felix, Trevor had left around his eighteenth birthday and had never returned to Lost Summit. There'd been some falling out with the father and son after Rat's wife had lost her battle to cancer, but Rat hadn't spoke of his son in years. From first appearances it seemed that Trevor had gone down the wrong path, but they wouldn't know more until he woke up. Rat's other two children lived in other states and returned for visits every couple of years.

This was such a waste of time that Mav's anger rose with each passing mile out to the turnoff for the campgrounds. He would have rather been by Henley's side as she helped Elijah, Lola, and her daughter up to the lodge. Henley had taken his Jeep as transportation with the thought that he'd catch a ride back with Felix. Ernie and Paul Lockton had taken what supplies the grocery store owner had kept for himself up to the lodge, allowing Stanley and his crew to clean out half of the shelves for their refuge. Everyone should have been able to effectively clear out of town, but here he was about to have another run-in with Ratliff.

"Just let me do the talking," Felix muttered, grabbing his sheriff's hat and positioning it on his head just so. "Rat was already agitated when he left town. This isn't going to make him any happier."

Mav didn't give a shit how Rat felt at the moment. The man was being a jackass for trying to prove he knew better than Tank. This wasn't a competition. This was about survival and the handful of people who followed Stanley's lead would end up dead if they didn't start to think for themselves very soon.

"Let's just get this over with." Mav got out of the car and went around to the back of Dylan's truck. Lo and behold, Trevor Ratliff was starting to come to. "Felix, he's coming round."

"Trevor, wake up. You're lucky you're alive after the stunt you just pulled." Mav could hear the sheriff talking to Rat and it wasn't long before both men were walking his way. Mav wanted answers and he wanted them before this man's father prevented it. "You want to tell me what you're doing here?"

"Damn, that hurts," Trevor muttered as he placed a hand to the side of his head. He squinted up at Jeremy, who rode in the bed of the truck to ensure that Trevor didn't come to and try to make a run for it. "You have a hell of a swing."

"You got what you deserved." Jeremy didn't seem too forgiving at the moment and it dawned on Mav that these two men must have known each other when they were boys in school. There didn't seem to be a lot of love lost though. Mav tilted his head to tell Jeremy to hurry this up. "Trevor, what are you doing back here? I didn't even recognize you."

"Jeremy Jenkins?" Trevor slowly sat up, wincing at the pain his movements caused. He gave Jeremy a curious look. "Shit, I didn't even know that was you. I just saw two armed men and I figured something had happened to the town. It's total chaos out there, man."

"Two?" Mav asked, knowing full well the only one who'd been stationed as a precaution at the front of town had been Jeremy. "Where did you see the other sentry?"

"He was around thirty feet from Jeremy but looked to be about six feet tall." Trevor's face was still clouded in pain, but a look of apprehension mingled into his features when Rat's voice became rather loud and the man himself came into view. Mav stepped back, still wanting answers but assuming these two needed a moment. "Dad. It's been a long time."

Stanley abruptly stopped a few yards away and he appeared sentimental for the first time since Mav had known Ratliff. He was always trying to one-up every other man in town and that had included his sons, from what Mav had heard. He hadn't been privy to what had made Trevor leave Lost Summit, but Mav understood the need to be home in times of a crisis. To Mav, that was here as well.

"Trevor." Stanley surveyed the crowd, not pleased that his son's homecoming was being witnessed by quite a few people. He didn't address it either, but awkwardly motioned with his hand toward Trevor's wound. "What happened to you?"

Mav stiffened and waited for the truth to come out, which would only perpetuate the tense situation they'd all been placed in. He glanced toward the mine's entrance, seeing that Stanley was currently having people take rations and other items inside the tunnel. Didn't he realize that he needed a fuel source, electricity, water, and heat, along with numerous other vital elements to be able to last in there for the length of time needed before the National Guard would be able to drop supplies off to the survivors?

"Nothing," Trevor said, sharing a look with Jeremy and slightly relieving Mav's stress. He wasn't sure why he would protect Jeremy, unless it was to prevent Rat from finding out that he'd been bested. Mav wanted answers as to where the other stranger had gone that was armed. "I must have slipped and hit my head. Jeremy helped me out and gave me a lift. Looks like you're holing up in the old Pine Peak Silver Mine."

"We are." Stanley appeared to be more composed now that his personal life wasn't on display and gave the sheriff, along with Mav, a look of disgust. "You've come just in time to lend a hand before the ash cloud arrives and it gets too bad around here."

"Stanley, your son should see Mary. I don't know if she's up at the lodge yet or if she got stuck at the hospital in

Metaline Falls, but his head took the brunt of the fall," Sheriff Ramsey said, keeping up with the pretenses as he stepped closer to show his sincerity. "Why don't you let me take him up to..."

"Trevor, I need to know who that other man is that you saw on the east side of town." Mav kept his voice as low as he could while Ramsey kept Stanley occupied. There was something wrong with this picture all the way around and Mav wouldn't feel comfortable with the security of their camp until Berke, Owen, Mason, and Van arrived. "Can you describe him?"

"He was tall, built, armed, and dressed in black." Trevor shrugged in regret at not being able to share more. At least, that's how it appeared to be. Mav still couldn't understand how Jeremy wouldn't have seen or heard someone else that close to his vantage point. He trusted Jeremy over Trevor Ratliff, but it appeared that was all the information that the boy was going to share. "That's all I can tell you. Sorry."

Black. The color clicked now, reminding Mav of Kellen Truman's outfit this morning. Mav had assumed Kellen had gone directly back to the lodge. Henley mentioned that he was aware that Fairchild wasn't accepting any more civilians, but that she hadn't seen him after that. Could Truman have some of his friends in the area like Mav suspected? He was glad Henley was armed, but he still felt the need to get back up to the lodge.

"Sheriff, we need to go," Mav announced, cutting into the

heated discussion that had risen to another level all because Stanley didn't want his son anywhere near Ernie. It was getting old and Mav certainly wasn't going to lose any sleep over Rat's poor choices. It was unfortunate it would be too late for the others by the time these people wised up. "Jeremy, you're welcome to ride with us or catch a ride with Dylan and Jason."

"I'm going to go with Dylan and Jason to help out their father with the rest of the animals. He's opening up the pastures and allowing them access to the higher ranges to the north, although we're transporting most of the chickens, a few pigs, and a couple of cows up to the lodge to help sustain us for the length of time we'll be up there."

"We'll need all the help we can get. Make sure to load up plenty of grain feed for the chickens," Mav replied, ignoring Stanley as he walked past him to the sheriff's vehicle. Felix was close behind him, removing his hat before he got in on the driver's side. Neither man spoke until they were on the main road and heading back toward town. "Someone is watching the town and they're armed. I have no idea if this has anything to do with Kellen Truman but we need to find out."

"He's not just going to come clean with us if he's behind something, Mav." Felix coasted through town, seeing if any of the townsfolk were still around and if they might need help. The only person they saw was Mr. Jenkins, who waved at them that he was fine and would meet up with them soon. Mav didn't need anything extra with regards to guarding the lodge now that everyone would be located in one area. He would put people on rotation twenty-four seven to provide security for those on the property, as well as one person monitoring the security cameras that Ernie had rigged around the key bunker security points. "Let me handle it until I inform everyone that I've deputized you."

Mav figured this was coming and accepted the offer with a handshake. Felix then concentrated on the drive back down the road, giving Mav time to think. According to Henley, Truman had made reservations for a cabin back in January. The first question that needed answered was if he'd known a natural disaster had been about to occur, along with how he would have gained that information. His timing couldn't have been more impeccable and that wasn't something to take frivolously.

"Tread lightly but don't push too hard," Mav suggested, thinking it might be better to keep an eye on Truman than it was to show their hand. "Maybe mention that someone caught sight of an armed man to see what his reaction is, but it's better to keep him in the dark of what we suspect."

"I'll play it by ear," Felix answered, not promising anything. He'd been around the block a time or two and Mav respected his experience. "Any word from Berke, Owen, Mason, or Van?"

"Not yet, but I haven't had time to monitor the HF radio." Mav spotted quite a few vehicles up near the lodge parking lot, but not as many per people due to limited amount of space. They'd suggested to everyone that it would be best to leave the majority of the cars and trucks in town. Ernie was standing near the entrance to the fishing lodge, which was where Felix pulled to a stop. "Where's Henley?"

"She's in the lodge assigning rooms to those who are older and the cabins to those who are younger and able to stand watch." Ernie waited to continue until both Felix and Mav were out of the car. He looked around the area and found the quiet unsettling. There were no signs of animals, nor was the wind blowing to give animation to the trees lining the edge of the forest. He glanced up at the sky, but nothing appeared abnormal. "We've done a headcount and have around twenty-eight people, with an additional eight that we're expecting. My boys and then Mabel's son, along with his wife and children."

"So that means Rat has roughly eight or ten townsfolk with him," Felix surmised, tipping his hat back and thinning his lips. Mav calculated that there were more people than supplies within the bunker should they need it, but there wouldn't be a choice as to who was left outside to fend for themselves. He and his team would sacrifice their lives for these people if need be, just as they had done when they were fighting for Mother Freedom in the green machine. "We lost quite a few people this morning who are headed for the border. Any chance they'll be able to make it back this way if they get spurned at the border?"

"The Canadians are protecting themselves," Ernie said in understanding, running his fingers down his mustache. "They'll be affected by this too and it is Canada's responsibility to take care of their own, not ours. Hell, there isn't a place on this earth that won't be touched by what is coming our way."

"Tank, Jeremy will be back with the other men once they clear out the rest of the farm. We spoke to them about guard shifts and they're pretty much all we have to work with. I'll conduct some firearms and sentry training once they get here. We can arm them with the M4s and a basic load out. I'll be in with Henley until then, but I'll show them the designated vantage points for guarding the area when they arrive and we get the basics out of the way."

Mav left Ernie and Felix to talk amongst themselves and headed toward the front of the lodge. The large heavy door opened before he could grab the handle and Henley stepped across the threshold. Her eyes were slightly bloodshot and there was a tinge of blue underneath her eyes to indicate her exhaustion, but to him she'd never looked more beautiful. He pulled her into his arms, not caring who could see them. Her warm body melded with his and he buried his face in the softness of her hair, which had come loose from her hair tie.

"How are you holding up?" Mav said after a while, pulling Henley only far enough away so that he could see her face. "Has anything happened while I was gone?"

"Just getting everyone sorted out, including Kellen. I told him to stay in the cabin he'd been assigned but I haven't seen him since we got back." Henley half smiled and then patted her hip where she was still carrying, her one hand remaining on his shoulder. He'd wished the last three years had been like this, but he wouldn't take this moment for granted. He wouldn't question the timing or the reason they'd communicated fully. Questioning created doubt and he was done with that. It certainly didn't fit into the future. "I had things covered here while Ernie was taking care of the perimeter. He mentioned he was waiting for you though."

"Yeah, I just spoke with him." Mav took Henley's hand and led her away from the lodge along the curved access road leading off toward the location of the bunker, a barn with a corral, and the NG Wellhead blockhouse. Kirk Parson must have been assigned the cabin closest to Truman's, which worked to Mav's advantage because he was currently unloading a suitcase from his car. Kirk was in his mid-fifties and ran the fish and bait shop in town. He could more than handle a firearm and he wouldn't ask questions if Mav were to request that he keep an eye on their guest. "I'm going to show Jeremy, Dylan, and Jason where I need them to set up during the night. Ernie, Felix, and I will take the dayshifts. Ernie and I will also backup the night shift as needed, at least until the rest of the guys get here."

Mav held Henley's hand on the short walk and it felt more natural than breathing. Her fingers laced perfectly against his and he found that he needed a minute alone with her, away from everyone and everything. He detoured away from the entrance to the bunker and guided her down to where she liked to sit sometimes near the barn. He'd caught her sitting on a specific boulder a time or two on his past visits and he wanted to share that with her.

The view was through the woods from behind the lodge to the south downhill side where the pond faced the four-season room. It was a lovely sight and it covered the entire southeast approach from any point lower in the valley toward the lodge or the NG Wellhead Blockhouse. This would certainly turn into one of their sentry posts.

"Shouldn't they have arrived by now?" Henley asked with worry etched into her voice. She didn't hesitate to fit herself in between his thighs when he positioned himself on the large rock. Once she was in place, he held her to him and wished he could ease her worries, but he couldn't. Technically Mason *should* have been here by now considering he'd been in Nebraska when word had spread about the eruption. "Is there no way we can get a hold of them?"

"Only if they stop long enough to set up a field expedient antennae for their HF radio, and we haven't been here to monitor for emergency transmissions," Mav said, looking out at the still water of the pond. It was too still, for usually small round wakes could be seen of passing water bugs treading across the surface or the occasional splash of a tail could be seen from the fish feeding at the surface. It wouldn't be long before some of the ash arrived. "That's where I'm headed, but I just wanted a quiet moment with you."

"I, um, gave away your cabin." Henley spoke the words matter-of-factly with the exception of a brief *um*. Mav smiled behind her, liking that she was comfortable enough with him to make that decision. It meant she was confident in him as well. "I thought we could put the guys in the bunker as their primary billeting since we don't have any more rooms or cabins left."

"That's a good idea," Mav approved, caressing the back of her hands that were resting on her knees, noticing that she didn't wait for his reaction regarding staying with her at her cabin. He wouldn't want to be anywhere else and there wasn't a point in talking about it when it was what they both wanted. "Did you give Mabel a cabin? I'm sure we can rig up some sleeping bags for the rest of her family when they arrive."

"I did. I also—" Henley broke off her sentence, causing Mav to brace for the reason why. He didn't see anything around them until she pointed it out. "Mav?"

Henley moved her fingers underneath his to catch his attention. A miniscule ash had settled onto the back of his hand, letting them know that time was running out. They both looked up into the sky, but didn't notice anything different than it was five minutes ago. This must have come from the high up in the atmosphere. It was a calling card and they'd been found.

CHAPTER SIXTEEN

THE NIGHT WAS quiet as Henley looked out the window into the dark, unable to see if any more ash had fallen. She and Mav had joined the others and spent the rest of the evening in the lodge's great room making decisions that the vast majority of the group had been comfortable with. The topics had ranged from shelter to food, and then to security.

Ernie and Mav agreed to take everyone through the bunker in small groups as time permitted. All the men were provided with an M4 with a basic 180 round load out. The women that had skill with firearms were provided M9 Beretta pistols with one extra fifteen round clip and a shoulder holster. Classes on firearm safety, the cleaning, and the operation of the various small arms carried by the camp's population would be conducted as needed. Everyone that was armed was told that they were to maintain possession of their weapon at all times and not to leave it anywhere for any reason.

By the time the sheriff had shared his thoughts and views, Ernie had also added on supplementary issues that no one had really thought of, such as group assignments and schedules for moving the entire contents of the outlying camp into the bunker based on milestone events. All in all, everyone was now on board with how the next few weeks or months would go until the National Guard was able to reach them with supplies. It was hard to imagine what the world would be like after they emerged from underground, provided that they were able to make it through the initial stage and transition into the mountain.

Henley and Mav had returned to her cabin after they had taken the time to eat the meal that Mabel had prepared for everyone in camp. Mabel was voted the official camp cook and in charge of meal preparation and food distribution. Mav had insisted that Henley eat something in the dining room as he explained to her that they had to take care of themselves if they were to be of any help to the others. It was strange to have dinner with him at their own table surrounded by the town's people. Even after they'd been intimate she hadn't contemplated coming out to the town about their relationship in quite so public a fashion. She'd mentioned that she'd never be the Martha Stewart type and he'd laughed, saying that was good because he definitely wasn't interested in the popular Susie Homemaker icon. The light moment hadn't eased the tension from what they were about to face, but it felt nice to take a minute for themselves over a nice hot meal.

A lot of things had changed in the course of a few days and it was as if Henley had been deposited into a different life. On one hand, she could have totally gotten used to this *playing house* thing since Mav had been by her side assisting in the meal lodge's preparations. On the other, she could have done without the apocalyptic event that was causing them to ration everything down to their food.

They met with the individuals that had been assigned the various duties to keep the camp operating. Guards had to be trained. They didn't have time to wash clothes or prepare their own meals. Animals needed to be fed, milked, and butchered. Rob Wicks was responsible for and handled those duties in an effort to do his part toward the group's goals. God knows they had enough producing chickens to last quite a while. The facilities needed to be maintained inside and outside the mountain. Ernie had spent his entire day going over things with Gage, the town's former garage mechanic, detailing how the various systems worked.

Everyone had kept the conversation light and not dwelling on the doomsday scenario they were facing. Henley discovered that she really liked Mav's sense of humor and discovering facts about him that she'd never known, such as his affinity for Payday bars. He'd made a face when she said she'd preferred anything with chocolate and caramel together.

They'd eaten lunch out of her refrigerator in the cabin earlier in the day, which were precooked chicken breasts that she'd had in a Tupperware dish. They'd made side dishes from the things that were the most perishable. Anything canned or boxed would be saved and carried to the lodge tomorrow. Mabel would make meals in the lodge starting tomorrow morning and everyone would eat as a group during designated hours. That's the mentality they needed and that's what they would implement in order to survive. Breakfast and dinner would provide the largest part of their substance. Only a light lunch would be provided to carry them through their busy days.

"We were able to get a lot of things sorted out today," Mav said, walking into the room after having taken a shower. Henley had done the same right after dinner and she was now wearing a pair of cut-off sweats and a faded red T-shirt that now appeared a dark shade of pink. She looked over her shoulder to see that he was only wearing a pair of jeans…nothing else. The temperature in the room began to slowly rise, surprising her that she could feel anything other than trepidation for what they were facing. It was a nice distraction, but he was anything but that. Mav had become her rock—her foundation that she'd come to rely on that had nothing to do with security. He was her emotional pillar that she'd always dreamed of but was forever afraid to have. "How are you feeling about the decisions made?"

"I'm confident in what's been decided because of who made them," Henley replied honestly, giving one last look out into the dark where not even the moon was shining through the clouds. At least, she hoped they were rain clouds and not ash. "Ernie and Felix have seen combat tours just like you. They know what it will take to endure the coming days and I trust you. You spoke up when you disagreed as to why and then the issue was debated."

"Do you?" Mav asked, slowly walking closer and holding out his hand. It was such a sweet gesture that Henley didn't resist or inquire about his question. She automatically slid her fingers into the palm of his hand. "Trust me, that is?"

"Yes," Henley replied, not wanting any doubts left between them. He pulled her close until their bodies were mere inches apart. She wanted him to know how she felt and why, without any reservations. She stepped away and then led him to the couch, waiting for him to take a seat and then sitting down beside him with one leg drawn underneath her. It gave her the ability to face him and read his reactions, which was what she'd always shied away from. "Mav, you and I both know that in any other circumstance…things would have gone slow. You probably would have continued on home to Chicago if the caldera hadn't exploded. I would have been left here to stew over my stupidity, along with having a sidekick who never would have let me live down that I kept allowing fear of other people's judgments to rule my life. You would have eventually called me, pretending that all was fine when it really wasn't. I might or might not have accepted that call because I was too embarrassed to admit that you were right. Then depending on the time frame and where both of us were at over the course of the year…we might have bridged the distance between us. I'd like to think we would have anyway, but I don't regret a single second of the last few days."

"Ernie would take offense at being considered a sidekick. He definitely thinks he's the main attraction." Mav gave her a small smile, but he did reach for her hand and lace their fingers together. He stared down at them while she had trouble focusing on anything other than his contoured chest. She'd been lucky to get those words out and there was still more that needed said. "Henley, we both handled things badly. I shouldn't have let things go for as long as I did, but you were right when you said three years was basically cut down to maybe five or six weeks overall between vacations and holidays. I kept up with your welfare through Tank because I could never get you off of my mind. I want to clarify a few things though."

"What would those be?" Henley relaxed a bit at Mav's willingness to talk and she rested her shoulder against the couch, still holding his hand. His brown eyes weren't as troubled as they were, but she couldn't help but get the feeling that he was keeping a part of himself hidden. They hadn't started a fire like she normally would have so that they could preserve the firewood for when the temperature plummeted, but being next to him gave her all the warmth she needed despite that lone cold shiver at whatever he was hiding. "Mav, if you're not—"

"It was wrong of me to compare you to my mother." Mav's fingers tightened on hers and she wasn't sure she was ready to hear the horrors he'd faced when he was younger. He said that his childhood had helped shaped him into the man he was today, along with the friendship of his team and the father figure Ernie had represented. All Henley could picture was an innocent, scared little boy seeing his mother passed out on the floor from the crack she'd purchased on the street that night. "You are nothing like her. The compassion you have for the people in this town astounds me. You saw the lines of vehicles leaving town today, so you witnessed what fear and panic can do when faced with adversity and you did your best to get them to see past that. My mother would have been the first one in a vehicle to save her own ass, with no thought to anyone else."

"These people are my family," Henley said, wishing he'd had the support that she'd had growing up. It dawned on her that she hadn't had a meltdown or a full blown panic attack at being placed in this dire situation, whereas a simple insult in her previous life would have resulted in her thinking she was having a heart attack. The reason that happened was because the community in her town supported one another, which was something Mav had never experienced until he'd gone into the Marines. "They're your family too. Blood doesn't make you family—it just means you're biologically related."

"Come here." Mav tugged lightly on her hand, pulling her into the crook of his arm and holding her the way she'd always wanted to be held. She snuggled against his warm skin, not wanting to take a single moment they had together for granted. "You're going to get both of us in trouble with your rationalizing that everyone is this town is cut from the same cloth. Some of them aren't who you think they are."

"If you're talking about Rat, he's just scared and letting

pride get in the way of reasonable judgment," Henley said, having known the man since she could remember. "Kellen is a little too quiet for my liking though, so I agree that we should continue to keep an eye out for him."

"I'm glad to hear it," Mav replied wryly, but she ignored the taunt. They both had different viewpoints on Stanley and that wasn't going to change. Honestly, Henley expected Stanley and those that had chosen to go with him to show up sooner rather than later. That would mean doubling up even more people, but no one would turn them away. "I have Kirk monitoring Truman's movements just in case he gets it in his head to try something. Jeremy, Dylan, and Jason are watching the access road into the lodge, while Ernie is currently in the bunker monitoring the HF transmissions."

"You're worried about the guys." Henley stated it because it was the truth. She'd seen the concern in Ernie's eyes as well, all of them knowing that Owen should have been here by now. There were numerous things that could have held him up and she did her best not to think of the negative ones. Mav had faith in them and so would she. "They'll all make it."

Mav gently stroked her arm in comfort and they must have stayed that way for over an hour before Henley needed more. She untangled herself from underneath his arm and slung her leg over his lap so that they were face to face. She ran her thumb over his eyebrow, wanting to erase the worry lines that were now etched there. His brown eyes searched hers and cupped his face, wishing she had the ability to make everything okay again. Instead, she would use her touch to give him a moment's peace.

Leaning in, Henley gently covered his mouth with hers while using her tongue to ask permission to deepen the kiss. He parted his lips, allowing her access and she took what she wanted. She slipped her fingers through the back of his hair and pulled him closer, reveling in his masculinity. She loved his strength and the hardness of his body. She hadn't had a chance to explore before, but she did now and would take total advantage of the time they'd been given.

"Take your pants off," Henley ordered against his mouth, not breaking their connection. She felt his gradual smile, which prompted her own. She finally kissed him one last time before drawing away. There was a sparkle in his eye that she hadn't seen since last night. "Don't tell me you have trouble taking orders from a woman."

"I listen to those placed in command, but I'm not so sure you're in that position." Mav ran the back of his fingers over her shirt, targeting her nipple and finding the hardened peak with no problem. She inhaled sharply, but wasn't about to lose this battle of wills when it meant that she would get to enjoy what she hadn't last time around. "Still a bit sensitive?"

Mav's question was tinged with laughter, but he somehow managed to keep a straight face. He knew exactly how sensitive she was after their first night together, but she was about to return the favor. She reached for the button and zipper on his jeans and tugged the material over his hips, loving the energy that materialized that had nothing to do with the static electricity generated from the movement of the fabric.

"This is my opportunity, Maverick."

Henley stood and was happy when Mav didn't resist the rest of her ministrations. By the time she was done he wasn't wearing a stitch of clothing. She leaned down and placed her hands on his legs, separating them enough so that she could stoop to her knees and have full access to what was in front of her. His cock was long and hard, but it was his width that she remembered from before. Her pussy still ached from having been strained, wanting to experience that again. She traced her fingers up the inside of his thighs and smiled when a vein popped out and throbbed in time with his heartbeat.

"Are you going to do something anytime soon?" Mav asked, his voice sounding kind of rough and sending shivers through her. Henley decided to make him wait even longer as a result, liking this magical influence she had over his body. "Sweetheart, the world's about to end and—"

Henley chuckled and then pulled her hand up to cover her mouth. She couldn't stop laughing even though she tried. She laughed even harder when she saw his raised eyebrow. This wasn't the most appropriate time to lose her composure when thirty seconds prior she was aroused to the point of severe aching, but the thought that he was actually trying to get her to move things along with the warning that the world was going to end was just too cliché not to enjoy.

"You have a tendency to give me complexes that aren't very good for my self-esteem, sweetheart," Mav said wryly, laying his head back against the couch with a half-smile on his face. It took a few more minutes for her to catch her breath before she was able to start touching him once more. His smooth flesh was a lot warmer than her palm and she looked down to find a small drop of pre-cum on the end of his cock, as if he was bestowing her with a present. As much as she wanted to taste him, she didn't want to go too fast. They had all night and this was exactly how she wanted to spend it. "Your touch is enchanting, Henley. It makes me forget about everything outside these four walls...as if time stood still."

"That's my goal," Henley whispered, taking her thumb and drawing it softly over his tip. "My answer is to stop time so we have forever."

Henley smeared his pre-cum around and around, utilizing his very own lubricant. She turned her hand and combined it with a flick of her wrist, wanting his every nerve ending to applaud her efforts. She moved her hand up and down once she got that area nice and wet, wanting to prolong his pleasure. Mav's chest had stopped moving as he watched her motions, almost as mesmerized as she was, although she didn't think it was possible to forget to breathe. She palmed his sac, massaging his two heavily laden balls until she elicited a guttural groan from him. She wanted him to feel every bit as aroused as she'd been last night, trapped with Mav between her legs relentlessly torturing her clit with his uniquely talented tongue and then some.

Henley continued to stroke him while she leaned in and circled his nipple with her tongue. Mav didn't have a lot of chest hair, most of it in the middle of his chest between his pecs. His sun-kissed skin practically seared her lips when she placed a kiss where she'd just licked. She did the same to his other side, but she had to stop when he brought his hand up to delve his fingers into her hair and bring her mouth up to his. Their kiss was unlike any other she'd experienced and was full of passion and need. They were both out of breath by the time he let her pause.

"You're going to find yourself undressed and on your back in under thirty seconds if you don't do something soon," Mav murmured in a weighty, hungry voice while holding her close enough that their foreheads touched. She stuttered out what air she had left in her lungs and nodded her understanding. She wasn't sure how much longer she was going to last either. "I need you, sweetheart."

Henley slowly pulled away from him, causing him to remove his grip of her hair. She gradually lowered herself until her lips were less than an inch from the tip of his cock. She was snuggled inside his legs and shifted so that she had a better angle to take him deep into her mouth. Taking her tongue, she licked his tip so that she could finally taste his essence. Salty, musky, and downright sinful were the only words to describe his flavor. She wanted more and opened her mouth wider to take more of him, sliding his cock over her tongue until she couldn't fit any more. She caressed the underside of his shaft and would have smiled if she'd had the ability, but his fingers had somehow found their tangled way around her strands once more.

"Damn, your mouth is so hot," Mav sighed, unknowingly leading her by his hold on her hair. Henley didn't mind at all and the tighter he gripped his fingers, the more she wanted to please him. She purposefully grazed her teeth gently over him when she pulled up. "Yes."

The word came out of Mav's mouth more like a hiss and she kept manipulating her tongue and teeth over his sensitive flesh, doing so in a slow fashion to prolong his pleasure. Henley continued to massage his sac until she sensed his flesh tightening, indicating he was drawing toward that inevitable moment of explosion. She wasn't ready to have this stop quite yet, so she brought her fingers up to the base of his shaft and gradually squeezed.

"That's not fair, sweetheart."

Mav had spoken in clipped words, letting Henley know exactly how that had affected him. She'd essentially delayed his gratification for her own purposes, just as he'd done to her last night. She wasn't doing so to get back at him, but to show him exactly how much she'd enjoyed that herself. The longer she'd been on the edge the more powerful her orgasm had eventually been.

Henley released her fingers leisurely, not wanting to have him right back where they'd started. It had just been a way to relieve his pressure and allow him to enjoy this a lot longer than five minutes. She had to press against his hand that was twisted in her hair so that she could continue to pleasure him, once again laving her tongue on his underside. She could hear her own breathing, sounding shallow in her ears, but it was his heartbeat that she felt when she rested her hand against his inner thigh.

Henley pulled up until she only had Mav's tip in her mouth and started to suckle lightly while brushing her tongue over his slit. With each draw on him, she worked her way down until her lips were pressing against the bottom of his shaft. She'd had to leave her throat open to accept the length of him and once she'd stopped, she paused and then swallowed.

Two things happened at once and Henley found herself fighting the urge to go into a fit of complete laughter once again as she leaned back onto her heels. Mav had just been about to come in her mouth when a knock sounded on the door. The string of cuss words that came out of him would have prompted an offended look from even the most nefarious sailor.

"I'll get it," Henley said in between trying to catch her breath and laughing. Mav was scrambling for his briefs and jeans, but she'd already risen and was heading to the door. She cracked it open just an inch to see Dylan standing there with a note in his hand. "Dylan, is everything all right?"

"Tank just wanted me to drop this off to Mav," Dylan replied, not even curious in the least as to why Henley didn't open the door wider. "He said it was something the two of you should know right away."

"Thanks, Dylan." There was nothing like being thrown back into reality. She said her goodnight and then closed the door, turning to find that Mav had already pulled his jeans back over his erection. The bulge he was sporting at this very moment made her not even want to know what was written down on the piece of paper still clutched in her hand. This end of the world crap was getting real old. "Well, Ernie would have called us on the radio if it was bad."

"Not if he was trying to keep things off of the community radio channels." Mav held out his hand as if he wasn't standing there with a raging hard-on and waited for her to give up the note. "Ernie doesn't trust Truman either, so it would make sense for him to send Dylan with any intel that we need kept private instead of broadcasting it over one of the channels."

Mav wasn't the only one who was still feeling the effects of their lovemaking. Henley's entire body was aroused to the point of throbbing and for once she wanted to be irresponsible, postponing finding out why they were needed. Instead, she walked around so that she was side by side with him when he unfolded the paper.

Owen is currently in New Mexico. He had no choice but to go south when the caldera erupted. His current plan is to get to the West Coast so that he can work his way north via the least congested roads.

"Owen never does what he's told," Mav exclaimed with a laugh, shaking his head more in awe than in disappointment. "He easily had time to make it north up near the border, but he must have waited too long."

"At least we know he's safe," Henley reminded him, wishing they knew the status on the other guys. "And Owen is in a place that he can set up a receiver to transmit those messages."

"Agreed," Mav said, crumbling up the paper in his fist and then pulling her toward him. Henley rested her cheek against his solid chest, allowing his warmth to surround her and take away the evening chill that had invaded from the outside interruption. It could have been horrific news, so she was grateful they'd heard something positive. It also gave them a moment to collect themselves, but she wasn't prepared for when he lifted her shirt over her head. "Now that I'm no longer in whatever spell you weaved through your sorcery, I think it's time we speed things up just a bit."

Henley would have choked out another laugh had Mav not spun her to face the door, lifting her hands up so that her palms were resting on the hard wood. He'd only ever been gentle with her, and she hadn't been prepared for her arousal to go from ten to hundred in under one point five seconds by his taking charge of the situation. Maverick had pulled down her cut-off sweats along with her panties before she even said his name and had them down around her ankles.

"You had me in the palm of your hand, sweetheart," Mav whispered against her ear, his now naked body up against hers. He must have taken his jeans off when she'd been catching her breath. The heat off of his body rivaled her own, creating a sauna that contained just the two of them. "It's rare that I'm in such a vulnerable state, which just goes to show how much I trust you."

"Take me, Maverick." Henley pressed her palms into the hard surface, loving the feeling of his fingers sliding between hers. She moved back against him, flicking her discarded clothes away to the side, arching to feel his cock as it nestled in her crevice. "Hard and fast."

"With pleasure."

Cold air washed over her body when Mav stepped back, but it did nothing to diminish the flames that were licking her skin. She heard a wrapper being torn and a crazy thought that they'd have to raid the grocery store soon crossed her mind, but that conversation was for another time. It didn't take him long to roll the condom over his tip and down his shaft. Within seconds his hands were on her waist, pulling on her hips so that she was perfectly bowed to accept him.

"Maverick!"

Henley had just separated her legs farther apart when he took the opportunity to bury himself inside of her with one wet thrust. She'd been aroused the entire time she was pleasuring him, so she was more than ready to accept him. It took a moment for her to adjust to his width, but was good by the time he'd pulled out and drove back into her.

"Take your right hand and slide it down the front of your body. Use your fingers to massage your clit and don't stop—even after you've come."

Henley felt the trigger of her orgasm just from his words alone and didn't think she'd need contact on her clit, but he was already taking her wrist and doing it for her. He helped swipe her fingers to gather her cream and then placed them on her sensitive and swollen tissue. It was such a naughty thing to do that she immediately felt another orgasm start.

"I can feel you coming," Mav said, the vibrations against her ear overwhelming. Her senses were besieged and it was if electricity was running through every part of her body. He manipulated her fingers so that they were currently moving in a circular motion, prolonging her orgasm until she was screaming out his name. "Now don't stop."

Mav firmly placed his hands on Henley's hips, using them as leverage as he continued to ferociously drive into her from behind. She had to rest her forehead on the door, knowing full well if he hadn't had such a good hold on her that her knees would have given out. She'd never been this wet and the sounds of their lovemaking echoed off of the walls, integrating with the cries that must have been coming from her.

Henley's fingers had taken a life of their own and were now rubbing hard against her swollen clit. The pressure alone had made it feel as if she'd never stopped coming and as another wave of her release crashed—it could have been her second, third, or fourth—it slammed into her. She didn't stop the circular motions and at one point, she would have sworn she was floating upward. The reverberations faded away, lights began twinkling behind her closed eyes, and the only thing her body felt was the ravaging pleasure Maverick was inflicting upon her mind.

Henley was vaguely aware of hearing Mav shout out her name, but it took quite a few minutes before she realized that he was talking to her. Little by little, everything became clear as he turned her around to face him. He had a boyish smile on his face that made her return one as they caught their breath.

"That was…"

Henley didn't have the words to describe what they'd just experienced and maybe it was best to leave it for what it was—intimacy in its purest form. Mav pulled her to him and turned so that his back was toward the door, bringing her into his comforting embrace. She remembered what he'd said last night about the bond they'd created and there was no doubt that they'd just fortified it.

"Um, Henley? Mav?" Dylan's discomfited voice came through the door, followed by a hesitant knock. Henley turned her face into Mav's chest in mortification at the thought that Dylan had returned to the sounds of their lovemaking and had purposefully waited until they were done before he interrupted. "Tank would like to see one of you in the bunker…in a minute or two."

"Tell him we'll both be there in a short bit," Mav called out without the slightest hint of embarrassment. She looked up at him to catch a glimmer of laughter in his eyes. He lowered his voice for only her to hear. "One of these days, we'll be given the time to hold and enjoy one another instead of being interrupted by end of the world updates. It's getting kind of tedious."

Henley laughed and welcomed the lighthearted comments. Her body still felt like it had been jolted with ten thousand volts of electricity, and yet somehow Mav was able to make everything okay with just a few words. She sighed and slowly pulled away from him, fortifying herself to face whatever was waiting for them on the other side of the door.

"Let me clean up and then we'll go see Tank." Mav placed a kiss on her forehead before leaning down to snatch his jeans off of the floor. Henley figured she never got those extra minutes to enjoy such a sight, so she took his place against the door and appreciated the view as he sauntered across the room. "Turnabout's fair play, sweetheart. Next time you can do a little catwalk just for me."

Mav waited until he was at the bedroom door before he turned around with a wink. Henley smiled, but it faded when he disappeared from view. How was it that she could be happy inside of this tiny cabin when so much misfortune was happening outside? What did Ernie need them for? Henley wasn't about to rehash her and Mav's past over and over. Instead, she vowed not to take one minute given to them for granted because their time just might be running out.

CHAPTER SEVENTEEN

"ARE YOU SURE?" Mav asked, probably having reiterated that question five times since last night. It was currently morning and while sporadic particles of ash would fall every now and then...the sun was still peering out from the scattered clouds and the atmosphere above them was relatively clear. He and Tank were walking the perimeter of the encampment, more so to keep prying ears from hearing what was being discussed. They'd left Henley to monitor the HF radio nets that Mav had established for emergency contact with the team, along with a frequency scanner set to only break squelch for a nearby transmission with a relatively higher signal strength. Ernie had wanted to note any local unencrypted radio traffic. It could give them a heads up of an approaching group and their possible intentions. With Henley secured inside the bunker, it allowed Mav to have one less thing to worry about. "I'd hate to open this place up to an experienced man who has us at a disadvantage. We're vulnerable until the others get here."

"I hear what you're saying," Ernie said in agreement, readjusting his ball cap as they started for the lodge. His wise eyes were taking in everything and everyone. A few of the lodge residents had taken a few trips back to town for more supplies and the occasional odd or end. They were systematically cleaning out the shops and hauling whatever they could up here to the lodge, with instructions that Ratliff have the same opportunity. Jeremy had taken a run down to the campgrounds to notify Rat before coming back to catch some sleep before starting another shift on sentry rotation this evening. "But I know how we would have reacted in Truman's situation had our guys been out there to fend for themselves."

"Fairchild AFB would not have turned away active personnel," Mav pointed out, still concerned with the safety of their camp. "Truman's men should have been able to have access and he should go down there with them."

"Truman isn't the typical military man that would have his name listed in a unit alpha roster," Ernie said as he slowed the pace. Elijah was sitting on the front porch of the lodge, his keen eyes observing everyone and everything. Mrs. Welsh—with her portable oxygen tank by her side—was keeping him company, but Kellen Truman was nowhere to be seen. "I gave him access to the HF radio remote control panel in my office, but he was unable to contact them—at least from what I heard. That means he's now aware that there is a radio room somewhere around here that he hasn't been given access to."

Mav understood what Ernie was saying. All it would take was for Truman to broadcast a code word over the radio net. Tank was absolutely right in the fact that they weren't dealing with run of the mill military unit. Kellen had Special Forces training written all over him and as painful as it was for Mav to admit...Truman would have had more training than Mav, making the man more dangerous and more of an unknown.

"I'll take another look at those here at the lodge," Mav said, studying Elijah and figuring he would be privy to the history of the men and women staying in the lodge. Age only factored in the physical aspect, but the mind was a beautiful thing. In fact, many of the older men and women were involved in the daily food preparation, as well as monitoring the shortwave and bringing meals to the guards on post. "We can give some of the older folks something to keep them busy and utilize them in keeping the lodge safe."

"Felix is keeping tabs on the town and ensuring that items are distributed evenly given the amount of people in each camp. While you figure out where we might have weaknesses, I'm going to catch a few hours of shuteye myself while Henley's at the radio. Now that's something she should train a couple of seniors on right there." Ernie started walking to his cabin before throwing a bit of advice over his shoulder. "You might want to go into town yourself, son. The grocery store is limited in their prophylactic section and I highly doubt that's on the runner's list."

Mav somehow maintained a straight face, turning to where Elijah was trying to do the same. Mrs. Welsh was fanning herself, a flush having come over her powdered cheeks. He ignored both of them as he made his way up the stairs with the intention of throwing his and Henley's clothes into the dryer on the second floor. He was still wearing his jeans from yesterday, but he did have on a clean shirt. He'd thrown in a load before breakfast, which consisted of Henley's hamper contents and his laundry bag. At least they didn't have to worry about water, given that the natural springs gave them access to an unlimited supply of fresh clean drinking water, which Ernie filtered and softened with a kinetic industrial softener. It made him aware of the fact that they didn't have anyone in place to monitor their natural resources. There were too many vulnerabilities exposed to a potential enemy from within.

"Truman headed down the access road around five minutes ago," Elijah said nonchalantly, resting his hands on a cane that Mrs. Nantri had given him yesterday. He made the statement as if he were sharing the weather for the day. Mav liked his style and was grateful to have him monitoring the comings and goings of people. "He had a pair of binoculars hanging around his neck."

"Thanks, Elijah."

Mav didn't waste time. He veered off the porch and made his way back to Henley's cabin. He used the key she'd given him to enter the small premises, ensuring that the invisible tape he'd placed high on the seal hadn't been broken. He then walked into the bedroom where he collected his M4 rifle, along with a pouch of extra magazines. Although he did have on his shoulder holster there wasn't a chance in hell he would take the chance of getting caught off guard.

It wasn't long after that Mav was on the heels of Truman, heading east toward the bunker and the NG wellhead blockhouse. There wasn't any sight of the man, so Mav kept walking carefully and quietly while managing to keep up a good pace. Five minutes was a good lead and Mav needed to close the distance between them.

Where could Truman be heading and why? Was he meeting his comrades? It still didn't make sense to Mav that Kellen would have known that a natural catastrophe was going to take place months in advance. If that was the case he would have hopped on a flight and headed to another country in the Southern Hemisphere where the percentage of survival was a hell of a lot higher than sticking it out here in the States.

The terrain became a little rockier as Mav continued to get farther and farther away from the lodge. The incline was steeper and he was grateful that he was still wearing his combat boots. He stopped to listen once he had enough coverage to camouflage his body. The wildlife had been relatively quiet since the eruption; probably moving north would be Mav's guess. The only sound that Mav could make out was the ruffling of the leaves from the light breeze coming in from the west. He ignored a flake of ash as it floated down in front of him. Tilting his head just right and waiting another eighty seconds finally rewarded him with the crack of a branch coming from his left.

Mav didn't move quite yet, not wanting to draw attention

to himself. It was a good two solid minutes before he redeployed and followed the route that Truman was taking. Damn if the man wasn't heading toward one of the natural mountain springs farther down the slope from the camp. Knowing that was the only resource up here and the only place where Truman could be heading, Mav broke off to his right and circled around the rough terrain to have a better advantage point from his flank.

It took around eight minutes for Mav to make to his destination. He would have said it was breathtaking had he been here for the visual. It was nature at its finest, with the vivid greenery overhanging the pool of water below. The water was so clear that the depth appeared to be endless. This spring along with several others fed Whispering Creek that ran down the western side of the valley the Lost Mountain Lodge was in. The one thing it was missing from the picture was the man who should have been here, which was exactly when Mav realized his mistake. Sun Tzu had taught him that if you wait by the stream long enough, the body of your enemy would float by. Mav had made a tactical error and assumed how Kellen would move, isolating himself and placing him exactly where he'd be expected.

"You're good." Truman's voice came about ten yards to Mav's left, but he didn't pull his weapon. He'd already be dead if that was this man's intention. He slowly turned to face Kellen, who had now made himself known. "I didn't realize that you were even on my tail until I stopped and used my glasses. I caught the rustling of some leaves around thirty yards back."

"You want to tell me what you're doing down this far?" Mav asked, noting that Truman hadn't pulled his weapon either.

"I wanted to see if anyone had been up this way, considering you left a viable resource unprotected." Mav didn't believe that for a second, but he went along with the excuse to see what other information could be gained. "You're wasting precious assets by having people watch me when they could be focused on areas like this."

Both men would have appeared completely relaxed to a stranger when underneath both of their pretenses radiated tension and unease. Mav thought carefully on how to reply, not wanting this to turn into anything other than a discovery of intel.

"Is there a reason you opted to come here yourself when you could have approached either Tank or myself with your concerns?" Mav widened his stance and settled in to hear what this man had to say. He also turned back on his two-way radio, which he'd turned off so that any incoming calls wouldn't be blasted through the terrain. "This would go a hell of a lot easier on both of us if you'd just come clean with me about who you are and how you lucked out being here on the day a world changing disaster occurred."

"Coincidence?" Truman offered up, the left half of his mouth turning up into what some would call a smile. Mav wasn't so sure it was. "You think I have the ability to see into the future?"

"I think you have the right connections to be informed had any of this been known beforehand." Mav kept his gaze connected with Truman's, all the while studying the type of binoculars he was holding in his hand. They appeared to be U.S. military issue—M24 7x28 Glasses with anti-reflective coating and a built in laser range finder. "I also noticed that you chose not to answer my question. Are you meeting someone near here?"

"I already told you that I'm part of a special unit out of Joint Special Operations Command at Fort Bragg. I'm not privy to say anything beyond that and honestly, it's not up to me to convince you. I just want to help. You can take it or leave it. I caught on early that you and Yates have military training, so it would make sense that you have some type of system to monitor this area. That doesn't mean someone can't get around it if they know what to look for. I thought I'd lend you a hand since the two of you are so busy taking care of the lodge." Truman finally broke their stare to look out over the natural mountain spring. "No one has been in this area for quite a while, except maybe a fair sized brown bear about a day ago. I haven't had a chance to thoroughly check out the boundaries, but I understand if you don't want my help."

"I don't trust you, Truman," Mav declared matter-of-factly, wishing like hell that Van were here. That man could spot ill intentions a mile away with just a glance. "You need to come clean about—"

"Mav," Henley's voice came through the two-way radio, cutting off what Mav had been about to say. "Someone or something just activated the alarm you set up near the bottom of the valley on the road. You've got PA-1 written over the light."

A loud and sharp snap resonated through the area, causing both men to draw their weapons. The sound came from the other side of the spring and it wasn't long after that they could hear someone running away. Truman signaled he would take one direction and while Mav still had reservations about him, he took the other path around the large pool of water. He didn't like that his attention had to be split in two directions, but there wasn't anything he could do about it.

"I'll check it out," Mav replied back to Henley before securing the transmitter back to the clip on his belt.

Mav made good time in getting to where the noise had originated from and he caught the racket the intruder was now making in his or her attempt to get away. Truman came through the brush and Mav gave him a hand signal to follow the person. Seeing as their target knew they were on his tail, Mav didn't hesitate to break out into a dead run to the left, knowing this mountain as good as those who hiked the area. He'd be able to cut him off at an angle to where this subject no doubt had some type of vehicle waiting for him on the main thoroughfare leading up to the lodge.

Mav slowed down upon reaching his destination, not

wanting to give up the coverage of the thick brush on the side of the road should this be some type of set-up. He proceeded cautiously with his weapon in hand but there was no one around. It wasn't until Truman stepped out of the shrubbery that he'd accepted they weren't going to locate who'd been up near the springs.

The rumbling of a vehicle could be heard from a ways and Mav was ready for when it finally cleared the bend in the road. He relaxed his stance when he saw that it was the sheriff's cruiser. Felix brought the car to a stop, his window already rolled down.

"Mav, what are you doing this far out from the lodge?"

"Just checking the area," Mav replied, sharing a look with Truman. They weren't sure where the target had gone, and he wasn't about to talk about it out here in the open. He would fill everyone in when he got back to camp. "Everything go okay in town?"

"Yes. You'll see the other vehicles soon. Everyone loaded up what they could, but we'll make a second trip once we get things unloaded."

"Truman and I will meet you up there after we do one more round of the perimeter." Mav's statement had Ramsey raising his eyebrow in question, but he went along with the conversation. Mav used the back window's reflection to see if anyone was behind him in the woods, but nothing moved to indicate someone was there. "I'll see you later."

Mav tapped the hood of the car and then stepped back,

allowing the sheriff to continue up the hill to the entrance of the camp. Truman finally joined him, having kept his distance as he monitored the area. At least that's what Mav thought he was doing. It crossed Mav's mind that Truman could have known the intruder and then helped him by directing him away from where Mav was trying to cut him off.

The more Mav thought about it though, it probably *wasn't* one of Truman's buddies. A special operator would have easily spotted the crude homemade, antipersonnel system and not tripped it in the first place.

"I'd like to use the radio again," Truman said, scanning the area and appearing quite tense. Too tense for a man who might have known whom the invader was. "My men are trained and can be of assistance if I can just get them here."

"You realize that I won't hesitate to put a bullet in your head if I find out that your intentions are to take over this camp," Mav said casually as he walked back into the woods, wanting to be clear of the road for a lot of reasons. "I'm careful like that."

"I bet you are," Truman replied with a touch of humor in his voice and if Mav was correct…a tad bit of respect. They hiked side by side while making their way back to the springs and Mav had to fight a smile at Truman's next words. "You might hate my guts, Beckett, but I think I could grow to like you."

CHAPTER EIGHTEEN

Henley made a note on the roster that held the names of those staying at the fishing lodge. Mav had given each of them a responsibility and the reactions had been very favorable. She studied the shifts as she sat on the porch alongside Elijah, who had requested in private that he be allowed to stay there to watch the others. He wasn't physically capable of walking long distances and he felt like he was providing a service. Mav had agreed, gave him with a two-way radio, and had even commended Elijah for the knowledge he had of the residents in camp.

Henley looked over Mr. Jenkins' rotation and wasn't sure that he should be on his feet for the eight hours listed. He'd said he wanted to help around the lodge, but Jeremy had been the one taking on more hours at the hardware shop so that his father could take it easy.

"Let me see that list," Elijah said gruffly, holding out his gnarled hand. Henley eyed him in curiosity, but she sighed as she handed it over when she realized he wasn't going to budge. She fiddled with the pen as she looked around the land and noticed that Mr. Wicks had managed to bring at least four of his horses up to the lodge. He was sharing a cabin with both of his sons, who'd made an appearance around ten minutes ago. They had a few hours before they were up on rotation to keep an eye on the entrance, but it appeared they were pulling more than their own weight by helping their father create a makeshift area for the horses to graze behind their cabin's clearing. "Pen, too."

"We have everything sorted out, Elijah," Henley exclaimed as she handed over the writing utensil. She sat forward, trying to see what he was writing down. It didn't look like anything other than a couple of marks next to some names. "Why did you single out Gage Dorian? He's in his mid-fifties and has run the garage since he took it over after his father passed away."

"Will you wait until I'm done, missy?"

Henley inhaled and counted to ten to prevent herself from snapping at the older man. Ernie called her *missy* when he wasn't pleased with something she did and she was damned tired of it. Mav came out of the lodge and walked over to where she was sitting right when she was about to ask Elijah to hand back the list. He surprised her when he leaned down and kissed her. He'd been tense ever since returning from his hike up to the hot springs, not that she could blame him. He'd taken quite a while to get back to her and let her know that the area was clear once she'd notified him that one of the perimeter alarms had been activated. They had no idea who'd been down there or why.

"Why do you have that look in your eye?" Mav inquired, keeping a hand on her shoulder.

"Because I won't give her the list back," Elijah muttered, finally finishing going through the twenty-eight names. Eleven of them were too elderly to do any hard labor, so after much discussion some of them were posted to the HF radios. The others were detailed to food preparation and kitchen duty. That left seventeen people who could be used for the harder tasks. Besides the ones who'd already been given their duties, Gage Dorian was assigned facilities maintenance. Rob Wicks was assigned to the livestock. Lola and her daughter, Missy, wanted to stick with what they knew—which was taking care of the running day-to-day operations of the lodge. The sheriff and Ernie, however, had managed to talk Missy into supervising the nighttime sentries, namely because she could outshoot the lot and had better organizational skills than any of the rest of them. Mabel had already staked claim on the kitchen. Mr. Jenkins had been given the task of battening down the lodge and cabins to ensure they could withstand ten centimeters of wet ash. Sherman Roan would run the grow room in the bunker while Terrell Vaughn would transport supplies and materials to whomever needed them. Kirk Parson would now maintain the natural mountain spring in the bunker as well as test the remaining springs in the valley for acid content. Henley would run logistics of the whole operation. "Here. The ones with the marks next to their names are the ones you have to worry about should the going get tough around here."

Elijah had handed the list back to Henley, but she held it up high enough for Mav to see as well. There was a star next to the names of Gage Dorian, Sherman Roan, Mrs. Nantri, and Reggie Thomas—who totally shocked Henley. The mayor? Elijah was telling them they needed to worry about the mayor?

"Reasons?" Mav got straight to the point, removing the paper from Henley's hand and folding it in half.

"The first two are selfish and will most likely start stealing rations when no one is looking. The third is here because of Ratliff, even if she did give me a damned good cane. As for the mayor, well, he'll pretend to hand over the reins to the sheriff while standing back and waiting for him to make a mistake. It's more pride, but that's the downfall of good men."

Henley scanned the area, ensuring that no one was close enough to hear them having this discussion. No wonder Mrs. Nantri had asked if she could learn the HF radio system. Mav had told Henley time and time again that people showed their true colors at times like these and she was utterly astounded that she'd read some of these people so wrong.

"I'll share this with Tank and the sheriff," Mav disclosed, giving Henley's shoulder a squeeze before he walked off of the porch and headed up the access road to the bunker. He turned back around before he got too far. "Tell Missy, Jeremy, Dylan, and Jason that I need to talk with them before they go on rotation. The sheriff is currently monitoring the entrance along with Parson but I'd like for someone to be on a higher elevation."

Henley stood and walked around Elijah, patting him on the shoulder. He might be a tad bit crotchety but he was sharp as a tack. The more they planned and the more everyone agreed on what was being decided, it made her confident they could survive what was coming their way. Worst-case scenario would be that the ash was too thick for these structures to take, which was highly unlikely due to the way Ernie had them constructed. If that did happen they would all move into the bunker for whatever the number of days needed before venturing out and seeing what was left. She had a feeling Mav would disagree with inviting certain outside individuals inside, but there wasn't a chance in hell she'd leave anyone out here to fend for themselves. After having gone over the capacity, they found they would be able to move more cots in specific areas but it wouldn't be for a ten-year span that way it was originally planned. There was plenty of space and supplies to go around for at least a couple of years if needed—it was better than nothing.

Henley made her way to where Dylan and Jason were helping their father with the horses, taking the time to look up at the sky. Once in a while ash would float down to the ground, but it wasn't much more than a reminder of what was coming their way. They would be ready. She was proud of what they'd accomplished in the last couple of days. With Ernie's well thought out plan and what they'd all referred to as his irrational hobby, they had a sustainable way of life here for as long as they needed until the infrastructure of the States rose out of the ashes.

It wasn't long after she'd passed on the instructions from Mav that Henley decided to stop by her cabin to grab a sweatshirt. The evening air had chilled a bit and since she was more than likely going to be out late this evening going over numbers with everyone, she'd like to be comfortable. She'd unlocked the cabin door, but instantly remembered the extra step that Mav had wanted her to take before entering. She looked up to where the strip of tape was located and saw that it was intact. She removed it and would have to replace it with another before she locked up for the evening.

Henley finally pushed the door open and then shut it behind her as she made her way across the living area and into the bedroom. She took time to use the bathroom and wash her hands before walking over to her dresser. She drew the shirt she was wearing over her head, opting instead for a thin long-sleeved shirt meant to be worn underneath something heavier. She'd just opened the drawer where she kept her sweatshirts when she thought she heard something in the living room.

Henley quickly turned, leaving the drawer open while her hand went to her holstered Beretta. She didn't move, but instead stayed where she was to see if she could hear anything else. Silence reigned and yet the air was heavy as if she wasn't the only living creature inside her cabin. Her heart rate sped up and blood rushed through her ears as she strained to listen. She'd lived here for three years and had never once been afraid.

She slowly took a step forward to the bedroom door, which she'd left open. She had a direct line of vision to the front door. It was ajar. Henley knew for a fact that she'd closed it behind her and she could have kicked herself that she hadn't locked it. It wasn't like there was anywhere to hide considering the layout of the cabin, but she was still too far away from the door to see the living area.

Henley soundlessly withdrew her weapon and quietly took a few more steps, bringing her closer to the threshold and giving her a better visual. She still couldn't see into the corners and she tightened her grip on the butt of the weapon, trying to ignore the perspiration that now coated her palms. Mav's words kept resonating in her head about the desperation people felt in these circumstances. Why would someone target her though?

"Henley, why is the door open?"

"Shit, Mav!"

Henley startled at the loud entrance Mav had made, his voice booming through the cabin. She lowered her gun, his gaze following and suddenly darkening in intensity. She swore her heart had rammed against her chest as the adrenaline had rushed through her and she leaned against the doorjamb for support. Her legs were now made of Jell-O and her fingers were trembling as she holstered her weapon.

"What the hell is going on?"

"I must not have locked the door after I came in—don't lecture me about it either—and I heard someone out here." Henley glanced uneasily around the room now that she had a full visual and didn't see anything out of place. "Do you think—"

Henley didn't finish her question since Mav was no longer in the cabin. He was through the door before she could stop him, although she did follow him outside. She kept her hand on her weapon as she stayed in the doorway and waited for him to return. It wasn't a good idea to go around the other side when he wasn't expecting it, catching him off guard. She scanned the area, but found nothing or no one in the vicinity of her cabin.

"Get what you need," Mav instructed as he rounded the corner, startling Henley once more. It was apparent he'd found something or else he wouldn't appear so heated. "We're calling a meeting and instructing everyone that they now have to patrol in twos. No one is to leave the main area without someone by their side."

"What did you find?" Henley asked, searching Mav's face for answers when he didn't reply right away. A sliver of fear ran up her back, replacing her earlier confidence that they had everything under control. "Mav?"

"We still have someone inside our camp. There are footprints leading away from the back of your cabin, but then they fade into the trees." Mav reached for her, rubbing his hands up and down her arms in what she assumed was reassurance. Unfortunately, the tension in his body caused her to recognize the danger they were in. "Whoever breached our security earlier today never left and now we're all targets."

CHAPTER NINETEEN

MAV CAMOUFLAGED HIMSELF against Henley's boulder, keeping his Rock River AR style rifle at the ready. Being next to her favorite place had him thinking of her and he was so grateful to have her by his side during this strange time. Her irritation at him joining the others to help with security was quite adorable, although he doubted she'd look at it like that. She was also a little peeved that he was out here while she was at the lodge accounting beans, bullets, and bandages. She did agree they needed someone inside that was well educated in weapons. The majority of the camp's group was holed up in the main lodge with the older generation. The other men and women were now doubled up and patrolling the immediate area above and below the encampment, east to the bunker and west to Whispering Creek. The sheriff had made a run down to the Pine Peak Silver Mine to have a conversation with Rat.

"I appreciate the use of the HF radio."

Mav glanced over to Kellen, who was his partner until Ramsey returned to camp. This way he could keep an eye on the man without leaving him to roam free. There were too many unknowns right now and the sheriff seemed to think that maybe Rat had someone staking out the place, but that didn't explain why the person entered Henley's cabin.

"That Special Forces team that you're with…how many of your men are out there?" Mav asked, keeping his tone casual. They might as well shoot the shit while monitoring the area. From their vantage point they'd be able to see someone coming a mile away down the slope—especially with those Northrup Grumman M24s. "I overheard you say you were at a fishing lodge, but you kept the coordinates off of the air."

"I've been nothing but honest with you since I set foot on this property," Kellen said as he continued to look through his glasses. He did pull them away to look over at Mav before he finished answering. "The team I'm with is made up of four men—including me—and one woman. There are only two on the West Coast, which is who I spoke with this evening. The other two were out of the States when Yellowstone erupted."

"So your team knew of your *vacation*?"

Kellen sighed and shifted his stance so that he could rest his elbow on his knee as he brought up his binoculars. Mav wasn't about to let this go, because there was no way in hell a man like Truman would take a fishing vacation packed the way he was. He was either hunting or scouting, but there was a damn good reason for his presence. Kellen finally pulled the M24s away from his face.

"Look, the team was granted leave and I had some personal business to take care of that I'd put off long enough. This area was convenient, that's all—a place where no questions would be asked. A base of operations that was out of the way." Kellen barked a laugh, more at himself than anything else. "Only someone with my luck would end up at a retired Marine's fishing lodge who just happened to be a prepper. To answer your question, my team is always well aware of my location. There wasn't a need to broadcast coordinates just for some schmuck to overhear and head this way. It appears we have enough trouble on our hands with the locals."

"This personal business you're talking about—I take it that it's still unresolved," Mav guessed, more comfortable now that the pieces of the puzzle were fitting together. What he wasn't too crazy about was that there weren't that many people around this area Truman could have personal business with. Did that mean that he was looking for someone who resided in Lost Summit? "Would you care to expand on that?"

"No."

Mav hadn't expected Truman to share his personal business and with Yellowstone erupting, it was highly doubtful that he would get whatever it was resolved anytime soon. They sat in silence, observing the area and taking note of anything that appeared out of the ordinary. An hour eventually passed before they saw headlights entering the camp and heard Jeremy's voice come over the two-way radio announcing Sheriff Ramsey's return.

"Do you really think that Ratliff has someone spying on the camp?" Kellen asked as they both stood and started to make their way over to the lodge. The horses' hooves could be heard prancing in the barn as they passed below the wooden structure. "What would there be to gain unless they were going to try to take it for themselves? Ratliff doesn't have that kind of manpower from what I saw at the community center. His two sidekicks have to be in their mid-eighties and the others that are staying with him at the camp don't appear to have what it takes to scale the valley's slope without having a heart attack."

Technically, Truman was spot on in his assumption. Mav wasn't so sure this had anything to do with Ratliff when it made more sense that it was someone in relation with Truman. It definitely required follow up questions.

"There's not a chance that this person you have personal business with happens to know you're here, would they?"

The clouds had hidden any moonlight that might have helped lead the way or shed light on Truman's reaction, but it was still easy to distinguish the shake of the man's head. Mav didn't like not knowing all the facts and whether or not he could trust Kellen Truman. It would make Mav's job a hell of a lot easier if he could.

"Mav, report."

Tank's voice came over Mav's two-way radio, so he unhooked the device and pressed the button in order to speak into the mic. There didn't seem to be an emergency, but Ernie happened to be in the bunker with access to the alarm panel.

"What do you have for me?"

"One of those communications we were waiting for came through from the East Coast. All is fine and ETA is expected to be another week."

So Van was still safe and working his way across the northern part of the States. The news came as a relief and yet it smacked of the hazards his friend must be dealing with. Ash had to have completely covered the Midwest, making it almost impossible to travel by car. Walking would require masks that could clog with ash and need to have the filter changed on it quite often. The hardships that Van would have to overcome would be difficult, but not insurmountable.

"Good to hear," Mav replied into the radio with satisfaction. "I'll get more details from you later after I've greeted our guest."

"It sounds as if part of my team will arrive before yours," Kellen said as they watched the sheriff climbing out of his car in front of the lodge. He surprised Mav by making an unusual proposal. "We can always divert my two members to help your buddies if they need a hand."

"I appreciate that." Mav wasn't sure if there were strings attached to that offer and he wouldn't take the chance. Trust was earned and not enough time had passed for that to happen. As for now they had problems of their own to deal with. They'd finally reached their destination. "Sheriff, were you able to speak with Ratliff?"

"Yes, but I kept the conversation rather vague." Felix adjusted his hat just so, regardless that it was nighttime. "I told them I was checking in on things before the ash cloud arrived to see if they needed anything or if they'd changed their minds and would rather come up here."

"What was his response to that?" Mav asked, already knowing the answer. Rat wasn't the type of man to admit defeat. He had to see by now that the abandoned mine he was dealing with was nothing like the one Ernie had outfitted by working on it for the last ten years. Hell, the people with him were intelligent men and women who had to see for themselves that they couldn't make it there on their own. The lack of a reliable power source meant the heat and electricity would be spotty. They would eventually be overcome by exposure. The fact that their immediate supply of rations wouldn't last more than a month limited their ability to stay where they were beyond that time. All of them would eventually end up on Ernie's doorstep. "And how is Trevor's concussion? It's really too bad that Mary hasn't been able to make it back up here from Metaline Falls. She would have been a tremendous asset."

"Rat basically told me what I could do with myself," Ramsey said with a touch of humor. It immediately faded when he shook his head at the futility of it all. "I tried talking sense into him, but it's useless. Jarrett seemed to be seeing reason and it wouldn't surprise me if he made his way here in a day or two, but I hope like hell it's before we're holed up inside. Speaking of Mary and her particular set of skills, it occurred to me that Milton Owain was an EMT back in the day. Since he's with Rat's group, that must be why Stanley felt that Trevor was fine other than a few residual headaches."

Mav glanced at the lodge behind Felix, seeing Elijah's empty chair. He'd turned in an hour ago, but would no doubt be up when the sun rose. They had another two days before the ash cloud arrived according to the shortwave radio. It was creating chaos around the world and no one appeared unaffected by its relentless onslaught.

"I've got to tell you, Mav," Sheriff Ramsey said, leaning back against his cruiser. "I don't think Rat has anything to do with this person who's breached our perimeter. Sure, he might complain a lot and run his mouth off to anyone who will listen, but we still have to take into consideration what Trevor said about that man he saw dressed in black near the access road into town."

"I've been thinking about that and I can't understand how Jeremy wouldn't have seen someone in that area." Mav leaned back slightly to look past Truman to where Jeremy was positioned by the road. Dylan was deeper into the woods with cover and Jason was located at a higher vantage point. All three were brought up hunting and fishing, so it wasn't as if they were novices out on that type of terrain. Had someone they knew come to town that no one knew about? "Did anyone report seeing—"

"Incoming!"

Mav's two-way radio crackled, but there was no need because he could hear Jeremy from where he was standing. All three men started jogging that way. The sheriff just got done saying that Rat was perfectly comfortable where he was, so it was highly doubtful he'd changed his mind in the span of thirty minutes. It could have been Jarrett, but that was unlikely from the looks of the vehicle. Was that an Expedition?

"I'll take lead," Mav instructed, noticing that the vehicle was slowing down upon seeing the men lined up and waiting. Kellen maneuvered to the side and down the edge to where he'd have visual of the back. Mav held up a hand and then made sure his voice carried. "Put the vehicle in park, roll down the windows, and show your hands."

Within seconds the driver of the vehicle had done what Mav had directed. Everyone stood at the ready and it wasn't until the man's voice drifted through the night air that Mav relaxed his stance.

"Derek?" Mav moved forward, indicating that it was all right for him and his family to exit the vehicle. "Jeremy, run and get Mabel."

"Let me do the honors," Ernie said with a smile, walking up from the access road where he must have exited through the front of the bunker right after his alert. He held out an arm and shook the man's hand. "Derek, it's good to see you."

"Same here, Tank." Derek looked over at Mav and nodded. "You too, Mav. I probably would have stayed if it weren't for you. We barely made it out in time as it was."

Ernie was smiling for the first time since Mav and the guys had arrived for their annual vacation. There hadn't been much to be happy about lately, but the fact that one of their own had made it through the turmoil that must be going on out there was nothing short of a miracle.

"Amy, it's good to see you." Derek's wife and two young children got out of the SUV and Mav realized the responsibility that these young boys would be. They had to be somewhere around the ages of five and eight if Mav remembered correctly. Amy had waved and then walked around to the opened back door, retrieving the youngest—Mabel's granddaughter, whom she kept showing pictures to her patrons at the diner. Lost Summit wasn't known as a family community anymore since there were no means of support, other than the tourist attractions of fishing, hunting, and camping. They would have to devise something for the children to keep them safe. "We've set it up for you to able to stay with Mabel in a cabin so that you can have some privacy."

"Derek?" Mabel's excited voice cut through the air as she came running down the lane, way ahead of Ernie who was following at a distance. "You made it! I knew you would. I just knew it."

Tears of joy were streaming down Mabel's face by the time she was in her son's arms. Derek held her, patting her on the back while telling her they were fine. Ernie came to stand by Mav, slapping him on the back as everyone stood there and watched the touching reunion. It was about time that something turned out right for a change. Mav turned back to look at the lodge, wishing that Henley would have come out to see this poignant exchange. Maybe, just maybe, this event was the start of things to come.

CHAPTER TWENTY

H ENLEY WAS TIRED and the only thing she wanted was to go back to her cabin, take a shower, make love with Mav, and then get some sleep. They got up way too early to be up this late at night and how Mav could even function on a security rotation was beyond her. She'd almost fallen asleep in the sitting area of the lodge on one of those overstuffed couches positioned in front of the fireplace, but Mrs. Welsh wouldn't stop talking about her knitting needles being back at her house in town. The mayor and the sheriff still had small groups retrieving supplies from town and Henley made a promise to herself that she would go on a run to get those damned needles.

Needing a break and wondering when Mav would return, Henley used the bathroom and then made her way into the kitchen for a glass of water. She reached down to adjust the volume on her two-way radio when she realized that she'd left it on the couch where she'd been sitting. She'd have to clip it back on her belt so that she didn't miss anything, like the sheriff returning to the lodge. Nothing had been said after that, so she assumed nothing had come of Felix's visit to Stanley's group.

Henley opened the cupboard for a glass when she spotted a garbage bag in the corner that Mabel must have put there for one of the men to take out. She was old-fashioned that way, but Henley wasn't one to let things set when she could do them herself. She placed her glass by the sink as she grabbed the top of the bag and started for the back door.

"Mabel?"

Henley heard Ernie call out only to hear Mabel answer. She smiled at the exchange, happy that Ernie and Mabel were getting closer now that they were in such an intimate proximity of each other. The front door of the lodge closed and Henley wondered at the safety of those two going outside so late at night when someone was on the property looking to cause trouble.

She lifted the garbage bag and opened the back door that led to the wraparound porch with stairs off the back leaving toward an enclosure that contained the trashcans. The garbage couldn't be left outside because the smell of food would attract the scavengers. The lodge was too far away for a trash service, so Ernie would load up the dozen fifty-five Rubbermaid garbage cans once a week into the back of his truck and take them over to the landfill over at the back of Wick's farm. The cans were getting full and Henley made a mental note to have them taken down to town before they couldn't travel anymore. Recycling would take on a whole new urgency before too long.

She lifted the cover and barely managed to fit the bag inside, pressing the top down on it to compact its contents. One couldn't leave the lids unsecured. Had she not been so determined to get it closed, she might have noticed that the outer door had been opened. Unfortunately, someone was already coming toward her by the time she turned to look. A hand slammed into her face and her body stumbled backward into the wall. Instinctively her hand went to her weapon but she immediately stilled when the blade of a knife dug into her throat.

"You so much as scream and I'll slice you without a second thought."

Trevor Ratliff's breath was rancid as he threatened her, but it was the wild look in his eyes that made Henley aware that he was unpredictable. He wouldn't think twice about killing her if he thought she would give him away. She frantically tried to think of a way to stall him so that someone would find them, but he was already removing her weapon and pushing her toward the enclosure's exit and away from the lodge.

"You're going to be our key to getting inside that bunker," Trevor muttered, steering her toward the woods in back toward her rock. Henley knew the location of the alarm on this side of the property and they couldn't avoid it, giving her hope that someone would reach them in time before Trevor got them off of the mountain. "Once I hand you over to my father, he'll be able to barter mine for mine."

Henley remained silent, not wanting to make Trevor more unstable than he already was. How was it that no one could see or hear them? The branches and leaves underneath them sounded like gunshots to her every time they took a step. He was still holding the blade to her throat, making it difficult to walk. She winced when it finally managed to cut her.

They had made it deep into the woods before Trevor steered them toward the main road. Henley knew that Jason was up here somewhere, but he might have been on the other side. Mav and Kellen had searched for hours near the hot springs for any sign of the intruder, but it was a large mountain and he or she could have gone anywhere. Now that she was aware it was Trevor…there had to be a way she could talk him out of this.

"Trevor, you don't have to do this," Henley spoke softly, grateful when he finally pushed her away from him. She wasn't far enough to make a break for it, but at least he no longer had a knife to her throat. She placed a hand to her skin only to come away with blood. "The sheriff has told your father many times that he and the group were more than welcome up here. As a matter of fact, Sheriff Ramsey went to see Stanley an hour ago."

"My father will never share lodging or supplies with Ernie Yates." Trevor pushed her shoulder when she'd slowed down. Henley wiped her fingers on her sweatshirt, lifting the neck a little higher to put pressure on the small cut that was stinging like little bees. "They hated each other when I left town and they hate each other now even more."

"You have to think this through," Henley urged, her fear

temporarily put on hold at the anticipation of coming up to where the alarm would be triggered. Trevor couldn't have known where the sensors were or else he wouldn't have activated the one on the other side of the perimeter. She tried to turn around to see if he was holding her gun or if he'd put it somewhere, but he pushed her shoulder when she'd tried to look. "The ash cloud is going to be here soon and no one is going to have an advantage if we're all fighting with each other."

"There won't be any fighting when my father shows up with you. Yates and his sidekick would do anything for you," Trevor boasted, walking right past the area that would send a signal back to the bunker. Henley could have cried, but she held it together as she thought of what she could do to keep them there. "I saw that for myself and my father will realize what an asset I am after I personally deliver you to him."

Henley stopped and spun around, catching Trevor off guard. He still held his knife but her gun was nowhere to be seen. The darkness made it hard to make out anything other than his shape and his extended arm holding a blade. She did her best to compute what he was saying, but now was the time to clarify. It would only add extra minutes for those to come and find who caused the sensors to go off.

"Are you saying that your dad doesn't know you're here?" Henley wished she could see his expression. He was still too close to her for her to make a run for it, but she kept an eye open for any opportunity. "Trevor, taking me hostage by knifepoint isn't the way to get his approval. We're talking about life or death here for a lot of people. You aren't the eighteen-year-old who left here because he didn't get along with his father. You're twen—"

"I was sixteen," Trevor growled out before advancing on her. Henley backed up, but because the terrain was slanted she slipped and went down hard. That was one way to buy time, but the pain in her wrist took her attention for the moment. That was until Trevor wrapped a hand around her arm and hauled her to her feet, pushing her once again in front of him. "Nothing ever pleased that man, but producing you will take care of a lot of issues. I don't plan on dying in a mine that doesn't have a setup like Yates' does. My father will see that this benefits all of us and I'll get back into the fold."

Henley cradled her wrist as they kept walking, all the while straining to hear any signs of someone behind them. She was choking back a sob that was more in anger than it was in fear by the time they'd reached the road. She'd given Trevor an opportunity to grab her when she should have been more careful.

There were several ways this could go—Stanley might see just how unstable his son was and right a wrong, Mav and Ernie might be able to get the people with Stanley to see reason, she could save herself and make it back to camp, or Trevor would lose what sanity he had left and actually follow through on his threat to kill her. She knew the odds weren't in her favor when she saw an abandoned vehicle tucked away from the road.

MAV AND THE others had gotten the notification that a second alarm had been triggered on the east side of the southern end of the valley. He and Kellen had immediately disbanded, leaving the sheriff jogging to his cruiser with the intention of driving out to the entrance in hopes of catching the intruder should he try to make a break for the main road. Jeremy, Dylan, and Jason stayed at their posts and Ernie proceeded to take everyone who'd been outside back into the lodge.

"This gatecrasher obviously didn't leave the area the first go round, so maybe he cut back this way and is trying to get out without any bloodshed," Kellen said, taking the lead and rounding the lodge to an open area right before the edge of the deep woods. Owen was their man for this, but Kellen would have to do since he undoubtedly had more training in this capacity than Mav. "There's no way it was Ratliff or anyone in his group if the sheriff vouched for them."

Mav didn't express his thoughts on that. Felix didn't necessarily say he'd taken a head count, so it was still possible that Ratliff was responsible. It was highly doubtful it was some random person seeking shelter. He or she would have revealed themselves and asked for help. There was definitely malice in the intentions of whoever the guilty party was.

Kellen finally stopped, kneeling down and flashing a light

onto the landscape below. Even Mav could see the imprint of two sets of boots among the foliage. One set was smaller than the others, which didn't make sense. They unquestionably had been looking for one person, according to the signs left on the soft ground near the mountain springs. Had this second person been hiding in the wings?

"We're looking for two individuals," Mav said carefully, taking a step back and holding his Rock River rifle at the ready. He scanned the area, unable to see more than twenty yards in front of him. He was in a vulnerable position if his conclusion had any merit. "One male, one female."

Kellen must have caught the edge in Mav's voice, because he stilled the motion of the flashlight and looked over his shoulder. There was reflection from the lone beam to aid in seeing the man's face. He appeared more wary than he did that of man who was caught in his own lies of deceit.

"Beckett, I don't know what you're thinking, but I've been upfront with you about everything," Kellen said softly, a sharpness invading his voice along with impatience. "Yes, I have a woman on my team who happens to be around a hundred miles from here with a good serviceman by her side. But I can assure you that these prints don't belong to them. Wrong boots."

"You were the one to follow the male down to the road while I cut around in hopes to cut off his path," Mav pointed out, keeping a very close eye on Kellen's hands. He was holding them away from his sides, the flashlight still on. "What would you have me think right about now, Truman?"

"I'll admit it doesn't look good," Kellen offered up, still not making a move for the weapon on his hip. "And if I were in your shoes…I'd probably be thinking the same thing."

Mav weighed his options. The longer they stayed in this position, the more time the two individuals had to make a clean getaway. The question was did they have what they wanted or would they eventually make their way back to try and take the bunker? He needed to make a decision and he needed to make it quick. "Henley's not in the lodge."

The words came through the two-way radio, even surprising Truman if his expression was anything to go by. Mav wanted to think he'd heard wrong, but Kellen turning his back on a weapon that was pointed his way told him another story all together. Fear like he'd never known descended over him and his chest compressed to the point of pain.

"Mav, are you copying? Henley is missing."

"Go," Mav barked to Truman, yanking the two-way radio off of his hip and responding. Kellen ran through the trees as fast as he could with the visibility given to them. "We're on their track heading down-slope. Have Ramsey cut them off, but for god's sake don't shoot."

Not even Mav would take a shot in the dark unless he was one hundred percent positive that he could hit his mark. Right now there was no way to make that guarantee. Ramsey would be making a crapshoot and Mav didn't like the fifty-fifty odds of it being Henley that got tagged.

They were three-quarters down to where the access road was located when they heard the rev of an engine pulling out. Mav veered to the left, knowing there was a drop off but taking the chance anyway. His feet slid out from underneath him and he let gravity pull him down, folding his rifle to his chest and keeping his elbows high enough to avoid injury. His back bore the brunt of the rocks and branches, but his feet hit their destination well before Truman made an appearance.

It didn't matter though. The vehicle's taillights could be seen from a distance, driving toward town. Mav spun on his boots and started walking the other way with a hell of a purpose and a promise that whoever had taken Henley would be dead upon sight. His country had trained him to close with and destroy the enemy by fire and close combat. They put him out in the field for one purpose and one purpose only—to eliminate the enemy by any means possible, rapidly overcoming his will to fight by fire and maneuver. Truman called his name, short on his heels but Mav kept walking until he finally caught sight of the one thing he needed. Sheriff Ramsey pulled his cruiser up and Mav opened the passenger door while Truman hopped in the back.

"A beat-up old piece of shit Dodge Ram pickup is headed toward town. He won't leave, so we need to find out where he's going before the skies open up and we're all buried in ash."

"How do you know they won't leave?" Ramsey asked, not bothering to look over at Mav as he stepped on the gas pedal.

He knew these roads like the back of his hand and could maneuver them better than any longtime resident.

"He has Henley and he wants the bunker," Mav stated bluntly, refusing to allow the fear of losing Henley to invade his mind. He said what made sense, and Truman grunted out an agreement. Mav would be of no use to Henley if he couldn't function and that wasn't an option, so he steeled himself for that he had to do. Whoever had taken her had made a fatal mistake and one he was about to face judgment for. "What he doesn't know is that he isn't getting either."

CHAPTER TWENTY-ONE

HENLEY FELT SOME relief at the horror that crossed Stanley Ratliff's face when he saw what Trevor had done. It was just the three of them standing outside of the mine's entrance, nothing at all like the mine up at the lodge. This was dilapidated and on the verge of caving in, and that was by just seeing the entry point. There was no way these people could survive here and she could convince Stanley of that if the look on his face was any indication.

"What the hell have you done, Trevor?"

"I heard you and Jarrett Moore talking this morning," Trevor said, wiping the sweat off of his forehead with the same hand he was still holding the knife with. Henley could now make out the bulge near the front of his jeans where the butt of her Berretta was sticking out. She'd never be able to get it from where she was standing without him stabbing her, so she talked herself into being patient. It was hard when all that was keeping her standing was the will to live. Her left wrist was practically twice its normal size and throbbed to the point of unbearable pain. The stinging on her throat had subsided, but it was a definite reminder of how far Trevor was willing to go to follow through with his plan. "This place isn't going to keep us alive, so we need to take Yates' bunker. There's only one way to do that."

"I know this girl, you fool," Stanley whispered harshly, looking over his shoulder as if he were afraid someone could hear them. "You can't just kidnap someone and expect to get something in return. I know Yates and his boys. They're more likely to put a bullet in your head than negotiate something like this."

"It's not like I can return her," Trevor sneered, waving the knife in her direction. Henley was standing not even two feet from him, but she would swear she could feel the blade cut through the air. "You said so yourself that the bunker can't hold everyone. So it makes sense to take it for ourselves and the only way to do that is barter for it."

"I was also in on those meetings and there's a good chance they won't need that bunker," Stanley pointed out, running a hand through his thick hair that had more oil in it than the vehicle they drove here in. Henley peered over Rat's shoulder, hoping Jarrett or someone would appear. They would see how crazy this was and put a stop to it. "Which is why I'm telling everyone we'll be fine here. We'll have to rough it out, seeing as we don't have natural gas or commercial generators like his, but we'll make do."

"Make do?" Trevor was losing his grip and Henley was the one who was going to get hurt. She looked around the open area; there was nowhere to run to that he couldn't catch her.

Her best bet was to either try for the entrance to the mine in hopes someone saw her or scream bloody murder until someone came to find out what was going on. "I'm not making do, *Dad*. These people think I left when I was eighteen years old. You threw me out the day I turned sixteen. There is no way I'm making *do* anymore. We make this barter happen and we'll all be in a better position."

"Son, you're not thinking clearly," Stanley said with a bit of despondence. That wasn't a good sign and Henley felt that wave of panic start to descend over her once more. "This isn't going to work. They'll be gunning for your head and—"

"Rat, are you out here?"

Both Stanley and Trevor shifted their gaze onto the entrance of the mine. Randy Bassett was coming their way and this was her chance. Henley quickly stepped away and opened her mouth, ready to scream as loud as she could when Trevor somehow reached her before she could yell. He'd grabbed a hold of her hair and yanked her head back until she swore her neck cracked. He moved fast and was able to get her behind the truck with the knife to her throat.

"Yeah, Randy. I was just looking for Trevor. He ran into town for me to get some things but he should be back shortly."

Stanley's voice seemed to fade as he walked farther away instead of standing where they'd left him. Trevor pulled the knife away from her throat and right when she would have turned around to make a grab for her weapon still tucked into his pants…everything went black.

"STOP HERE," MAV ordered, the rage inside his blood boiling as he witnessed the vehicle turn left into Ratliff's campground. Henley was in that car and as of right now, there wasn't a damned thing he could do about it. The sheriff had turned his lights off once they'd caught sight of the other vehicle. It was a good thing this man knew the roads like he did, or else they'd be stuck in a ditch somewhere for how dark it was without the moonlight escaping through the clouds. "Don't get any closer."

"Well, we have our answer," Truman offered up from the back seat. "I take it this is where Ratliff is holed up?"

"Yes, but I know that man—as bad-tempered as he can get, he wouldn't have done this," Ramsey said, drumming his fingers on the steering wheel. "I also know Henley and she wouldn't have come here willingly."

"No, she wouldn't." Mav watched as the taillights faded around the turn of the road that would lead to the entrance of the old mine. Felix and Kellen continued to talk while Mav thought this through. There was no way in hell he was going to allow them to take over the bunker and it would be over his dead body before they hurt Henley in an attempt to get their way. In all honesty it didn't matter who had been the one responsible for abducting Henley. The entire group was now accomplices as far as Mav was concerned. He had a decision to make and he needed to make it fast. He glanced over in the seat to see Ramsey's two-way radio and he grabbed it before holding it over his shoulder for Kellen to take. "Truman, I need you to stay here and monitor the situation. Ramsey and I will head back to camp, getting the weapons and people that we need in order put an end to this."

Truman took the two-way radio without a word, opening the back door and stepping out into the cool night air. He quietly closed the door until a small latching sound could be heard and then he faded into the dark. Mav hoped like hell he just hadn't made a mistake.

"I take it you have a plan," Ramsey said, not even bothering to word that statement as a question. He put the cruiser back into drive and then did a U-turn in the middle of the road, taking them back into the direction of the fishing lodge. Mav was busy going over strategies in his head but he finally nodded his answer. "You realize that we're under martial law and I still need to do my job."

"Then do it," Mav instructed, not wanting to hear about rules and laws. He'd do what he had to in order to get Henley back safely and up to the lodge. "You make sure they pay for the crimes they committed and I'll do what I have to do to make things right."

The remainder of the ride was made in silence, Mav still planning and organizing the best way to enter the campgrounds and retrieve Henley without any bloodshed. That probably wouldn't happen, but it would only be by those who put up a fight. Mav was out of the vehicle before Felix had put it in park. Jeremy came hurrying from his place near the front while Ernie was already waiting for them.

"Rat has Henley," Mav said, taking the keys that Ernie was dangling from his hands. It was to his entrance into the armory within the bunker. "We'll go in at daybreak, so switch out Dylan and Jason so they can get some sleep. Jeremy, that means you too. Leave Missy in charge here with the others just in case this is a setup. Give her instructions to do what is necessary to protect what is ours."

"We might have a slight problem, son," Ernie said, managing to keep up with Mav's strides.

They marched into the main entrance to the bunker. The security door was high strength steel alloy with a cypher-lock keypad. The entrance opened up to reveal a well-lit main cavern with several structures built inside. A security office was on the left and a large equipment barn filled the right side. Two major tunnels granted access to the mine. One was leading off to the left where additional shelter could be seen and the rumble of the generators was heard. Heading down the corridor straight ahead, they passed the freight elevator and several golf carts with equipment racks on the back. There were multiple corridors and rooms off the main hall leading left and right, but they bore right around to the security billeting and the armory stores. Mav had hardly managed to pause to unlock the armory vault door when Ernie finally delivered the bad news.

"An announcement was made on the shortwave radio around twenty minutes ago. The wind current has picked up steam and the ash cloud is set to arrive by eight hundred hours."

Mav clenched his teeth at the glitch they'd have to overcome, but it wouldn't stop him from tactically carrying this plan out to his satisfaction. It was the best strategy of attack and they needed to be able to see their enemy. He didn't stop moving because to do so would allow his emotions to break free from the vessel he'd closed them into.

"We stick to the plan—first light." Mav came to the cage where the equipment racks held the various weapons and equipment that guaranteed their victory. Before them was a fully functional armory. The pistols and tactical rifles glistened in their racks. Magazines and ammo cans were stacked high. A weapon's smith couldn't have asked for a better-equipped workbench, stacks of reloading equipment, and two progressing load presses. Cabinets marked several powder types and another listing multiple size primers. Mav began to choose several ammo cans with .223 rounds loaded into stripper clips. He grabbed load bearing equipment and smoke grenades for everyone that would be a part of the recovery team. They already had their M4s except Kellen, and Mav pulled one off the rack for him as well as a magazine pouch with extra loaded magazines and a speed loader. By the time he was done, this act alone gave him satisfaction that this mission would be successful. There was only one thing left they needed to take with them. "Tank, we'll need those 40mm NBC gas mask filters."

CHAPTER TWENTY-TWO

HENLEY BLINKED, TRYING to adjust her eyesight against the throbbing at the back of her head. She took her time, careful not to move in case she jarred the pain worse than what it already was. It wasn't like what she read in books, where pieces came to a person slowly after they'd been knocked unconscious. No. Not at all. She was well aware of what happened and the emotional toll was wearing her thin. The sharp pain faded her heightened fear and now it fed into an anger that would see her come out alive at the end of this.

"You did what?" Stanley asked, his voice dropping to a rough and somewhat panicked whisper. Henley felt a sense of satisfaction that he was rattled about what his son had done. Rat would have put a stop to this immediately if he'd been any type of man. It was still dark, but it must be close to morning from the way the dimness shined through. "Milton will sell us out in a heartbeat. That ash cloud is arriving sooner than anyone expected and they're all panicking. We can make it here. I know we can, but you've messed this up, kid. You're certainly your mother's son. Everything you touch turns to shit."

"You never had faith in me or Mom and now isn't any different. Milton took one of the vehicles up the access road and delivered my message," Trevor said, confidence lining his voice while it only disgusted Henley that he thought this was okay to do. He was exactly the type of people that Mav had always been talking about. Rat was just as bad, letting a boy who'd made some very bad decisions carry out his plan. "It shouldn't be long now. They'll come down here with their tail between their legs, begging us not to hurt their *Henley Varano*. I listened to every word you said when I arrived. She's some kind of celebrity who came home after her mental breakdown, unable to cope with people looking at her all the time. What kind of shit is that?"

Henley could tell from the way their voices carried that they were facing away from her. She finally managed to open her eyes all the way, figuring out that she was lying in the back seat of the pickup truck that they'd arrived in. She leaned her head back, making out the two figures. She took advantage of their distraction and reach down to the floorboard with her left hand, almost crying out when she the pain in her left wrist shot up her arm as if she'd been shot. She bit her lip until she tasted blood, the agony fading bit by bit.

She quietly rolled to her side, all the while keeping an eye on Trevor and Stanley. Henley wasn't sure what they were looking for, but she hoped they continued to do so. Leaning down, she used her right hand to feel around the floor for anything she could use as a weapon. The only thing she came up with was a box of tissues, which she would have used for her tears had she had time. Mav had to know by now that she was missing and this was the only likely place she could be. Was he out there somewhere? Was he just waiting for a chance like she was?

"I don't think that darkness coming in from the west is rain clouds." Stanley took a few steps farther away. Trevor followed and Henley figured she'd have to make a break for it. She wasn't any good to them dead, so it was highly unlikely Trevor would flat out kill her before negotiations even began. Cradling her left wrist to her chest, she slowly inched her way to the open truck door when something in between the front seats caught her eye. Was that a pocketknife? "We heard on the shortwave radio that the ash cloud would roll in sometime this morning."

"Then my timing couldn't have been more perfect." Trevor turned back around only to find Henley standing next to the vehicle. She'd caught herself from fleeing just in time and stood her ground, keeping her right hand behind her back. "Look who's awake. It sucks having that pounding headache, doesn't it? Jeremy Jenkins got in that lucky shot and I can tell you that it hurts like a bitch from personal experience."

"There was never another man that day, was there?" Henley asked, taking her eyes off of Trevor long enough to see Rat turn around. She purposefully ignored the ominous dark cloud that Stanley had referred to because it would only sidetrack her with more fear. It was becoming a constant thing to be afraid and she was grateful for the sanctuary Ernie had provided. She just needed to do her best to get back there before that ash cloud descended on them. "You made it up as a distraction to get the focus off of you."

"What do you mean Jeremy Jenkins was responsible for your injury?" Rat asked angrily, putting a hand on Trevor's arm and turning him around. "You couldn't even take that boy down by surprise?"

"What's going on? The others are making their way deeper into the mine before the ash cloud arrives," Jarrett Moore said, his voice coming from the other side of the vehicle. She glanced over her shoulder, his surprise at seeing her evident. "Henley? What are you doing here?"

"There's been a change in plans," Trevor announced, taking his knife out and holding it down to his side. Henley didn't want to miss her chance, so she turned back around to face him and Stanley. Jarrett was a smart enough man to figure this out and he might be her only chance out of here. There was a slight problem with the fact that the ash had started to fall intermittently, Mother Nature letting everyone know she'd arrived at their doorstep. "Tell everyone we're moving up to the bunker that Yates has waiting for us."

"Don't you say a thing to them," Stanley warned, pointing his finger at Jarrett. "Trevor, we're staying here. You can right this wrong by taking Henley back up there, but we're sticking to our original plans. You made this mess so you clean it up. I'm tired of cleaning up your shit, boy. Both you and your mother together weren't worth a plugged nickel."

Henley had a feeling that Stanley had just pushed his son a little too far. Everything happened at once, but Henley wasn't about to lose the advantage. With more strength than she realized she possessed, she swung the pocketknife from behind her back at the same time that Trevor raised his blade and multiple shadows came toward them. She felt more than heard the sickening thud of her short knife entering the man's neck. It was unlike anything she'd ever experienced and never wanted to again.

Mav had always told her it was easy to say one could take another's life in self-defense, but it was another to actually follow through with it. Henley had no doubt that Trevor would have killed his father in that moment, and then her if he'd had the chance. She hadn't spent days preparing to live out a catastrophic event only to have it end here at the hands of a desperate and selfish young man.

"You bitch," Trevor yelled and to her amazement, his blade still kept coming down toward Stanley.

Henley shoved the older man to the ground as gunshots rang out and she covered him with her body. She tried frantically to look back underneath the truck to ensure that Jarrett hadn't been hit, but she couldn't see anything…just empty space. Stanley was mumbling something, but the blood rushing through her ears was preventing her from hearing anything he had to say. She whipped her head around to the other side and caught sight of Trevor falling straight down.

When he finally landed with his head turned toward her, his eyes were wide open, pupils fully dilated in death with half his head missing. It was a sight she would see again and again in her nightmares for many nights ahead.

MAV USED HAND signals to advance that Truman and Ernie understood perfectly. He'd explained them to Jeremy, Dylan, and Jason during the ride down here. Each of them had pouches on their right sides with gas masks and another on their left with additional ammunition. Mav had determined that the load bearing vests wouldn't restrict their movement too much. They hadn't originally known what they were up against until Milton had shown up an hour ago. It turned out that Trevor had something to prove to his father he could carry his weight and thought the way to do that was by taking Henley to trade for the bunker. He couldn't have been more wrong.

Trevor and Stanley were currently standing by the Dodge Ram pickup sitting at the bottom of the road. Mav was able to see Henley using Kellen's M24s in the back seat of the super cab through the open truck door. His relief was palpable that she appeared to be moving. She was making her way out of the vehicle when it would have been best for her to stay inside, but there wasn't any way she could know that. Mav and the men continued forward, using the coverage of the opposing tree line. By the time they reached the edge of the roadbed, Henley was standing beside the truck, having caught the attention of Stanley and Trevor. This heightened Mav's tension, but he needed to concentrate on the task at hand.

Mav was about to indicate they were a go to converge on their target when Jarrett came up from behind the truck, possibly causing a problem with the plan. He had everyone stay where they were until it was evident that their situation was about to go south. He signaled and together they moved forward as one, crushing the small flakes of ash that had landed on the shoulder of the road. He was close enough to hear and see what was going on, so he wasn't surprised when Trevor turned on his father and Henley.

"You bitch!"

Mav was at the ready and had pulled his rifle up to his cheek, taking aim through his Trijicon ACOG 4x32 scope. Henley must have had some type of weapon in her hand, because she had brought it forward with all of her might and landed it directly in Trevor's neck. Pride overwhelmed him at her ability to fend for herself, but that wasn't about to stop a man hyped up on adrenaline, so Mav did what he had to do. He pulled the trigger and put one .223 caliber 68-grain hollow point boat tailed slug into his head. A couple more shots were taken, but they were warnings for those up at the entrance of the mine farther up the valley...not that they were needed. Everyone stood there in shock at what had just transpired, but Mav allowed the others to deal with them. His one and only focus was Henley.

"Henley?" Mav quickly shifted the strap of the rifle so that the weapon rested on his back while he physically lifted her body off of Stanley's. He was already mumbling and making excuses, saying he had nothing to do with Trevor's plan. Mav didn't give a shit and pulled Henley to him, holding her tight. "You scared me, sweetheart. I don't think I've ever felt such a terror like that before."

"Mav, I knew you'd come for me," Henley whispered against his neck, holding on to him as forcefully as he was to her. He also knew her nature was to immediately defend those of this town, but he really wasn't ready for that quite yet. That didn't stop her though. "Trevor was behind it all. Stanley didn't know until we got back to their camp. He's telling the truth, just ask Jarrett."

"Henley, could we focus on you right now?" Mav asked, pulling her away so that he could look her over. He couldn't see any fresh blood other than what was on her hands, but he wasn't sure he would with the way the ash was falling right now. Henley was definitely in pain and he needed to find its source. "Where are you hurt?"

"My wrist," Henley answered vaguely, turning her head to look at the others with a wince. That tell told him she was hurt somewhere else, but she was being too damn stubborn to admit it. Her eyes skimmed over Trevor's body, but she obstinately held true to what she believed. He had no doubt the reality of what had happened here today would sink in and he would be there for her. "We need to get everyone up to the lodge now."

Mav had already released her and had pulled his backpack off while setting his rifle on the deck. He withdrew her gasmask pouch, handing Henley hers as she continued to ask if they had enough for everyone here. He would have laughed at the absurdity of it all, but all he could do was take a moment by placing his hands on his knees. She literally had no idea the worry and terror that he'd experienced thinking that he couldn't save her. He took a deep breath, trying to steady what nerves he had left.

"Mav? Did you hear me? The ash is starting to come down and we need to get everyone up to the camp."

"Henley, give the man a minute," Ernie instructed with a bark, walking up to them and slapping Mav on the back. He managed to stand and shoot the old man a warning look. It didn't help in the least. "He just saved the woman he loves. That'll take something out of a man—hell, he'll be greyer than me by the time you're through with him. I will say I'm downright proud of you, girl. You fought like a champ and came out the victor."

"Yates," Ratliff called out, making his way over through the thickening air. Henley was right when she said they needed to start clearing the area, but Mav couldn't take his eyes off of her face. She was smiling brighter than any sun he'd ever had the pleasure of seeing and would no doubt not see for a very long time. He didn't need to with her by his side. "Could we talk?"

"The man lost his son, Ernie," Henley spoke softly, her eyes never leaving Mav's face. "Go easy."

Ernie grumbled as he walked away and Truman took over in getting the remaining people in the vehicles he had brought up by the other team members. The ash was coming down but it wasn't thick enough to clog the engines before reaching the lodge. Ramsey had come in through the access road and would take care of Trevor's body, leaving Mav and Henley to their own devices.

"You could have just told me you loved me," Henley said after she'd taken one of the gas masks that Mav held in his hand. He picked up his pack and rifle, slinging it over his one shoulder so that he could wrap his other arm around her. She was cradling the mask to her chest with her right hand while protecting her left. He wasn't sure he'd be able to let her out of his sight for a while, but that wasn't going to be an issue for some time to come. "Letting an old man do your dirty work isn't like you, Maverick."

Mav laughed, grateful for this weightlessness that came over them. This was the Henley he'd met three years ago, the one who kept him on his toes and loved taunting him with mocking scoffs that got under his skin. The thing of it was…he liked it. Hell, Ernie was right—he loved it.

"Are you going to wait another three years to say it or are you going to hide in that cabin of yours until the sun starts to shine again?" Mav asked, pressing a kiss on top of Henley's head as he led her to Ramsey's cruiser. The sheriff would have to use that shitty old POS Dodge to transport the body to a burial ground. The ash was still falling lightly, giving everyone time to get the things done they needed to do. It was heavy enough though that had they had to walk any farther in distance, he would have had her put the mask on. "We all know how long it takes for you to make up your mind."

Mav released Henley to open the passenger side door of the cruiser and then looked down at her when she didn't immediately get in. She was looking up at him with those green eyes of hers, ashes settling on her upturned face. Her answer was already shining bright.

"I do love you, Maverick Beckett. And it's a good thing too," Henley said, carefully sitting down into the passenger seat. "Who else is going to keep you on your toes and give you something to do around this one horse town?"

Mav stored his pack and rifle in the back seat before kneeling in to kiss her as tenderly as he could. It was more than apparent by the pain in her eyes that she was hurting and he didn't want to add to that. He finally pulled back, making sure she was paying attention to every word he said.

"I can think of many things we could do that will keep us on our toes, sweetheart. Many, many things. After all…it's the end of the world."

CHAPTER TWENTY-THREE

MAV ENTERED THE cabin two days later and waited until he'd shut the door to remove his mask. He had already brushed himself off with the whiskbroom before he entered. He leaned against the door and rested his head against the wood. He was bone tired, but very satisfied with how things were turning out. Ernie had been right about the location being protected from the elements and the ash falling here was not as significant as the vast majority of the United States, allowing them to continue to stay in the lodge and the cabins. They'd managed to get some of the older townsfolk into the bunker while making room for Stanley and the others that had come back with them in the lodge. The gas masks were used to get from point A to point B, no one wanting to take the chance of getting ash into their lungs.

"It took you long enough," Henley called out from the bedroom. "Do me a favor and have a seat in the overstuffed chair in front of you."

Mav frowned when he noticed that their furniture had been rearranged. The chair she was referring to was positioned right in front of him, totally out of place. The back of the couch was to his left and the coffee table was turned on its side on his right. What the hell was she doing when she was supposed to be resting?

"Henley, what the hell are you doing?"

Mav finally gave up when she didn't answer right away. He used the time to remove his boots, not wanting to get ash anywhere within the cabin. He also took off his jacket and coveralls, hanging them up on a hook he'd installed the other day. There was a side table there for his two-way radio along with his sidearm. His rifle he hung from the other hook. That left him in nothing but his T-shirt, cammies, and stocking feet before he gratefully fell into the chair in a heap. He looked over to his left, finally noticing that she had a fire roaring in the fireplace, making the whole cabin very toasty.

Transmissions had been received from Berke, Owen, Mason, and Van. All four were headed here and should arrive any day now. They'd made an agreement to transmit every evening at twenty-one hundred hours so that Mav and Ernie were aware of their locations and progress. Truman's team of two had shown up this morning and both were a hell of a lot nicer and freer with information than their leader was. They would make a great fit to the security team and were currently bunking in with Kellen.

Stanley was staying out of Ernie's way and it was more than apparent who Mabel was fonder of, considering she saved a little extra dessert for Ernie every evening. It wouldn't surprise Mav if one morning he woke up to Mabel living at

Ernie's cabin. The man was certainly one to talk about taking one's time, but the irony was lost on him.

The thumping of bass rhythm music could be heard coming from the bedroom, causing Mav to open his tired eyes and see what she was up to. He might have fallen asleep there for a moment, but the sensual vision before him certainly woke him up in a hurry. Henley was in some type of long black slip that formed to her body like a lover's caress. She had her hair down around her shoulders with make-up done as if she were doing a live runway walk. Mav straightened in his chair as the blood rushed from his upper body straight to his cock.

"I think you mentioned a catwalk the last time we made love," Henley said in a suggestive tone that covered him warmly and slowly as if her words had been made of molasses. "You certainly gave me one and I aim to return the favor."

Mav certainly wasn't going to argue and had to acknowledge her initiative for the way she'd staged this. It had been the sole reason for their hang-up and after having gone through what they'd gone through this last week…it was obviously her way of saying nothing else mattered except that they were both here to enjoy and love one another.

"You'll have three choices to choose from," Henley said, stating the ground rules as she started to saunter his way. Her hips swayed back and forth like a psychiatrist's stopwatch used to hypnotize his patient and damned if he wasn't already mesmerized. "This first one is a little black number that falls to my ankles in a sultry manner that will leave your woman feeling very sensual. You'll find the color matches the brace on my wrist for the appeal of the total package."

Mav's gaze eased over her, taking in every curve and glisten the material displayed as it shifted with her movements over her naked body beneath. He ignored her little injection of humor as he was otherwise engaged. It wasn't until he'd lowered his eyes to her ankles that he spotted the stiletto heels. The slit on the side gave him access to view her toned calf and he almost protested as she turned away and sashayed her hips in the opposite direction. It was the wrong direction, because she should have kept walking toward him.

"Intermission for lingerie number two."

Mav didn't hesitate and pulled his T-shirt over his head, tossing it down beside the chair. He'd unbuttoned his cammies, but didn't have time to do anything else before she made another appearance. The flush on her face told him how much she loved doing this for him.

"This is a white spaghetti-strapped slip, edged with black lace and slit along the right side for easy access to please your woman," Henley relayed, her voice barely above a whisper. It was unequivocally the sexiest voice he'd ever heard on a woman and he was blessed to have her by his side. "Do you like this one, Maverick?"

"Yes, very much," Mav replied, watching her get closer and anticipating what would happen when she reached the chair. Unfortunately, she must have anticipated that he wasn't going to let her go because she turned a little bit earlier than the last time, strolling back to the bedroom with a flick of her hair. "That wasn't nice."

Henley's laughter filled the air and Mav was pleased that she was feeling better. She'd had headaches on and off for the past couple of days from the bump that she was still sporting on her head from where Trevor had knocked her unconscious. Mav still had deep-seated anger at what the man had done, but this wasn't the time or place to let it interfere with the pleasure his woman was deriving by driving him insane.

Mav took the spare minute and removed his pants and briefs, making sure to pull out a condom. Ernie had handed him a cardboard box the other day with enough boxes to last them a year. Mav would have to make a run somewhere and somehow reload their supply when they ran out because there wasn't a chance in hell they were going to stop making love to each other.

"Allow me to describe this little number," Henley said, pulling his gaze to the bedroom where she was standing there looking more beautiful than he'd ever seen. Her arm was flush with the doorjamb and her hip was arched just right. Her olive skin appeared darker with the color of the lingerie and the matching lipstick made him want to kiss her until her natural shade appeared. She leisurely walked toward him, the sensual movement of her hips almost more than he could take. "You see, this half slip was made in the color of candied red apples for the sole purpose of sexual enticement."

Henley walked closer, giving Mav time to rip the wrapper

with his teeth. Her green eyes darkened as she took in his actions, managing to hike his own arousal. He could play her game and managed to roll on the condom as slowly as she was strolling toward him. It was hell, but the end result would be well worth it.

"The satin provides the ability for me to pull it up over my skin, allowing me to straddle you," Henley murmured, getting closer enough that he could see she wasn't wearing any panties underneath that red little number. She had shaved her pubic mound smooth, allowing her swollen clit and engorged labia to make their first appearance. Mav's eyes were glued to her hands as her fingers worked the silky material up and over her hips. "Shall we try it?"

"With pleasure," Mav replied, pleased when he was finally able to touch her. He wrapped his fingers around her waist, guiding her over him. It was easy to see that she was ready for him, her cream glistening between her inner thighs. The smooth material felt warm against his skin, but it was nothing compared to the feel of her pussy stretching around his cock. He had to close his eyes and even out his breathing to prevent himself from coming far too soon. "I'd say the designer did a fantastic job of creating a slip that allows this, sweetheart."

Henley hummed in appreciation, letting her head fall back as she rested her forearms on his shoulders. The chair was big enough that it allowed her knees to tuck in beside his tight thighs, which she used for leverage as she continued to ride him at her own leisure.

Mav was in awe of watching her expressions, those red lips parting in a smile rich with pleasure. His main goal was to hold out until she received her orgasm, but it was going to be damn close unless he helped her along. Holding one hand on her back so that she had some support, he brought his other hand around and tucked it under the fabric between them so that his fingers brushed against her wet, exposed, and swollen clit.

"Maverick, make me come," Henley pleaded, her eyes fluttering open and meeting his gaze. She could ask for the moon and he would somehow manage to give it to her. "Please."

"You don't have to beg," Mav replied, giving her what she needed as he helped her quicken the pace. It meant holding on to her waist with both hands, but hearing her cries was well worth it. "Come for me, sweetheart."

Henley exploded in his arms and he wasn't far behind. He pulled her tightly to him as he buried his face in her hair and inhaled her fragrance. She'd become his everything and nothing of this world would ever take her from him. Mav finally loosened his hold on her, not wanting to cause her headache to come back. It wasn't until he was lightly stroking her arms that he realized she'd tensed.

"Are you okay?" Mav asked, leaning back so that he could look at her face. Henley was smiling and held a hand to her ear. He laughed and shook his head. "You don't hear anything because I left strict instructions not to interrupt us unless the

West Coast was about to fall into the water."

"Hmmm, don't jinx us," Henley chuckled lightly, relaxing into him and resting her head on his shoulder. It appeared she didn't have any plans to move, but since his semi-hard cock was still nestled inside of her...he was more than okay with that. "We have enough to deal with."

"As long as you love me half as much as I love you, we can get through anything." Mav closed his eyes and took time to treasure the woman in his arms. They had all night before another day of survival started that would keep them alert, defending what was theirs.

"I couldn't agree more, Maverick."

They stayed that way for quite a while, both cherishing what they'd been given during these hard times. The saying was true about the sun still shining during dark times and the proof was in his arms. An essential beginning had taken place in more ways than one.

The End

Continue on in the Surviving Ashes series with...
Hidden Ashes (Surviving Ashes, Book Two)

There were a few things that got Owen Quade through his multiple combat tours. One was the dream of riding a custom motorcycle on a winding mountain road. The former Marine had finally managed to complete that goal, and along the way he'd gained his own bike shop and the mechanic to go with it. She was a rare beauty, and he wasn't talking about his bike either.

Prue Whitaker preferred working on engines over rubbing shoulders with people, and that included her boss. She'd learned the hard way that men weren't as reliable as the hogs she could repair and she kept her distance from those who didn't feel the same way. She'd been successful until she'd recently shared a scorching kiss with Owen.

One phone call had changed everything. A catastrophic event is on the verge of occurring, forcing them to pack up and leave everything behind. Prue is driven to trust Owen, who's given his word that he can get her to safety. Through the endless days of darkness, passion and intrigue await them as they make their way through ashes and into the flames of tomorrow.

BOOKS BY KENNEDY LAYNE

Surviving Ashes Series

Essential Beginnings (Surviving Ashes, Book One)

Hidden Ashes (Surviving Ashes, Book Two)

CSA Case Files Series

Captured Innocence (CSA Case Files 1)

Sinful Resurrection (CSA Case Files 2)

Renewed Faith (CSA Case Files 3)

Campaign of Desire (CSA Case Files 4)

Internal Temptation (CSA Case Files 5)

Radiant Surrender (CSA Case Files 6)

Red Starr Series

Starr's Awakening (Red Starr, The Prequel)

Hearths of Fire (Red Starr, Book One)

Targets Entangled (Red Starr, Book Two)

Igniting Passion (Red Starr, Book Three)

ABOUT THE AUTHOR

First and foremost, I love life. I love that I'm a wife, mother, daughter, sister… and a writer.

I am one of the lucky women in this world who gets to do what makes them happy. As long as I have a cup of coffee (maybe two or three) and my laptop, the stories evolve themselves and I try to do them justice. I draw my inspiration from a retired Marine Master Sergeant that swept me off of my feet and has drawn me into a world that fulfills all of my deepest and darkest desires. Erotic romance, military men, intrigue, with a little bit of kinky chili pepper (his recipe), fill my head and there is nothing more satisfying than making the hero and heroine fulfill their destinies.

Thank you for having joined me on their journeys…

Email: kennedylayneauthor@gmail.com

Facebook: www.facebook.com/kennedy.layne.94

Twitter: twitter.com/KennedyL_Author

Website: www.kennedylayne.com

Newsletter: www.kennedylayne.com/newsletter.html